I0608553

ARCHITECTS OF ARMAGEDDON

Architects of Armageddon

A Kate Dawson Mystery

John L. Flynn

INTEGRATED MEDIA
NEW YORK

All rights reserved, including without limitation the right to reproduce this book or any portion thereof in any form or by any means, whether electronic or mechanical, now known or hereinafter invented, without the express written permission of the publisher.

This is a work of fiction. Names, characters, places, events, and incidents either are the product of the author's imagination or are used fictitiously. Any resemblance to actual persons, living or dead, businesses, companies, events, or locales is entirely coincidental.

Copyright © 2017 by John L Flynn

ISBN: 978-1-5040-8420-8

This edition published in 2023 by Open Road Integrated Media, Inc.
180 Maiden Lane
New York, NY 10038
www.openroadmedia.com

To my brother Bob and our late mother Norma Jean,
with love.

ARCHITECTS OF ARMAGEDDON

PROLOGUE

Thirty-four-year-old Wendy Ross walked into the backyard. Clad in a white satin, ankle-length skirt and lacey, white blouse, she climbed a small stepladder standing next to a tree, wrapped one end of a nylon rope around a tree limb and made a slipknot in the other end. She placed the noose around her neck, tightened it, and drew a white satin pillowcase over her head. For a few heartbeats, she struggled to maintain her balance, then stepped off the ladder to her death.

Twenty-three minutes earlier . . .

Wendy Ross had come in from the small, postage sized backyard and gathered her five children into the living room of their Noe Valley home in San Francisco.

The house was small, much too small for a large family of seven, but it was all they could afford. The Ross family had hoped their move from Sioux Falls, South Dakota, to the City by the Bay would have yielded better employment opportunities, but both Wendy and her husband, Philip, experienced difficulty finding jobs.

Apparently, systems engineers were a dime-a-dozen in San

Francisco, Oakland, and the nearby Silicon Valley. When the dot-com boom went bust, it produced the largest number of unemployed computer workers and technologists in the country. Things had gotten worse in the intervening years.

Now, most of those earning six-figure salaries were forced to work minimum-wage jobs while their resumes probed markets in the rest of the country or overseas.

Wendy and Philip had missed the 'gold rush' and were counted among those underemployed, working menial jobs at a local restaurant and home-improvement store. If it hadn't been for the charity of fellow church members, they might have found themselves living on the street with their five children.

Wendy lit a small white candle, which seemed to chase away the tomb-like darkness of the room, and took the family Bible down off the mantle. She opened it to the last book, Revelation, and placed it on the living room table. She raised her hands with palms facing upward, and turned her gaze to the ceiling, her eyes unblinking as she stared at the reflection cast by the candlelight.

"Our Father which art in Heaven," she said, reciting the first few words of the Lord's Prayer. She paused for a moment, waiting for her children to catch up, then continued, "Hallowed be thy name . . ."

Back in her youth, Wendy attended the First Baptist Church in Sioux Falls, but she was never confirmed as a member. Like many God-fearing Christians, she accompanied her parents to church twice a year, once at Christmas and then again on Easter Sunday. She knew her parents were not church-goers and saw little point in attending service every week. The sermon was always the same, and she felt the Baptist minister did not make an effort to mitigate his message of fire-and-brimstone with any words of comfort or love. She knew she was damned, so what was the point in being reminded every week of her final destination.

When the small sectarian church opened its chapel doors in the evening to host a youth group, Wendy joined the teenagers who came each night to sing and read scriptures, because her boyfriend and future husband, Philip Ross, was the group's leader, not for any religious reasons. Then, one fateful night, she was listening with the others to an audiocassette tape and heard a preacher's message that made sense to her. He talked a great deal about the End Times and preparing an army for the Lord. The message just resonated with her because it was a hopeful one. Wendy realized that she and the others were more than just a bunch of young college and high school-aged kids. They were the Chosen Ones, destined by God to inherit the earth, and she had an important mission to fulfill. She no longer felt damned.

"For thine is the kingdom, and the power, and the glory, forever. Amen," Wendy Ross said aloud, concluding the prayer.

She waited patiently for the four oldest children to say "Amen," then crouched next to the toddler to listen to his gurgled version that included the well-punctuated "hayman" at the end. They had all worked so hard to learn their Sunday school lessons. She felt pride over each one of them, especially her youngest, Connor, who always tried to keep pace with his sisters.

As she looked at them, one child to the next, Wendy forced back a tear. Her religion did not permit crying. The church elders believed it was a sin to cry. They would say a person who cried lost their joy and the privilege of eternal salvation. Wendy knew the rules all too well and did everything in her power to raise the perfect little Christian family. That was why it was twice as hard for her to hold back the tears now or, for that matter, break into hysterics over what she had to do. But Wendy was, first and foremost, an obedient woman unto God. If He commanded her, like Abraham, to take the life of her first-born son, or all of her children, she would do so, with no hesitation or tears. She owed her life and the lives of her family to God, and there was nothing more sacred to her than that bond.

"My darlings, the kingdom of the Lord is upon us," she said with a faint but reassuring smile. "We are all being called home by God and will dwell in a very special place He has made just for us."

The Ross children sat together on the couch with little or no sound, listening to their mother talk. They ranged in age from six years down to eighteen months. Each child had been dressed in a beatific manner, all in white.

Other than the lovely silk ribbon that bound their hands with a bow, they looked ready for church. Sarah, the eldest, set the example for the others by sitting up straight, the pleats in her dress perfectly aligned, not a wrinkle in the bodice outlined with tiny little roses. Hope and Charity wore matching white, satin dresses; the twins looked like little cherubs in a Michelangelo-painting with their rosy cheeks and bright smiles. Rachel struggled to keep from picking her nose; even with hands bound in front, she could not help raising them to her face then wiping them on her white, ruffled Chiffon petti-skirt. And Connor, dressed in a white linen suit and tie like his father, sat with his feet tucked under him on the couch. They could easily be mistaken for Stepford-children if this had been any other city but San Francisco.

"Will Daddy be coming with us, Mommy?" Hope asked with a sugary-sweet temperament.

"Yes, but not right away, sweetheart," Wendy could see this response did not satisfy her daughter, and added, "because Daddy has an important task that was given to him by the Lord, and he must complete it before he follows. So, we will be going on ahead of him."

Charity asked, "Will we have to go really far away, Mommy?"

"No, my love. Just into the backyard," Wendy answered. She then looked at all of them, and said, "Do you remember the story I told you about Ezekiel and his fiery chariots? Well, the Lord has sent a chariot for each one of you, but you will have to close your eyes really tight and let me tie you into the chariot, lest you fall as it takes you on your journey to Heaven."

Except for Connor, they all nodded in unison. When the toddler realized he had missed something, he nodded, too.

Wendy swallowed a deep breath then slowly exhaled. "Do you remember the song 'Jesus Loves Me?'" She waited a moment for them to acknowledge her query with a nod then looked at her eldest. "Well, I've asked Sarah to lead us off, then we'll all join in, singing it together while I take you, one at a time, to your chariot."

All at once, Sarah sat forward, opposite her siblings, and started singing with a beautiful angelic voice. "Jesus loves me, this I know, for the Bible tells me so. Little ones to Him belong . . ."

". . . they are weak, but He is strong," the rest of the children joined the sing-along.

Wendy gathered the littlest and weakest member of her family, Connor, into her arms and carried him over to his sisters for one last hug and kiss. Then, with the toddler's eyes closed and his body held tight against her chest, she made the short journey from the family's living room to the back door. She paused on the steps and felt her rapid heartbeat rise in her throat. As she glanced around the backyard, waiting for the queasy sensation to go away, she couldn't shake the feeling that Philip was standing right there with the church elders, hidden in the dark shadows, watching her, judging her actions. She strained to see him in the darkness, but she only saw their ill kept grounds. Trash, half-emptied garbage bags, forgotten leaves, discarded tree limbs, and broken toys littered the yard like a junk-heap on Skid Row. An oak tree stood at the back of the yard on a small hill overgrown with tall, prickly weeds—the kind that grew on gravestones and forgotten highways.

For an instant, Wendy thought about tucking her toddler under her arm and running as far as she could manage on her own. Maybe she would go back to Sioux Falls, stay with her parents, and start her life over again. She imagined that Abraham must have had similar thoughts when he reached the summit of Mount Moriah with his son Isaac. Otherwise, what was God's purpose for gifting man with free will?

Then, as her thoughts turned back to her other children and Philip, she realized there was no place to run.

They were everywhere, and if the prophecy was true, the End Times were truly upon her. She had a responsibility to Connor and her other darlings to spare them the horror and devastation to come. Wendy pulled her toddler tight around her neck and hugged him one final time with an intensity of emotion and feeling that surprised even her. She continued down the back stairs and out across the small yard before she could lose her nerve again.

Wendy climbed the small stepladder, with Connor still in her arms, and made fast work of tying the nylon rope off and placing the noose-like slipknot around the toddler's neck. She then kissed his forehead, placed a satin pillowcase over his head, and released him into the night air. He floated for an instant, caught in that moment between the tick and the tock of a clock, then plunged to his death.

Other than some instinctive struggling, legs flailing back and forth in a vain attempt to touch the ground, Connor died in a matter of seconds. When he finally stopped moving, Wendy's heart sank. There had been no heavenly army of angels charging to Connor's rescue; no booming voice of God commanding her to spare his life, just the dead silence of the city at night. Again, her resolve wavered.

She climbed down the stepladder and sat on the lowest rung, her head in her hands. *What on earth have I done?* She asked herself as the two-year-old's body swung gently back and forth in the evening breeze. *Is this really happening, or am I stuck in the middle of some horrible nightmare, struggling to wake up?* Just then, she heard soft angelic voices filling the air with song: "Jesus loves me, this I know, for the Bible tells me so. Little ones to Him belong . . ." She listened up and could hear her other children singing with precious innocence. They were not afraid, and repeated, over and over, how they placed their trust in the Lord.

Wendy climbed to her feet, and as if held under a spell, readjusted the stepladder relative to the tree. She then marched across the yard and returned to the house alone for her youngest daughter. Wendy recited the words to "Jesus Loves Me" as she walked into the living room, adding her voice to her children's chorus to hide the fact that she was dying inside. Expressionless, she gathered Rachel into her arms, carried her over to the other girls for one last hug and kiss, and exited the house through the back door. In the backyard, she made swift work of hanging her daughter from the tree.

After Connor and Rachel, it got easier. One by one, Wendy Ross took each child into the backyard, hanging them from the tree with a nylon rope. She shut down, but she continued with her grisly work as though programmed to carry out a task and one task alone, on an automated assembly line.

On her sixth and final trip, she returned to the house alone, empty-handed and serene, her five children now dead.

Wendy marched like an automaton into the family kitchen and tied an apron around her waist. She reached out for a pot, soaking in a sink of soapy water, and scrubbed it clean without passion or emotion. Her movements measured, almost practiced. She cleaned the remaining pots and pans, and placed them upside down on strainer for them to dry. She appeared to be nothing more than a scarecrow, her body stuffed with straw.

With her breathing shallow and as silent as the grave, Wendy turned away from the kitchen sink and untied her apron. She hung it over the handle on the stove, for the last time, and marched out into the back yard. She sucked the cold, damp air into her lungs and felt a momentary chill wash over her body. Then she climbed the six steps of the small stepladder that stood next to the tree. She looked away from her children, swinging from their respective ropes, and proceeded to tie another nylon rope to a limb. Wendy put her head in the noose and after pulling on the satin hood, she stepped off the ladder to her death.

When she stopped kicking, toes pointed down and feet four inches from the ground, her body slowly revolved in the wind.

As the first rays of the morning sunlight came through the front window of the modest Noe Valley home, a thin man emerged from the shadows and dialed 911 on the house-phone.

The operator responded, "911, what is the nature of your emergency?"

"I'd like to report a suicide," he replied. "Suicide?"

"Yes, it's my wife," he added. "It appears she has also taken the lives of our five children . . ."

CHAPTER ONE

For the fourth time that week, Kate had downed a bottle of whiskey to help her sleep, then spent the night tossing and turning in her twin-sized bed. The inspector for the San Francisco Police Department had forgotten what it was like to get eight-hours' rest, and it was beginning to take a toll on her. She had tried just about every over-the-counter sleep-aid and prescription drug to help her cope with the insomnia. When all of those failed, she turned to homespun remedies, like drinking warm milk or taking hot baths before bedtime, but they didn't work either. She gave acupressure and meditation a chance; then she smoked pot, took barbiturates, and tried a healthy dose of melatonin to turn herself off. Nothing seemed to work as effectively or quickly as the sour mash. And now, even that was no longer working.

Kate pulled the pillow over her head and struggled to bury her face in the two-hundre-threadcount percale pillowcase.

Maybe if she suffocated, she'd finally get the rest she needed. But her alcohol-addled brain continued to race on, like a high-speed train traveling through a never-ending tunnel of degrading images. Condemned to re-visit the nightmare that existed in the twisted kaleidoscope that filled her mind every night, she was a real mess. The tangle of deformed and distorted images of John Monroe, Crystal Rose, Bradley Rutherford, Stephen Collins, and the others, took on a reality of their own playing out like a low-budget, splatter film directed by the criminally insane. Kate was back in the dungeon, chained inside the Iron Maiden, forced to stare at the dismembered corpses and watch the beheadings and ravenous cannibals feeding on the living; horned beast-men raping and scourging slave women—sickening images of depravity from Dante's lowest circle of Hell.

Somewhere in her mind, Kate knew the images weren't real. They were the product of the madness that John Monroe inflicted on her and members of the public during his reign of terror as the Angel of Death. The psychology-professor-turned-serial-killer had been responsible for the deaths of seven men, six of whom were powerful and influential in the city, and the other one, her partner, Frank Miller. She surmised that he must have had an agenda that went beyond the murders themselves because he was a brilliant man; everything he did had a purpose behind it. Perhaps his agenda was collecting documents that he pieced together himself, revealing corruption at the highest levels of city government. Or perhaps Monroe just wanted to see if he was clever enough to get away with the perfect murder.

"Kate, when did you first find out?" John Monroe whispered in her ear.

Kate stirred in her bed, uneasy. The images running like miles of unedited film spooling through a Moviola and coalescing into a single, dominant image—that of John Monroe. She thought she heard his voice in her head . . . but no, it couldn't be because she put three slugs in him from a .38 caliber Smith and Wesson®. John Monroe was dead. The phantasm that visited her nightly was nothing more than the piece of him she still carried around inside her heart. She was determined to prove it to herself, if only she could awaken.

"When did you realize you could take a human life?"

He taunted her with the sweet lyrics of his refined, cultivated speech. Kate once thought she could listen to that voice read random names out of a phonebook and never grow tired of it. Even now, as she heard it again, those feelings of love and desire she fought to suppress washed over her in a cold sweat.

"Never again. Never again," she repeated to herself.

Kate struggled to move, to rouse herself from the nightmare, but her body was paralyzed. She felt awake, but she couldn't move a muscle in her body or speak. Lying in bed, she fought to make the steep climb to consciousness, aware of a presence in her bedroom. She watched and listened helplessly as John emerged from the shadows and walked around to the head of her bed.

He leaned over and whispered in her ear, "You know, Kate, we all have it in us." His hot breath hit the back of her neck. "Ten thousand years of evolution separates us from our beastly ancestors, but when you come right down to it, the mindless primitive is always there. We pretend that we have civilized the 'beast' with our laws, our religious beliefs, and our culture, but all we've done is enraged, inflamed and frustrated it."

She strained against the crushing weight on her body that pinned her to the bed.

"Until that day, when it strikes and goes on a rampage killing twenty children and six adults at an elementary school," Monroe continued, "we delude ourselves by asking all of the wrong questions, such as, what happened and why; when we should be asking, *what stops five billion people from doing the same thing*? That's the question that should keep you up at night. What's going to happen on the day when we all realize we can no longer control the beast?"

"I don't know," she snarled, struggling, still trapped in that zone between wakefulness and dreams, "but you had better thank your sorry ass that it won't be today."

Then Kate threw everything into wrestling the weight of the elephant off her chest, determined once and for all to take control. She had had enough bullshit for one night.

She knew it was time to wake up and sound the alarm.

And then, almost on cue, her phone rang.

She awoke to the guitar riff on Eric Clapton's first five bars of *Layla*. As the ring tone on her iPhone repeated, Kate lunged for it as if it were her only lifeline to reality.

The words she heard from the other end of the telephone were coarse and unpolished; they were also some of the best words that she had ever heard in her life. When she first picked up the receiver, Kate had half expected it was a collect call that John Monroe had placed from hell. Now, she couldn't put a name to the voice, but she knew the instant she heard, it belonged to a fellow cop.

The policeman barked out a few terse sentences, but since her intoxicated brain had not yet fully connected with her higher brain functions, the words 'murder' and 'suicide' were the only two words that registered with her. She scribbled down the address at Cesar Chavez Street in Noe Valley and turned to wrap up her call.

"Yeah, okay," she said, not entirely awake. "I'll be there as soon as I can."

Kate went to her small bathroom and splashed cold water in her face. She hunched over the sink and looked at the image in the mirror. She almost didn't recognize the reflection of her own face that starred back. She looked pale and drawn, the flesh around her eyes loose and sallow.

"Holy shit!" she said to her own reflection.

A few moments passed before she had managed the strength and wherewithal to get herself together and out the door.

Kate lived in a small studio apartment at Bayside Village in the heart of San Francisco's South Beach; one of the city's trendiest neighborhoods. She had always wanted to live there, a few steps from the water's edge. So, when her marriage ended with her daughter's death, she managed to call in every last favor that the boys down at the precinct owed her to make the dream a reality.

But she soon learned that dreams like hers came with a hefty price tag. No matter how hard Kate tried to enjoy her early morning strolls along the Embarcadero or the Giants' games at nearby AT&T Park or the convenient shopping for fruit and vegetables at the market, she still felt empty inside.

The events of the last several months hadn't made things any better for her. In particular, the death of her partner at the hands of the serial killer, who she both loved and feared.

She blamed herself for Frank Miller's death and for the death of that poor, twisted college girl, Rosemary Murphy. And no matter how many medals they wanted to pin on her for stopping Dr. John Monroe, Kate didn't feel like a hero. She felt more like the professor's last victim.

As Kate walked down the stairs from her third-floor apartment to street level, she pulled on a pair of $1200 Louis Vuitton sunglasses she bought at the flea market for twenty-five dollars. She needed them to shield her eyes and evidence of a hangover from the harsh light of day.

The trendy sunglasses, constructed out of a lightweight titanium, looked stylish on her face. A way for Kate to hide the way she felt on the inside, looking put together on the outside. She knew they were cheap knockoffs when she bought them, but she figured that no one else would know, or if they did, say anything about it. On an inspector's salary, Kate could not afford most of the finer things in life, but that did not mean she had to look as though she shopped at a discount store.

Kate was also smart enough to know that in a city like San Francisco, where the eligible single women outnumbered the men by six to one, she needed every advantage she could muster. Not only to compete with women her own age, but those ten and fifteen years younger as well. So, for outward appearances, her clothes were Versace or Marc Jacobs, shoes were Stuart Weitzman, handbag Fendi, fragrance by Coco Chanel, and an Omega timepiece. These were accessories to an expensive costume.

When her credit was good, she would reinvent herself into someone other than the real woman inside. She also carried a twelve-shot .9-millimeter Beretta in a triple-draw holster under her left arm and was trained in martial-arts to deliver a blow of deadly force.

Kate continued walking along the sidewalk to her car. Attractive, but not the woman that most men would have crossed the street and regarded with a second glance, her looks came more from effort than nature. After all, she had had a child in her twenties and never recovered the figure she once had. Her expensive haircut, cosmetic features, and designer suits masked an urban woman living on the edge.

As Kate approached the spot on the street where she had parked her expensive 5-series BMW the night before, she pulled out her keys and pressed the "unlock" button of her key-fob instinctively. When her car failed to chirp in response, she pressed it again. Only then did she realize that her titanium-silver BMW 5.25i coupe had been replaced by a Silver Birch Aston Martin, which was roughly about the same size and shape and color.

"Dammit!" she shouted, blowing her cool demeanor.

"Of all the freakin' days for this to happen!"

She was silent for a minute or two, standing at the edge of the curb, looking up and down the street for some sign that her worst nightmare wasn't true. But she could not find it. The finance company had repossessed her car again during the night, she conceded. It was her own damn fault.

She could not manage to keep her personal affairs in order.

How difficult was it to write a check once a month and put it in the mail or to have an automatic deduction from her account? She shook her head then pounded on the roof of the Aston Martin, like a child throwing a temper tantrum.

Her tantrum triggered the car's security system, and a loud honking sound was blasting the street with noise, alerting everyone in a three-block range.

"Hey! Hey, what are you doing!" a middle-aged, African-American man shouted, waving his right fist at her.

"That's my car."

Kate sobered up. She stopped pounding on the car roof and straightened her back. She felt there were dozens of eyes looking at her, watching her every movement, and she wasn't too far off the mark. Several shopkeepers, pedestrians, bicyclists, and even a taxi driver had stopped to see what the racket was all about. Kate caught a glimpse of their reflections in the window.

"Shit," Kate said to herself.

She turned and nodded to the Aston Martin owner as if he was an old friend or acquaintance she expected to meet.

"I'm really sorry," Kate replied, playing to the bystanders. "This is where I parked last night, and I thought it was my car."

"This is *my* car, lady," he snarled, clicking the button on his remote access key to turn off the security alarm. He inspected the vehicle for damage, first surveying the roof for any signs of a scratch or dent and next moved to examine the body for dings to the car's original paint scheme. "I'd be very surprised if your car looks anything like this one."

"Look, I said I was sorry," she repeated.

The man pumped his chest up, like a proud father.

"Less than one hundred and twenty-five of these were produced by hand and came off the assembly line during the production years 1963 to 1965," he explained, gliding his right hand over the hood of the car. "This is a vintage 1964 Aston Martin DB-5 coupe with all of its original equipment in perfect working order. It has a magnesium-alloy body, an all-aluminum 4.0-liter engine, a robust three-speed Borg-Warner DG automatic transmission, and three SU carburetors which produce 282 brake horsepower, and a top speed of 145 miles per hour. It is highly unlikely that you have ever seen a vehicle like this one, outside a museum or an automobile show."

For an instant, he reminded Kate of her former partner, Frank Miller, and a smile came across her face.

That's exactly the way Frank used to talk about the Victorian home he had purchased in Pacific Heights with his retirement fund. Well, maybe not the same words and phrases, but clearly that same sense of pride and accomplishment at having worked a lifetime to acquire the one thing that gave life meaning. She didn't have that in her life, and perhaps never would. But as she stared at the man's dark features, which had grown weathered and worn with age, she could see it in his face. She recalled what Frank Miller told her about the limited opportunities that he had as a black man growing up, and how much he wanted to live in a Victorian mansion, not just serve in one.

Kate listened, imagining how this man must have felt when he first saw this car in his youth. Probably devoted a lifetime of scrimping, saving, and doing without, so one day he would own a car just like it. She looked down at the man's feet, and nodded, acknowledging the old wing-tipped Oxford loafers *he* wore and Frank *used* to wear. She surmised that the man had an old rumpled trench coat hanging on his back door at home, as well.

"You're right, Frank. It's got character," she said, still in her reverie, recalling the first conversation they had had about the old Victorian.

"My name is not Frank," he replied, "and you've not heard a single word I've said."

"I'm sorry. You remind me of someone I used to know."

"Yeah, I'm sure. We must all look alike to people like you," he admonished, his eyes flashing at Kate. With a half-a-dozen onlookers recording everything with their cell phone cameras, the man played right into the hands of his audience. He exaggerated his movements as he conducted one final inspection of the car, and then he turned back to her. "I'd appreciate it now if you'd just back away from my car and go about your business. The show's over."

"Look, if there are any damages to your car, I'd be more than happy to reimburse you for them."

"Lady, I don't want your money. I never want to take another dime from someone like you again," he said with a huff, a huge chip weighing heavily upon his shoulder. The man climbed into the driver's seat, cranked it, put the car in gear, and pulled away from the curb without a backward glance.

Kate stood there dumbfounded as the vehicle accelerated down the street. She was ashamed to admit that her life was such a mess and that it took the actions of a perfect stranger to put it all into perspective.

For months, she had blamed herself for Frank Miller's death and had wallowed in her own self-loathing, like an over-stuffed pig in mud. If Miller were still alive, he would have set her straight. Now she had a very clear choice of her own: she could either keep feeling sorry for herself, or do something about it. At long last, she decided it was time to get her act together and make Frank proud.

Kate reached for her cell phone and dialed a familiar number. "Hello, Clark, could you send a car for me?" she said into the receiver. "Yeah, I'm having car trouble again."

Forty minutes later, the black-and-white squad car turned the corner at Church and Cesar Chavez and pulled up next to another police car parked along the 3900 block of the street. Inspector Dawson leaned over the front seat to thank the two patrol cops for the lift and looked right up at the small, brown split-level home through the windshield.

She found the familiar crime-scene carnival.

Uniformed police officers were erecting a makeshift barrier to contain neighbors and other interested bystanders, while dozens of other uniformed cops and plain-clothed detectives moved in and out of the house. Several of the tech guys were gathering samples. At the same time, a police spokesman was talking with reporters. Police cruisers were parked everywhere, and the atmosphere was charged with the static of police radios that echoed through the quiet neighborhood.

Inspector Dawson climbed out of the back seat of the squad car and stepped onto the pavement. She looked up and down the street and surveyed the crime scene. The neighborhood had seen more than its fair share of crime in the last ten or twelve years, with robberies and rapes at the top of the list. But she could not recall the last time a homicide took place here, much less a multiple homicide.

Things were changing, and not for the better.

Like so many other neighborhoods in the city, Noe Valley

started out as a working-class neighborhood for families that lived and worked in the area's once-thriving blue-collar economy. It was developed as a sub-division just after the 1906 Earthquake, with its borders set between twenty-second and thirtieth streets with Dolores Street to the East and Grand View Avenue to the west. The neighborhood welcomed poor and lower-income residents who were not afraid to get their hands dirty working manual labor jobs ten hours a day. Noe Valley, at one point in time, had the highest concentration of row houses in the city, with streets having four to six and sometimes as many as a dozen on the same side of the street. The rest of the homes were a mixture of the classic Victorian and Edwardian residential architecture for which San Francisco is famous.

For nearly a hundred years, the residents lived, worked, and died within these ten blocks. They were traditionally conservative, Catholic, and kept pretty much to themselves.

The children all attended the same elementary school and high school their parents and grandparents once attended; then on Sundays, the pews of St. Paul's Catholic Church were filled to capacity at each of the five services.

But in the last twenty years, as wealthy speculators bought up property in the less prosperous community and bulldozed row homes to build mansions, the move toward gentrification changed the make-up of the neighborhood.

Many of the lower-income residents could no longer afford to live in the community as home prices and property taxes climbed. That forced them to seek cheaper residences in the nearby Mission District and other locales. Still, others fought to hold onto the property that had been in their family for years, resisting the temptation to sell out to developers who planned to build one- and two-million-dollar homes for urban professionals. Noe Valley was clearly a neighborhood in transition, with upscale homes built adjacent to the old Victorians. A clash of cultures was inevitable as the old gave way to the new, and the rich displaced the poor.

With her badge worn conspicuously on her hip, Kate pushed her way past the police at the front door and nodded at several uniformed officers she passed in the foyer.

She noticed the husband sitting next to a friend or neighbor in the living room with hands on his head under the watchful eyes of a uniformed cop. Kate paused briefly to look at the "friend." He was ruggedly handsome but seemed to be completely out of place, sitting there with the Bible open in front of him. She didn't know where he belonged, but he definitely didn't belong there.

She followed the coroner's investigators out to the backyard where she found Dr. Edgar Brogan, a portly medical examiner with windblown cheeks and bloodshot eyes, working the bodies one at a time. Mikhail and a couple other homicide detectives stood huddled in a corner, listening to William go over his notes with them. Some forensics guys were sifting through the trash in the yard for evidence, while a police photographer snapped pictures.

Jorge handed Kate a cup of coffee. "I figured you could use some caffeine, partner," he said, his face pale, like a white, linen shroud. The young inspector looked like he was the one who really needed a good stiff drink, and not just coffee. "*Madre de dios.* What demon would have possessed a woman like that to murder her five children and then take her own life?"

"I don't know," Kate replied, taking a sip of coffee, "but I guess that's what we are here to find out."

"*Cuando el diablo no tiene que hacer con el rabo mata moscas,*" he said, looking at Kate. Then, when Jorge realized that she had not understood him, he repeated, "In my culture, we say, 'the devil finds work for idle hands' to remind people to keep busy. But it also has another meaning, a deeper meaning. Those who sit around all day, doing nothing—no hobby, no running errands, no care for children, no attempt to better themselves—are pressed into service by the devil's spawn to do something wrong. This is the work of a very bad demon."

"Let's not get all weirded-out now, Jorge," Kate said, patting his back. "We have no reason to think there are supernatural forces at work here; just a few murders and a suicide."

"You're right," he confessed, putting on a calm demeanor.

"Frank used to say that every crime scene has its own story to tell," she said, with a distant look in her face.

"We just have to slow ourselves down and listen very carefully to the whispers of truth it has to offer." Kate paused for a moment and listened. "Do you feel you've calmed down now? Are you ready to listen for those whispers of truth?"

Jorge shrugged his square shoulders.

"Good," she replied, "Now let's put our ears to the ground and see if we turn up something the others haven't found yet, like motive."

"Right," Jorge agreed. He smiled warmly at her and walked down the cement path toward the murder scene.

Kate was eager to join him, but she lingered just long enough to swallow down the rest of her coffee. For the last hour or so she fought a headache from the booze and lack of sleep, so caffeine became her drug of choice. If she could work out the science behind it, she could inject the coffee directly into her bloodstream. She figured it was likely to be a long morning, and her body would have never made it without some kind of stimulant. She was about to set the cup down when two large, calloused hands took it from her grasp.

"You've been drinking again," Lieutenant James Roberts said.

The head of Homicide brought the empty cup to his nose and sniffed inside, then ran a finger around the bottom of the cup for trace evidence.

"Just coffee," she replied.

"Don't fuck with me today, Dawson. I'm in no mood."

Startled by his tone, Kate took a step back.

Roberts was a big, hulking man who towered over her, like a modern-day Goliath. She had never liked the Lieutenant, but she attributed that more to the fact that her late partner often clashed with him over departmental operations rather than a personal, deep-seated dislike. James Roberts had no imagination. He was such a slave to the job's routine that he never thought outside the box, and that's where, Kate reasoned, most good, investigative police-work happened. She had a name for men like him: pragmatist. He was the very model of a pragmatist, a person with all four feet on the ground.

"Okay, if you must know, I had a drink last night, maybe two," she confessed, without guilt. "I don't recall reading any regulations that prohibit a cop from having a drink or two when they're off duty."

"A homicide detective is never off duty," he said.

"Well, if that's true, then maybe you should take that up with my union rep. I'm sure he'd have something to say about that."

Roberts scratched the stubble of beard that was growing on his face and then reached up to adjust the small horned-rim glasses on the end of his nose as if to bring the microscopic image of the female police inspector into focus. "Your union contract states that you're supposed to be physically fit and ready to work your shift on time, every day," he reminded her. "You were late again this morning. Christ, how many times does it make this week? Three? Four? I've lost track."

"I had car trouble," she protested.

"You can only claim to have car trouble if you actually have a car. Impounded cars don't count."

Kate nodded. "I'll have that fixed this afternoon."

Roberts shot her one of his patented steely looks. "I can also spot a hangover from a mile away," he said, with a sense of pride. "Your eyes are so bloodshot you can barely see out of them."

Kate folded her arms across her chest and looked down.

"Must have been one helluva party last night, Inspector," he concluded, raising his hands above his head, shaking them like tambourines and dancing a two-step. "Let them Wild Turkey chasers flow."

She was silent for long moment then said, "What would you know about it, sir?"

"Nothing. Not a damn thing," he replied.

"Personally, I don't give a fuck if you drink alcohol every night and wake up every morning feeling like shit. But as long as you carry a gun and a badge, I expect you to be the model of the perfect police officer between eight a.m. and five p.m. You got that?"

"Yes, sir."

"Keep your eleven o'clock."

"Now, wait a minute, Lieutenant," she said, knowing that her protest would set him off. "Do you want me to work the crime scene, or do you want me to meet with the fucking department shrink?"

"I want you to do what I tell you to do," he snorted, then pushed his way past her. Thumping his chest, Roberts added, loud enough for everyone to hear, "The last time I checked my name was on the door as the head of the department, not yours. You do what I tell you to do, or you find yourself another job."

"This is bullshit, Lieutenant!" Kate blurted out, unaware that their private conversation had turned public. As she turned and looked around, she saw everyone had stopped what they were doing and were watching the two of them. She straightened up, brushed the folds out of her Versace blazer, and tried to pull the rest of herself together.

"You only have yourself to blame for that, Dawson."

Lieutenant Roberts walked away from her, starting down the concrete path that led from the back of the house to the large oak tree. He barked out several orders, and all at once, the crime scene was a flurry of activity again. The forensics team returned to sifting through the trash in the yard for evidence, while the police photographer continued to snap pictures of the crime scene. Mikhail had pulled Jorge into a conversation and was arguing with the other two homicide detectives, while his partner William Clark scribbled a few notes into his notebook. Two uniformed cops stood around talking, not in any hurry to return to their beat.

Neither was the Lieutenant. Roberts just stood back and watched the action unfold, his chest pumped up, his hands raised in the air like a conductor before a symphony orchestra.

"Asshole," she whispered under her breath. Then she caught a glimpse of something out of the corner of her eye.

In the shadow of the oak tree, just beyond the hustle and bustle of the scene-of-the-crime boys, Kate watched as two members of the coroner's office took the bodies of the children down from the tree. Yet, when laying them out on the ground, the team treated them with gentleness; in order of birth, from the youngest to the oldest.

One by one, they untied the knot and removed the nylon rope from around the child's neck then carried the child between them, placing the small body on a simple white cotton sheet. Each body was then covered with another white cotton sheet.

Kate's bloodshot eyes misted over, and a tear ran down the

side of her cheek as the five little angels were laid to rest. She thought about her own daughter and started to recite the Lord's Prayer to herself when Roberts's bombastic hollering made her jump and crashed the solemnity of the scene when calling his team of investigators together.

"Okay, so what have we got?" he demanded.

Clark waved his notebook in the air. "All five victims were children, aged six years to eighteen months," he said, reading from the page. He stepped gingerly over their little bodies, identifying each one as he spoke. "Sarah was the eldest. Then Hope and Charity were the twins, followed by Rachel and Connor. They are related by blood as siblings and members of the Ross family."

Kate flashed raised eyebrows at Jorge, standing buddy-buddy with Mikhail and the other two homicide detectives, as she crossed to join Clark on the opposite side of the yard. She hunched down over the bodies of the children and pulled back the white shroud that covered the eldest, Sarah. The bright morning sunlight cast a warm glow on the child's pale cheeks. She seemed to flush and come to life, but only for a moment. Kate covered the face of the little girl with the shroud and stood up. "How long have the children been dead?"

"Their skin turns gray when I press it. This kind of discoloration is about right for eight to ten hours," the medical examiner replied.

He looked down at the dial on the thermometer he placed in the mother's abdomen and checked his watch.

"Eighty-nine degrees, give or take an hour for each degree, places the time of death around eleven p.m., plus or minus."

"We might as well make it official," the Lieutenant said, addressing Brogan but looking into the faces of each of his detectives. "We can speculate all we want, but I want the cause of death entered into the record."

"Physical evidence suggests the children died from asphyxia due to hanging. It is consistent with the injuries to the neck and the overall condition of the bodies." Dr. Brogan concluded. "In laymen's terms, when the ligature—rope—tightened around the child's neck, it choked off or forced the closure of the carotid artery, causing cerebral ischemia. Cerebral ischemia is the condition where there is insufficient blood flow to meet the metabolic demands of the brain, and that lack of oxygenated blood is why a victim loses consciousness and expires. Each of the children probably expired in a manner of minutes."

"What about the mother?" William Clark asked, pencil in hand, ready to add the transcript to his notes.

"I'm afraid to say that things are not as clear cut for her," Brogan said, with a deep sigh, "and I would be lying if I told you, with one hundred percent certainty, this was a suicide."

"Are you saying it wasn't a suicide?" Roberts asked.

"I'm saying, I don't know," the medical examiner replied. With much effort, the chubby man squatted down over the mother's body and pulled a hand out from under the white shroud. He pointed to the woman's fingers. "The fingers on both of Wendy's hands are badly bruised, and the fingernails are cyanotic—blue."

"Blue," Mikhail repeated.

"When I first examined Wendy Ross, the injuries to the neck and body were consistent with a woman who killed each one of her children without resistance and then put a noose around her own neck and jumped to her death," he said, counting each of the points on his hand. "The body was hanging there from the tree, right next to the branch she used to hang her toddler. Her arms dangling at her side, her feet—the toes pointed straight down—were about four inches from the ground. She was dead as a doornail, having suffered the same asphyxiation as her children. By all intents and purposes, it appears she planned and executed her own death flawlessly. End of story."

"But . . ." Roberts interjected.

"But the physical evidence suggests that Wendy Ross might have had a change of heart about committing suicide or struggled against someone who wanted to make it look like she committed suicide. In a possible last-minute attempt to break free of her strangulation, the thirty-four-year-old woman must have reached up with both hands and put her fingers between her neck and the noose. The compression on the fingers would account for the bruised knuckles and the cyanotic fingernails I found. With her brain slowly dying due to lack of oxygen, she may have realized that she only had a couple of minutes, more or less, to force the rope over her neck before she lost consciousness and died. She must have tried everything she could think of to break free. But in the end, the weight of her body and the force of gravity were far too much for her to overcome."

"But if you found her arms dangling free, someone must have tampered with the body," Kate said.

"Exactly," Brogan replied. "We should have found the fingers from both of Wendy's hands between the rope and her neck, not dangling at her side. That's why most people who are hanged have their hands tied behind their back."

"The husband?" Mikhail suggested.

Lieutenant Roberts nodded his head. "You've got a better suspect?"

"No, but then I'm fresh out of motives, too," Mikhail said. "I can't figure out why a woman would murder her entire family, and then take her own life?"

"Why would a father kill all of his children and then try to frame his wife for the children's murders?" Clark asked.

"*Madre de dios*," Jorge said and made the sign of the cross. "This is truly the work of a demon."

Mikhail turned to Jorge. "You said it, brother."

"Suppose the husband didn't do it," Kate countered, pacing, pulling her thoughts together. For an instant, she glimpsed the Lieutenant watching her. His determined blue eyes were unsettling, like beams from these great searchlights of truth that swept over her face, penetrating her brain and reading her thoughts. She tried her best to shake them off and stick to the point. "Why would he care if it looked like his wife had second thoughts about what she was doing? More importantly, why did he sit on his hands for ten hours before he called 911?"

"Yeah, come to think of it, why didn't he call 911 sooner?"

"Far too many questions—" Mikhail began to say.

"—and not enough answers!" Clark finished his partner's sentence.

The Lieutenant scratched the stubble of beard growing on his face, thinking, then said, "Wasn't there a recent murder-suicide in Oakland that bears some of the same characteristics as this one?"

Inspector Clark nodded, thumbing back through his notes. "It didn't get much play in the press, but I remember taking a note about it. Yes, here it is. Sixty-nine-year-old Gladys Stevens poisoned her four grandchildren and herself in an apparent murder-suicide."

"But it wasn't a murder-suicide," Kate said. "That's right," Mikhail said, jabbing his partner in the ribs, while Clark rifled through his notes.

"The old woman poisoned her grandchildren, but it turned out to be a mistake, nothing more," she added.

"Well, what about it, Clark?" Roberts asked. "The Alameda County coroner initially ruled it as a murder-suicide," Clark reported, reading from his notes. "But upon further investigation of the crime scene—and with the cooperation of the children's parents—he determined the deaths were accidental."

Kate tried not to frown, but the look was all over her face. "Ms. Gladys Stevens stored rat poison in the same pantry she kept her baking goods," Kate explained. "She had problems with glaucoma, and her eyes were not as sharp as they once were. So, when she went to make chocolate chip cookies as a treat for her grandkids, she reached in the pantry for sugar and came up with poison."

"*Madre de dios,*" Jorge repeated. "Good grief!"

Mikhail exclaimed.

"I can't imagine the grief those parents must have felt coming home to find their children dead," she said.

Kate's train of thought was trying to connect the dots. "As a matter of record, we should run down all the other apparent murder-suicides within the Bay area, see if there's any connection."

"Clark, see to it," Roberts ordered. "Gimme everything you can find, say, in the last month or so."

"Do you want me to include that bizarre house fire up in Walnut Creek?" Clark asked. "You know the one, where the six children died of smoke inhalation, but the parents escaped with only minor injuries."

"Sure. Just report anything out of the ordinary," Roberts added.

"Affirmative."

Lieutenant James Roberts walked over and tapped Jorge on the shoulder. "Ramirez, I want you to bring Philip Ross in for questioning. Make it look routine, and for Christ's sake, keep it quiet. We don't want a media circus down at the precinct," Roberts explained, "And we certainly don't want them polluting our investigation with a lot of unsupported rumors and half-assed opinions from Monday morning quarter-backs. If anybody asks you, just say it's routine, and leave it at that."

"Understood, sir." Jorge nodded.

"Clark, I want you and Dawson to do the interview."

Lt. Roberts was desperate for answers, and regardless of his personal feelings about the female inspector in his department, he knew Kate was the best at interrogating suspects. "Get him first thing in the morning before he's had his breakfast. That should soften him up a bit, and make him more anxious to talk with us."

"Agreed," William said, noting the time in his notebook.

"Thanks, Lieutenant," she said.

"Don't thank me, Dawson," he replied sourly. "Just be there on time, and for Pete's sake, be sober."

CHAPTER TWO

Booking at the Central Booking office was a tedious process that morning because the suspects had to be processed by hand. There were electrical outages all over the building, and most of the computers were down. Kate suspected the power grid for most of the city's buildings hadn't been updated in years, and they were just one major disaster away from the Stone Age. The extra time it took to photograph the suspects for their mug shots with print film, fingerprint with ink, and take saliva swabs for a DNA test cost the department time they didn't have. Kate and her partner Jorge had to wade through the slow process of handwritten paperwork just so they could question Philip.

By the time Dawson huffed and puffed the three flights of stairs to the police psychiatrist's office on the sixth floor of the Hall of Justice, San Francisco Police Department headquarters, the clock was showing eleven-fourteen a.m. Outside the door, she bent over and put her head between her knees, trying to catch her breath, drinking in deep gulps of air between clenched teeth. She knew she was out of shape—the booze and sleepless nights—but didn't realize how bad it was until she found the elevator out and forced herself to run up the stairs. *Thank God, she cast out a secret prayer, Roberts had not seen me fight to catch my breath or he would have pulled my badge for sure.*

She watched the digital clock click over to eleven-fifteen a.m., and reached for the office door. "I'm sorry, Dr. Glass," Kate said as she pushed into his office. "I got hung up at Booking and just lost track of the time."

Kate seemed more upset at her tardiness than the staff psychiatrist did. Dr. Barry Glass was leaning back in his great leather chair, eyes closed, listening to Don Giovanni on his iPod, oblivious to everything around him. At fifty-nine years, the balding 1970s Berkeley graduate had been with the department for nearly thirty years. Not once did he breach ethics or have one departmental policy violation in all the time he served the SFPD. Dr. Glass was the model of professionalism, even though his appearance and dress were unconventional for a member of the police department.

He sported a white beard kept neatly trimmed, and put what was left of his hair in a long white ponytail. He also preferred wearing loud, flashy Hawaiian shirts from Tommy Bahama to a suit and tie. At one-hundred-fifty dollars per shirt, Kate knew they were too rich for her pocketbook, but then she recalled that besides working as the department shrink, Barry Glass consulted at San Francisco General and was an honorary board member on the State Board of Psychiatric Health in Napa. In addition to his real passion, which was opera, Glass had filled his office with photographs of his wife, six children, and thirteen grandchildren.

Kate was caught off guard looking at the pictures of Dr. Glass' family when the staff psychiatrist leaned forward in his chair. "You've not hid your feelings about this process," Glass said, removing the ear buds from his head. "I'm really not too surprised about your being late. A little passive-aggressive behavior?"

"No, I was caught up in Booking," she replied.

He nodded, as if genuinely satisfied by her answer.

"Okay, that's fine," the doctor said. "Why don't you sit down? We'll talk, have a cup of tea, and just relax. No harm in that."

Kate shrugged.

Like most cops, she had never cared much for shrinks and had harbored doubt lurking deep down inside of her about the practice of psychiatry. She felt it was demeaning to be forced to talk about her feelings with a stranger who was most likely going to go home and jerk off over something she revealed. After her recent experience with Dr. John Monroe, she had grown to despise the way they played head games to trick you into saying something you had no intention to say. She also felt there was something downright creepy about being able to look into a person's soul and tell them what they were thinking.

After her daughter's death, she spent a few months with a therapist, trying to pull the pieces back together, and was prescribed Trazodone, an anti-depressant that made her weak and vulnerable. Kate spent a lot of time crying and feeling restless, down about herself, and suicidal. When she finally stopped taking the drug, she vowed that she would never let another person get that far into her head again . . . and then she met John Monroe.

Folding her arms across her chest, she sat down hard on the couch. Kate didn't want to be there, and her body language said it all. Dr. Glass looked at her crossed arms. She was self-protective and closed-off. *Her defenses are up, he concluded. She has a great deal of anxiety, likely driven by a lack of trust and sense of vulnerability.*

"How do you feel?" Dr. Glass asked, folding his hands on the table.

"That's a loaded question," she replied.

"Not at all. I want to know how you are feeling."

"I'm never sure how I'm supposed to respond to that question. Do I pretend and say I'm 'fine' and get thrown into the booby hatch because you think I'm delusional? Or do I answer honestly and tell you that I'm feeling shitty and end up in the hospital with tubes in and out the yin-yang on a seventy-two-hour deathwatch?"

"Naturally, I would prefer it if you answered honestly," he replied.

"Okay, I'm fine."

"Fine?"

"Come on, Dr. Glass!" she protested, sitting up straight on the couch. "That's the kind of head games that Monroe used to play with me. He would lure me into a very safe place within myself then ask me these open-ended questions that would make me feel very vulnerable before he pounced."

"Is that what you think I'm doing?"

"Yeah, I do."

Dr. Barry Glass paused for a moment, and leaned back in his chair. He put his hands together and created a point with his two forefingers. Then he balanced his head on the point, thinking.

"Why don't you let me make you a nice cup of tea? Chamomile will relax you, and refresh your spirit."

Kate shook her head. "I don't want to be relaxed. I like being on the edge. It's what keeps me alive. Without an edge, I'm weak and vulnerable."

"Well, the sooner we get through these sessions, the sooner you'll be able to put them behind you. You know as well as I do, I don't make the policy."

"The policy is bullshit, Dr. Glass. It lets people like you dissect me, cut open old wounds."

The doctor smiled knowingly. "Nearly every cop who has ever been sent to my office for psychiatric evaluation has said the same thing, but it couldn't be further from the truth. I am not your enemy here. Anything you tell me stays right here in this office and never leaves this room."

"Really?"

"Let's put our cards on the table, shall we?" Dr.Glass asked, leaning forward in his chair. "These sessions are mandated by Internal Affairs. It's standard procedure for any cop who's been through a traumatic experience. Plus, in this instance, a suspect was shot during the course of the investigation."

"Rosemary Murphy was not just shot, Dr. Glass," Kate corrected him. "I killed her. I emptied all six shots of my service revolver into that poor girl's body without hesitation. You know what a .38 caliber round does to a person. She was dead even before she hit the ground."

"So you feel guilty?"

Kate was silent for a long moment, and then said, "Yes, I can't imagine feeling any other way. Who wouldn't feel guilty?"

"That's very healthy."

"You know, I knew you were going to say that," she replied sarcastically. "And then next you're going to be telling me that, as a police officer, I have a responsibility to the community I serve to protect it from violent offenders, even if it means the use of lethal force."

Dr. Glass bobbed his head in acknowledgement.

"Rosemary Murphy wasn't a violent offender," Kate said, in order to set the record straight once and for all. "She was a sick, twisted little girl who had been abused years earlier by a child molester. Then, she was so manipulated by John Monroe, she became the perfect patsy in his serial murder spree. I was so convinced she was another 'Crystal Rose' that when I broke down his apartment door and saw Rosemary Murphy standing there striking him with a whip, I reacted. I didn't think. I just saw John in danger and reacted."

The doctor made some notes in Kate's file, open on the desk in front of him. He wrote longhand on an electronic pad connected to his computer and translated it into a Word file. He was silent and focused when he wrote and paused only to check the time before he resumed his notes. "Are you sure I can't offer you some tea?"

"No thanks, Doc," she repeated.

Dr. Glass reviewed the notes he had written in her file.

"Trauma of this type manifests itself in other areas of our lives and makes things more difficult to handle than they need be. For example, are you having any trouble sleeping? Do you find yourself given over to impulsive acts? Are you hearing voices, or are you otherwise troubled by memories of the past? Anything like that? Because I can prescribe something to help you cope with those issues."

Kate was experiencing all of those things, but she felt if she was honest with him she'd find herself on another anti-depressant and then staring down the barrel of her own gun. "No," she lied.

"What about your personal life? Anything to report? Anything you'd like to tell me about?"

"My personal life?" Kate repeated the question back to him, and then realized that he was asking about her sex life. She paused and smiled to herself. There really was no point in lying to him. "My personal life is shit. I work ten-hour shifts every day, five days a week, and then on Saturdays I catch up on all the paperwork that I didn't get finished during the week. There's no time left over to have a personal life. I consider myself lucky if I can squeeze in a one-night stand from time to time."

"Drinking? What about alcohol, Kate?" he probed.

"Yes, I have a drink every so often," she lied, "but it's no big deal."

Dr. Glass picked up the file folder from his desk and looked inside. "I have a report here from your supervisor," he said. "Lieutenant James Roberts says you drink to excess and report to work drunk or with a hangover."

"That happened once," she lied, again. "What about drugs?"

"Nothing."

"No coke?"

"No coke. No amphetamines," Kate said emphatically. "Dr. Glass, I told you I work my ass off six days a week. I don't have time for drugs. I don't even have time for a personal life."

The doctor paused a moment before replying. "Let's get something straight, Inspector. I don't have a beef to pick with you. I'm not here to trip you up, and I'm not working with Internal Affairs to get you fired. Frankly, I prefer to find people in perfect mental health."

Kate nodded. "Okay then," she replied. "Will you tell them I'm all right? That I'm just your average, healthy, overworked and underpaid civil servant."

Barry Glass smiled warmly. "Sure, no problem."

Kate climbed to her feet and started for the door.

"I'll see you next week, Kate," the doctor said, "at the same time."

"But—" she started to raise a protest.

"These sessions are mandated, you know," Dr. Glass interrupted, then took her file in hand and started to sort the materials on his desk into the file folder. "As long as Internal Affairs wants you to meet with me, we'll meet on a regular basis and talk about how things are going. Maybe next time you'll even have that cup of tea."

Kate and Glass exchanged glances, like the crossing of swords, and then she pushed her way out of his office.

At five-fifteen p.m., Kate and her partner Jorge saddled up to the bar at McGinty's Public House and ordered a couple of drinks. They were joined a few minutes later by William, Mikhail, and a few of the other members of the Homicide Bureau. Kate was still feeling vulnerable after her run-in with Lieutenant Roberts earlier in the day, as well as the department shrink, but she tried to hide her feelings behind a mask of fun. Not everything was as dour as it seemed. She accomplished something by settling the debt on her car and arranging a loan through the Police Credit Union. She was growing up. For two years, Kate struggled to keep her car on the road. That was something worth celebrating, and on her tab she ordered the first round for her friends.

McGinty's Public House was a bar located a few blocks from the Hall of Justice and was favored by members of the San Francisco Police Department for its hospitality.

The Irish-owned and managed bar was modeled after the traditional pubs in Ireland, Scotland, and Wales, and it sold hard drinks to the older, more conservative law-and-order crowd. They specialized in hamburger sliders, deep-fried chicken wings, and greasy fries. Even though McGinty's Public House was a one of a kind, every city had a bar just like it; a place where cops could go to have a couple of drinks with friends, throw a few darts at the dart board, and just unwind after a hard day of protecting the city.

Johnnie O'Flynn, a third generation Irish-American, poured the drinks at the bar in much the same way that his father and grandfather poured before him. Straight up shots of bourbon and full-bodied beers filled the counter for the thirsty patrons.

With both hands, Kate picked up her shot of Wild Turkey and the beer chaser and followed William, Mikhail, and Jorge with their drinks to an empty table. She sat down, with her back to the bar, and took a sip of the bourbon before slugging back half of the beer in one gulp. "Ahhhhhhhhhhh," she exhaled in satisfaction and licked her lips. It tasted mighty good to her.

"Now, tell me again, Clark," she asked, feeling good, "why you think the wife did it and not the husband."

"Because statistics show that more mothers than fathers kill their children under five years of age," he replied, without looking at his notes. "More than two hundred women kill their children each year. I know this is supposed to be shocking—the idea that a mother could possibly be of greater danger to her kids than big, bad dad—but statistics don't lie. Homicide is one of the leading causes of death of children under the age five, and when you look at the rolls of women who are currently on death row, eleven of the forty-nine are there because they killed their children."

"But your statistics don't explain the reason why," she said.

"They're not my statistics," Clark said, defending himself. He took a good stiff drink of his caffeine-free Sprite and put the glass down. "The explanation seems obvious enough: it's because women are usually the primary caregiver in any household and thus more likely to be dealing with demanding children throughout the day. If you couple that with an absentee father, the stress is that much higher and the likelihood of violence that much more."

Mikhail spoke up. "My money is still on the father.

He seemed awfully cool and collected for a guy ho had just come home from a prayer meeting to find his wife and children dead."

"You noticed that, too," Kate said, taking another sip of the bourbon and swigging the strong brown beer down as if she needed it to sustain her very existence. She smacked her lips and quickly downed another.

"The father," Jorge added, "didn't seem to be in much hurry to make that 911 call. I say he was possessed by a demon."

"Say that one more time," Mikhail cautioned, "and I'm getting an exorcist."

"You making fun of me?"

"No, never," Mikhail said, and then smiled a big, toothy grin.

Clark leaned forward in his chair and said, "Did any of you get a good look at the guy Ross called for spiritual advice? He looked like some backwoodsman who had just come in from chopping down trees. I would have never taken him for some Bible-thumper. Maybe Paul Bunyan, but not a Bible-thumper."

"I thought he was really hot," Kate sighed, remembering him.

"He looked like that crazy guy, Euell Gibbons. You know, the one who was always out in the woods eating the bark off trees," Mikhail laughed.

"Better looking," Clark said, for the record. Mikhail winked at Kate from across the table.

"Well, I'm sure Kate wouldn't mind getting down on her knees with him, Bible-thumper or not."

"Fuck you, Jawara," she replied.

"Any time, sweetheart," he said, drawing the first two fingers on his right hand into a V and sticking his tongue through several times in rapid succession.

"Oh," she groaned, "you're disgusting."

"What do you plan to do about it?" Mikhail demanded.

With that, each of them squared off, across the table, like two gunslingers in a showdown at the O.K. Corral. She squinted at Mikhail, and he squinted back at her, hands ready at their sides, low on the hip. But instead of drawing six-shooters, they grabbed their drinks off the table, tossed them back, and slapped the empty glasses face down on tabletop. A draw! They looked at each other laughing out loud together. Kate was not feeling any pain, and for the first time in months she was having a good time.

She couldn't remember the last time she had laughed, much less smiled. They continued laughing and joking and drinking.

"No matter how you cut it," William said, with the nod of his head, "we've got a real freak show on our hands."

Everyone stopped laughing.

"A real freak show," Mikhail repeated.

"This word 'freak.' It means the same as 'demon,' right?" Jorge said with his tongue firmly planted against his cheek.

"No!" Mikhail shouted.

Kate was drunk. She put her finger in the air and pointed it at Clark. "Just once, I'd like to walk into a normal crime scene, whatever the hell that is," she bellowed out loud, slurring the words, "and find an arrow pointing at the scumbag's prints and his DNA all over the place."

"How about catching him red-handed with the murder weapon?"

"I'll drink to that, Clark," Kate said and raised the glass to her lips. She drained her drink then wiped her mouth with the back of her sleeve and waved the empty glass at the bartender. "Hey, Johnnie, how about another round here?"

"Sure thing, Kate," said the bartender.

Johnnie O'Flynn put a fresh glass up on the counter and filled it with a shot of bourbon, but then he didn't deliver it to their table. Instead, carried on a fresh gust of wind that blew from the open door through the bar, Lieutenant Roberts scooped the drink up and walked it over to the table.

"Here's your drink, Inspector," Roberts said, taunting her with the alcoholic beverage. "Bottoms up!"

Kate sobered up. She took the drink but didn't bother to look up at him. She had seen that look of disgust in the Lieutenant's steely glare before and knew she was likely to see it again.

"We're discussing the case, Jim," Clark said. "Why don't you pull up a chair and join us?"

"No, thanks," he replied, an old sourpuss. "I stopped by to make sure my team was ready for tomorrow. We can't afford to make any mistakes. The story made the late edition of the paper. By tomorrow afternoon, we'll have every nut in town wanting to confess or dropping into Central Booking to be part of the circus."

"Yeah, yeah, do you remember that creep that used to come in once a month and confess to be the Zodiac killer? Only he would have been like three years old when the first victim was killed," Mikhail said. "Turned out he was on welfare, and his meds would run out before he could cash his monthly check and renew them."

"Arthur Davidson," Clark recalled.

"Damn! How do you remember shit like that?"

Mikhail added. "Partner, we should put your ass on Jeopardy and double-down on all those daily doubles. Watch out, Alex Trebek."

"I have an eidetic memory," Clark confessed. "I know it's kind of weird, but I remember every moment of my life in perfect detail, right down to the precise location and timing of my footsteps. The problem is that, when I try to remember details from other people's lives or their crime scenes, they get cross-wired with my own. That's why I take notes."

"You just remember to get your ass to the station on time

tomorrow morning—and sober," the Lieutenant replied gruffly to Clark, while eyeballing Kate.

"This is a soft-drink, sir, not hard liquor," Clark said, with a sigh.

Kate swallowed her drink down hard and glanced over her shoulder at Roberts with fire in her eyes. He was standing there, like a great big hulk of a man, looking back at her. She knew the comment was meant for her, not Clark, and fought to restrain herself from striking back.

"I'm off duty, Lieutenant," she said, struggling to control the rising anger in her voice. "You hear that? I'm off duty. I'm here having a drink and discussing the case with my partner and two fellow detectives. If you've got a problem with that, then you'd better write me up and file a formal complaint with my union. Otherwise, get off my back."

The Lieutenant took a deep breath, as if that alone would extinguish the anger he felt toward his female inspector. He let the air out slowly, through clenched teeth.

"I'll see you first thing in the morning," he said as he turned away to leave.

"Holy shit!" Mikhail exclaimed. "Where the fuck did he come from?"

"Out of thin air," Clark said.

"No, he's been dogging me for a while now. Ever since we wrapped the case on John Monroe," Kate said, feeling a bit uneasy. She glanced around the room to make sure he was gone. "I'm almost afraid to take a crap without first checking to see if he's in the stall right next to me."

"Take it easy, partner," Jorge said.

"It's not you, Dawson," William added. "The Lieutenant's been riding us all pretty hard since Miller's death."

Mikhail was suddenly sober and reflective. "When that fucking butch-dyke filed charges against me for slapping her around, Roberts chewed my ass right up and spit it out," he said. "I landed in that god-forsaken hole they call Records and spent the worst three weeks of my life there!"

"Kate, I got suspended for three days, without pay, for sharing a classified file with someone who was on suspension," Jorge reported.

"Yeah, I heard. I'm really sorry about that, Ramirez."

Jorge shrugged his shoulders. "No *importa*."

"See what I said? It's not just you," William repeated. "We've each had our turn at bat, playing his private whipping boy, even me. None of us liked it, but it's just the way things are. Now it's your turn."

"That's just what I wanted to hear," she said, with a hint of sarcasm.

Kate pushed her chair back away from the table and stood up. She swallowed down the last of her Wild Turkey and licked her lips one last time. The drink still tasted good, almost as good as it had an hour ago. She gathered up her personal effects and then counted out a handful of bills.

"You leaving?" Mikhail asked her.

"Yeah, we've all got a big day ahead of us tomorrow, so I thought I'd call it an early night. You know, go home and get some rest."

"Let me ask you something, Kate," he said.

"The answer's no, Mikhail," she replied, folding her arms across her breasts, as if erecting an invisible barrier between the two of them with her action. "I may be a little tipsy, but I'm not that drunk."

Mikhail got right in her face. "And what makes you think I want to fuck that boney white ass of yours, anyway?"

"You mean, you don't want to fuck me?"

He took Kate by the arm and pulled her away from the table.

When they reached a safe distance, he whispered, "Scuttlebutt around the office is that you're seeing the department shrink."

She looked at him sharply. "What the hell?"

"Don't pretend you didn't hear me."

"I heard you," she said, with a raised eyebrow.

Kate glanced at the two detectives who were seated at the table and figured they were already a couple of steps ahead of her. "I hate my life being part of the rumor mill. Does everyone know?"

Mikhail bobbed his head.

"Son-of-a-bitch," she swore, under her breath.

"Look. I need to warn you about Dr. Glass," he confided.

"Don't say anything more."

Kate turned away from him and walked back to the table. Her two fellow detectives were still there, nursing drinks.

"Anyone *else* need a ride?" she asked, looking from William to Jorge. She tapped her fingernails on the tabletop, waiting for each man to decline her offer, and when they did, she tossed some bills on the table. "Take care of my tab, Ramirez, would you? And have one on me." Kate then marched right over to Mikhail, hooked her arm into his, and steered him toward the exit.

The blast of cool night air struck Kate in the face. For the moment, she wrestled with her worst fears about Glass as she and Mikhail crossed the parking lot to the spot where she had parked her car. She had vowed never to let another shrink get under her skin, and yet, here was another one, gnawing at the edges of her reality, trying to find what was buried deep within her. She opened her car but kept the door between her and her fellow detective.

"This had better be on the level, Jawara," she said, "and not some juvenile ruse to get me alone."

"Christ! You got walls up in front of the walls," he said, moving his arms and legs wide as he spoke. "That psycho doctor sure done a real number on you, and here I was having one bitch kitty of a time trying tune into my white sister."

Kate didn't think much of his joke. "Stop the shuckin' and jivin', this isn't *Soul Train*," she insisted. "Just tell me what you know."

Mikhail smiled, but there was no amusement in his eyes. "Well, after that dust off with Purdy Spriggs—fuckin' butch-dyke—I was ordered by Internal Affairs to get some professional help for my anger, 'professional help'," he said.

"They call it 'anger management'. Who knew? I thought it was the title of a fuckin' TV series, not some fancied-up twelve-step program."

"Get to the point, Jawara," Kate said, her patience growing thin.

"Okay, okay," he replied, putting his hands out, trying to simmer her down. "So, they hook me up with Dr. Glass, and they warn me if I miss a session, I'm off the force. Fine, no problem. I've got this, right? But then, you know what happens? First time I'm in his office, he gets right in my face and tells me I'm an angry man. Can you believe that shit? We just met five minutes ago—five minutes! And the fuckin' doctor thinks he's got me all figured out—me?"

"Imagine that," Kate said.

"Yeah, I couldn't believe it either. What the fuck would this cracker know about being black? Sure, I swallow down a lot of rage, but it's because assholes like him keep dishing it out day after fuckin' day. And yeah, I also got a low tolerance for frustration, but then, when you put up with all the bullshit I put up with, you got to be frustrated by it all."

Kate could feel her own frustration rising. "Besides anger issues, what else did he find wrong with you?"

"I ain't got no anger management issues," Mikhail said. "I don't like fuckin' dykes! That's all it is. And here she was getting all in my face, disrespecting me. If she wants to act like a man, she better grow a pair, or get the fuck out of my way!"

"Simmer down, Mikhail," she advised. "Don't get so bent out of shape about it. Nobody cares what some shrink thinks."

They held each other's gaze for a moment, then Mikhail nodded at her and took a couple of deep breaths of the night air. A patrol car pulled into the parking spot next to Kate's BMW and deposited two uniformed policemen who nodded and said 'hello' as they walked toward door. A detective from vice walked by and winked at Kate on his way to an unmarked sedan. She turned away with a groan, trying to erase the memory of their one-night stand from her thoughts. Mikhail broke the silence between them.

"So, maybe I got issues with anger management," he confessed.

"We all got issues, my friend. That's what makes us human."

"Yeah, I suppose you're right."

"What else did Glass say to you," she asked.

"Oh, just that I hate my father," he replied, with a bewildered, faraway look in his eyes. "I didn't know it, but he says I do."

Kate flashed him a reassuring smile. "For my money, Jawara, there's nothing wrong with you. You sound like your average fucked-up cop."

"You think I make the grade?"

"Yeah, I think you make the grade."

Kate climbed into the front seat of her car and closed the door behind her. She pulled the safety belt over her body and snapped it into place then started the ignition. She was about to drive away when Mikhail signaled her to roll down the window.

"What's wrong? Do you *really* need a lift?" she asked, with a smile.

"No, thanks."

"Okay then, I should get going."

Mikhail crouched down to her eye level and put his hands on the window ledge of the car to stable himself. He looked to the right and to the left. "Listen, Kate," he whispered, "watch what you say to Dr. Glass. He's not what he appears to be."

"What are you saying?" Kate asked.

"I'm just saying that if you don't want your secrets known to Internal Affairs, I'd be careful of what I said to Glass. He's not known for his discretion."

Kate was nearing the Embarcadero, and the turn-off for Bayside Village, when she realized that she had spent the last thirty minutes in traffic, obsessing over the word 'discretion' as she drove home. What was it about that word that bothered her so much? The word was linked to its root word 'discrete', which meant 'showing discernment or good judgment'. She wanted to believe that anyone in a position of authority, like Glass, must have exercised some degree of good judgment, or he wouldn't have lasted as long as he had as the police psychiatrist. She tried to mitigate her feelings about the subject by telling herself that Mikhail, like every other cop she knew, feared what a trained shrink would discover lurking in the dark recesses of his mind.

She had many of the same fears. The thought that Glass would submit his report about her to IA terrified her, but there was nothing she could do about it right now. She would have to be on guard at her next appointment and bury her feelings.

She was still obsessing when she pulled into a parking spot in front of her building and turned the ignition off. She patted the dashboard of her BMW and climbed out of the car. She managed to get one thing right that day, and so worked on exchanging paranoid thoughts about Glass for a more positive outlook.

She climbed the steps to the third floor and walked down the length of the corridor. As she approached Lenny Provolone's apartment, she paused for a moment outside his door. She had not seen him in over a month, and she found that to be rather strange, even for Lenny. For the last several months, he had obsessed over her, following her every move to the point of tasking an experimental surveillance satellite he built for Northrop-Grumman to track her. And then—nothing. It was like he had fallen off the face of the planet. She hoped that he was all right.

Kate wondered when the last time she had seen him was. It was the movies. She had agreed to accompany him to see a restored print of *Star Trek II: The Wrath of Khan* at the Historic Balboa Theatre. She fell asleep during the final act when Spock sacrificed his life for the rest of the *Enterprise* crew. She woke up during the closing credits to Lenny berating her for sleeping through "one of the cinema's most climatic moments." She spent the rest of the night listening to Lenny go over the last few scenes of the movie in painstaking detail while he dripped mustard and onions from his hamburger into his bushy white beard.

She wasn't a fan of *Star Trek* or science fiction, and certainly didn't understand how robots, space ships and little green men had such a hold on the male population. Lenny was obsessed with this niche of popular culture. He would dress up in costume and take on the identity of science fiction characters at his conventions. She envied the fact that he had one thing that gave his life meaning. She didn't have that in her own life, and made a conscious choice to be less critical of his interests. He was odd and quirky, but he was a good friend nonetheless. And he made her laugh.

She knocked on his front door. "Lenny, this is Kate. Are you okay? Is everything all right?"

"Who is it? What do you want?" he asked. He sounded dazed like he woke from a sound sleep.

"It's Kate. Open the door, Lenny."

"What's wrong? What's the matter, Kate?" he replied, cracking the door and peeking out through the crack. "You're not here to borrow my car again, are you?"

"No, I don't need your car," she replied with a smile. "I haven't seen you for a while, and I wanted to know you were okay."

Lenny nodded with his head hung low and stepped back away to open the door for her. She stepped through the threshold and was overwhelmed by pungent odors. Lenny's apartment smelled worse than the public toilets down on Skid Row. Kate stormed into his kitchen and started bagging up the rotted food covering the counter and floor. "What the hell happened?" she demanded, wading into the mess.

In his dingy gray t-shirt and briefs, Lenny shuffled across the floor, like a dead man walking, and dropped hard into a chair near the kitchen. "I'm a pathetic loser," he said.

"What's wrong?"

"The love of my life just broke up with me."

Kate shot him a sideways glance. She stopped bagging trash and stood there for a moment. Had she fallen through one of Lenny's science fiction wormholes and landed in a parallel universe where he had a girlfriend. *Love of his life? Who just broke up with him?* Kate counted the days since their movie date. It was just over a month. How was it possible for her friend to have met someone, fallen in love, and gone through a devastating break-up in thirty-seven days? This was one story she had to hear, if only for her own personal amusement.

"The love of your life, Lenny?" she asked.

"Yes. Rebecca was *the one*," he replied, somewhat dramatically with a flourish that made her think that trumpets were now going to start blowing. "My heart is broken, and I have no emotional hit points left for love."

Kate bit her lower lip to keep from laughing. "You know, Lenny, it takes time to fall in love, even more time to become friends with someone. Most men I know become friends first with a woman before they try to take her to bed."

"She woke up in my bed next to me."

"No, no, no. You must realize how crazy that sounds," she objected. "Most women just don't wake up in bed with some guy they don't know. Even the professionals I've met over the years like to work out payment arrangements first."

Lenny waved off her objection. "Oh, sure, it happens all the time at science fiction conventions," he explained. He sketched it out on an imaginary white board that stood between the two of them. "You see, when a big science fiction convention, like BayCon or WesterCon, comes to a city like San Francisco, they negotiate to get the cheapest rates from the big hotels. That cheap rate means that a hotel room that costs two-fifty a night will only cost a hundred."

"I still don't understand how cheaper rates for hotel rooms would result with a strange woman in your bed."

He raised the palm of his hand to stop her from saying anything more and continued, "Enter the average science fiction fan who attends ten to twelve of these conventions per year, that's a hefty amount to pay. So, one fan books a room and then tries to fill it with as many of his friends as possible. People share the beds, while others sleep on the floor. Maybe one person sleeps in the bathtub. I can remember one time, at a BayCon years ago, we squeezed as many as twelve people in one room, and one guy who was a vampire slept with his arms folded across his chest in the closet."

"A vampire?" Kate shook her head in disbelief. "Who am I to judge? The point is, we try to cram as many people into the room as we can," he said. "Okay, okay, I think I understand," Kate said, sealing the third trash bag she had filled and putting it to one side. "But that still does not explain how the love of your life ended up in your bed."

Lenny yawned and stretched out on the comfortable leather chair, extending his arms out at his sides. The corners of his eyes dropped ever so slightly with fatigue.

"Well, the room at the World Fantasy Convention was my room. I lined up a bunch of friends to share the costs with me, but we had room for a few extras. So, when I passed by Filthy Pierre's Voodoo Board earlier in the day, I posted a note saying I had crash space."

"And she saw the note and took you up on your offer," Kate added.

"More or less. But then, as I said, this sort of thing happens all the time. She probably came in late, saw there was space on the bed, and climbed in."

"Talk about a fantasy!" Kate was incredulous.

"Lenny, I must confess that your account borders on the fantastic. I just can't believe a woman in her right mind would go into a perfect stranger's room and climb in his bed."

"It's true! I swear it really happened."

"Are you sure this—what did you say her name was?— 'Rebecca' wasn't put up to this by somebody wanting to play a trick on you?"

"No," Lenny said emphatically.

"Did Rebecca ever try to shake you down for money?"

"*No*. Do you trust *anybody*?"

"I don't believe a word of this story," she said and returned to cleaning Lenny's kitchen, opening several drawers and cabinets looking for an additional supply of trash bags. When she found it, she pulled several bags out and started filling them again with moldy pizza crusts and day-old French fries.

"You know I got friends down at the department that would slap your ass into a lie detector if I asked them to."

"I'm telling you the truth," Lenny pleaded. "So, tell me what happened next."

"Well, we woke up in each other's arms, and she said, 'I'm pleased to meet you and your excited friend,'" he said, relating the details of the event like they happened yesterday. "I guess you could say we were a captive audience."

"Just stick to the facts," Kate said rolling her eyes.

Lenny smiled, his own knowing smile, and continued, "Rebecca and I laid there together looking into each other's eyes, waiting for everyone to clear out of the room. Then, when we were alone, we did a lot of kissing and hugging and touching. It was nice. I had never had a girlfriend in high school, but here I was feeling like a teenager, making out with my sweetheart."

Kate tightened the seal on the last trash bag and rolled up her sleeves to tackle the sink full of dirty dishes.

She wanted to do a quick rinse and stack them in his dishwasher, provided she could find a clean sponge and some detergent. She looked up from the kitchen sink and focused her attention back on Lenny's tale of woe.

"And we continued to stay in touch after the convention through emails and text messages. She was much better at writing the long, loving emails than I was. For every six or seven emails I got from her, I may have sent her one or two in response. I have never been very good with follow-up."

Kate managed to tear herself away from the sink.

"Now, wait a minute. Let me try to understand this. After the convention, you exchanged emails and texts, but you never tried to call her? You never sent her flowers? You never tried to get together for dinner and a movie? You just sent emails and texts? Where the hell does this Rebecca live? On the dark side of the moon?"

"No, Sacramento."

"Lenny, Sacramento is only an hour and a half away!"

"Yeah, well, I was busy."

Kate resumed her work, stacking the newly-rinsed dishes in the dishwasher. "So, when did you know it was over?"

"I was just getting to that, Kate," he replied with another yawn. "Last week, I texted her about going to WesterCon with me, and she didn't reply right away. I left a bunch of messages on her cell phone and sent emails. When she finally did return my text, she told me she had met a new boyfriend, someone closer to her own age."

"I guess in the course of this investigation," she said, mocking her own sloppy police work, "I failed to establish the perpetrator's age."

"Rebecca is twenty-three."

"Oh my gosh, Lenny, she's way too young for you!"

"Sixteen years, that's not a big difference," he said. "I've never been attracted to women much older than Rebecca. Women over thirty are old and wrinkled and have lost their spontaneity. You're the oldest woman I've ever been out with, and that wasn't really a date."

She looked at Lenny as he spoke, then she sighed.

"My friend, you are a true one-of-a-kind. They broke the mold when they made you."

"You think I'm special?" he asked, fishing for a compliment.

"Absolutely!" Kate replied, putting the last of the flat wear in the dishwasher and rolling down her sleeves. She closed the door tight, turned the cycle to wash, came out of the kitchen, and stood in front of him. "Rebecca sounds like she wasn't wound too tight, and you should consider yourself lucky that she broke up with you."

Lenny put his head in his hands and began to cry.

"It's the story of my life. I always seem to attract the mental cases, while the normal ones run screaming into the night."

Kate flashed him a make-believe frown. She started toward the door, and turned. "Do you know that old Supremes' song, 'You Can't Hurry Love'?"

He shook his head.

"Well, Google it, and listen to the words," Kate advised as she took the handle on the door and cracked it open. "No matter how much you want love to come into your life, you can't hurry it along. Love takes its own sweet time to happen, and it will often find you when you least expect it."

"Well, maybe that's true for other people, but not me," Lenny said with a sniffle. "I told you once already that I don't have any emotional hit points left for love."

"Keep saying that, and you will make it come true."

"Kate, I know you're just trying to help, but you don't understand. You'll never understand what it's like to be me."

She opened the door wide and made ready to leave.

"Good night, Lenny. Try to get some rest," she said waiting for a reply that never came.

Kate closed the door and lingered in front of Lenny's apartment for a moment. She was worried about him, but she had been unable to reach that part of him that needed reaching. Kate felt very uneasy as she walked down the corridor to her apartment and another night of troubled sleep.

CHAPTER THREE

The next morning, Kate found Jorge outside police headquarters on Bryant Street. He was leaning against the crumpled fender of his late-model Ford pick-up truck, eating a sugared donut and drinking a cup of coffee from Dynamo Donuts. The powdered sugar was all over his face.

To Kate, he looked like the subject of a documentary about cops and donuts.

Back in the day, Frank Miller told her not many places would stay open twenty-four hours; just a few diners and donut shops would be open during pre-dawn hours. Cops who were up all night working the third shift would end up eating at the donut shops because that's what they had to choose from. In time, the erroneous notion that police officers only ate donuts and drank coffee stuck to them like an albatross around a seaman's neck, and it became a stereotype.

"Good, you came to meet me early, Kate," he said, crumpling up the greasy bag from the donut shop and tossing it into the back of his truck. The flat bed was full of discarded breakfast and lunch bags. It was hard to keep his truck clean because he was so damn busy with his new assignment in

Homicide and with his brand-new infant son at home, or so he told himself.

"You had better have saved one for me," she said, crossing the street, "or you're in for one serious beating."

Jorge nodded his head, smiling. He then reached over the side of his truck, and produced a separate bag of greasy donuts, opened it wide, and held it out for her.

Licking her lips, Kate looked inside the bag, pulled one out with a wax-paper wrapping and took a big bite.

"Sticky buns," she said with a sigh, as she swallowed it down. "My favorite." Kate took another bite of the donut and reflected, "The only thing that would make this perfect is a good cup of coffee."

Jorge nodded again, and reached over the side of his truck a second time. He produced a paper cup with a lid.

"Coffee, extra lite with sugar," he said, handing the cup to her.

"Perfect," she replied, taking a sip.

Jorge smiled then swallowed down a drink of his coffee.

Kate finished eating the first sticky bun, had another sip of her coffee, and began devouring the second. The sticky bun was rolled dough, spread with sugar and nuts, and then sliced and baked in muffin tins with honey on the bottom. The honey made it sticky. The taste was mother's home-cooking and heaven.

"Do you remember Winchell's Donuts?" she asked, savoring the last bite.

"*Si*, I would stop there as a patrolman."

"Their donuts were always so fresh," Kate recalled.

"Best cinnamon crumb donut I ever had. So much better than the ones, today, all fluff and no substance."

Jorge nodded his head.

"So, partner, what's this all about? I mean, you didn't text me an hour ago just to feed me sticky buns and watch me drink coffee."

"I'm concerned about you," he said.

"First, Jawara. Now, you," she said with a frown.

Kate figured that William would be the next one to reach out and express his concern for her, but only if he checked his notebook first. "With all this concern about my well-being, how could a girl lose?"

"*Claro*," he agreed, missing her sarcasm.

Kate wagged her sticky finger at Jorge. "I don't need anybody looking out for me. I'm capable of looking out for myself. You got that? Stop treating me like I'm helpless! I'm an Inspector with the SFPD."

"*Mierda*, what did I say?" Jorge pleaded.

She stared hard at him struggling to read the innocent look of bewilderment in his face. He was convinced he did the right thing. How could he not know how demeaning his actions were? Was it a cultural thing? Something related to his Latino roots? Or was it pure machismo—that age-old belief that men were superior to women? Kate was angry.

She had proven her worth many times and was damn tired of having to prove it again and again with her peers.

Jorge put out his hand to touch her, to reassure her if he could, but she refused to be comforted. She brushed his hand away, and unable to look at him, she turned inward.

Kate was silent for a long moment then drank down the last of her coffee and crumpled the cup into the bag, squashing the remaining sticky bun. At the first trashcan in front of the Hall of Justice, she disposed of the bag and started up the steps of the police station. Jorge followed, trailing behind, still trying to understand what he did wrong.

At the top of the steps, near the front door, they ran into William and Mikhail. They were an odd couple. Clark wore a button-down shirt and tie, looking square in a Navy polyester blazer, while Mikhail wore a black turtleneck under a classic gray suit. They were opposites in their demeanor as well. Clark had been walking with his head down, buried in his notes, and nearly ran into the other two detectives, while his partner was gregarious. They both scrambled to open the glass door. William won.

"Good morning. How are you doing on this fine day?" he asked, with a broad smile, taking hold of the door handle.

"What's goin' down, detectives?" Mikhail asked.

Kate glared at them both.

"Fuck off!" she said, and then continued into the building.

"What did I say?" William asked, turning from Mikhail to Jorge.

Jorge looked at him and shook his head, feeling pity for William. "When you discover what it is, let me know," he replied.

Mikhail shrugged, disappointed. "The Inspector just has a bug up her ass this morning. That's all."

They laughed and followed her through the door and down the corridor.

Kate pushed her way through the bottleneck of civilians and police officers at the information desk and turned the corner, heading to the bank of elevators. When she reached her elevator, she punched the up button, wanting to kill someone. Kate punched it again, and then again. She punched it several times until the elevator doors slid open, and she stepped in and waited for the doors to close.

No sooner had she made her floor selection, Kate eased back against the wall of the elevator and breathed a deep sigh of relief as she watched the doors sweep closed. She was hoping to have the elevator to herself to enjoy a few minutes of peace before she started her day. But Mikhail, who had been just a few footsteps behind her in the corridor, put his hand out and stopped them from closing. He and William and Jorge and two uniformed cops piled into the small car with Kate. They each took turns selecting their floors before the doors closed.

The elevator car moved slowly.

Unlike most days when the conversation was loud and the clamor kept most people from hearing themselves think, the atmosphere of this ride was silent and thick with tension. Kate held her breath and let it out slowly between clenched teeth. The others could feel the tension, too, and shifted in place, moving their stance from one side to the other.

Mikhail was first to break the silence. "Hey, Dawson," he said, "you know we got nothing but love for you."

"Thanks, Mikhail," she replied with a deep sigh.

"What he says," Jorge whispered, "goes double for me."

Kate nodded her head.

William said, "Inspector, you're an important part of the team. We couldn't function effectively without you."

"Thanks, guys," she replied, softening.

The two uniformed officers looked at each with raised eyebrows, but said nothing.

The elevator groaned upwards, heading to the Homicide Bureau and the floors directly above. But on its way up to the next floor, it shuddered like a great behemoth colliding with another one of its kind, and came to a dead stop between floors. The power went out, and the emergency lighting kicked on.

"Son-of-a-bitch, not again!" One of the uniformed cops exclaimed.

"Third time this month," the second uniformed cop remarked, quite agitated.

Clark said, "I should have taken the stairs."

"No shit," Mikhail replied. "The city's power grid is all fucked up. And until those assholes downtown agree to pay for a major overhaul of the entire system, we should all be taking the stairs."

"You mean, until the Mayor gets his head out of his ass, and starts listening to city engineers instead of those pinko, tree-loving liberals," the second uniformed policeman corrected. "What the fuck do those ass-wipes know about anything mechanical?"

"Right on, brother," Mikhail agreed.

"All these mechanical failures make me think of those creatures—you know the ones—that get into our machines and gum up the works," the first cop speculated.

"Gremlins?" William said.

"You mean demons," Jorge tried to correct him. "No, I mean gremlins," William repeated, without checking his notebook. "My grandfather who flew bomber missions over Germany during World War II used to tell us stories about those mischievous little creatures. Gremlins, not human error, were responsible for all of the mechanical troubles and mishaps of American and British aircrafts during the war."

"Y'know, those A-rabs, they've been shippin' them over here for a while now," the first cop said. "They put 'em in cars, they put 'em in your TVs. They put 'em in stereos and those little radios you stick in your ears."

William shook his head. "That's nonsense. It wouldn't take much for some foreign nation to crash our power grid," he said, with cool authority, "but they wouldn't need gremlins to do it. They'd hack into our mainframes with their own computers and send us back to the Stone Age."

"Foreign nation, shit!" The second cop interjected.

"We've got enough home-grown terrorist groups that want to bring us down, and they're a damn-sight closer and more dangerous than those Ayatollahs in the Middle East."

"Cyber-terrorism," Mikhail said, "can happen at any time and be targeted at us from any location."

"C'mon guys, this isn't funny," Kate stammered, reaching out and pushing every button on the elevator's control panel. She repeated her actions, pushing each button several times again. "All this talk about gloom and doom, and we're stuck in a fuckin' elevator."

"Take it easy, Dawson. Everything is okay," Mikhail said.

Kate struggled to keep a level head, yet her heart was pounding. She took several deep breaths and fought to swallow each one of them down like chunks of undigested pork. *What would calm me down? A shot of whiskey with a beer chaser might do it.* She reached down into her pockets but came up empty—nothing but fuzz. She had spent the last of her money getting her car back. Kate wondered what was left on her credit. Her face turned pale and she began to sweat. *A stiff drink, yes.* She began to shake. She wasn't sure how much longer she was going to be able to keep it together.

The lights flickered to life, and the elevator lurched forward. It rose and resumed its long and arduous journey upward.

When the elevator reached the fifth floor, the doors opened and Kate staggered out, like a drunk on a drinking binge, but she hadn't had a drink in over thirteen hours.

She'd never convince the Lieutenant otherwise if he caught her stumbling over her own feet. The color had returned to her face, and she was breathing again—short, deep breaths.

She needed to straighten herself up and get down the hall.

William was right behind her, a few paces away, followed close at hand by Mikhail and Jorge. He looked concerned and a little hurt as he reached out, grabbing Kate under one arm, attempting to help her straighten up and walk straight, but she resisted his help.

"What is your problem?" he asked, fighting to be her Good Samaritan. He was starting to lose his own balance.

"I'm trying to help you. Why won't you let anyone help you, Dawson?"

Kate tore her arm free from his grasp. She continued down the corridor under her own steam, struggling with each step. "I don't want your help. I don't need any help. Do you understand me?"

They all stopped in the corridor and stared at her.

"Yes, you do," William insisted. "Something's going on with you. We've all seen it, and we've all watched it take its toll on you. You may be able to fool the brass, but you can't fool us. We're your friends."

She stopped walking and turned. "I don't need anybody looking out for me. I'm going through a lot of shit right now. I need space to think. Some of it, I don't even understand myself. Believe me when I say I'm grateful to have friends like you who've got my back, but this is something I've got to do myself. For my own, I don't know, sense of well-being or some shit like that."

"Understood," William said.

"We're here if you need us," Mikhail added.

"*Tu eres mi amiga*," Jorge said, holding a hand to his heart, and reminding her of the bond they shared.

She gathered them together for a group hug, more for them than for her. "Okay, then," she said. "Let's go catch some bad guys."

Fifteen minutes later, Kate was sitting across the table from Philip Ross with his file open in front of her. She sipped her second cup of hot coffee, while William paced the length of the interrogation room in a pair of new Florsheim shoes that squeaked. Kate looked at his shoes and thought about the sky-blue heels she wanted. They were two hundred dollars. *Maybe the next paycheck.*

The room was very cold and dark, not unlike an empty waiting room at the city morgue, and was thinly furnished with a table, couple of chairs upholstered in black vinyl, and waste-paper basket from the Department of Public Works. Ross stared into the large two-way mirror without blinking an eye. To Kate, he seemed to be unusually cool and collected for a suspect in a murder investigation.

"Mr. Ross, this session is being recorded," said Kate, stating the obvious. "For the record, would you please state your name and age?"

"Philip P. Ross, thirty-five," he said. "The P is for Paul."

"You're not a native Californian," she remarked, first glancing at his file and then looking him square in the eyes.

Ross shook his head. "No. My wife and I are from Sioux Falls, South Dakota."

"Nice place?"

"Yes, I guess. We never lived any place else, so it was home for us. But like most cities, Sioux Falls was hit hard by the economic downturn of the last ten years; a lot of unemployment and no jobs."

"So, is it fair to say you came to San Francisco for work?"

"Yes," he said, with a nod. "We're both trained as systems engineers and hold advanced degrees in computers and technology."

Kate turned back to his file and read the box marked 'occupation'. She hadn't noticed it the first time around, but there it was in black and white: Systems Engineer. Her suspect happened to be a well-educated professional, polished and refined. Over the years, most suspects who had sat across from her were mechanics and construction workers, salespeople, civil servants, and the occasional healthcare worker, bank teller, and accountant. They were generally not educated and had turned to crime as an easy way out of their troubles. In her mind, the well-educated ones, like John Monroe, and now perhaps Philip Ross, were the most dangerous.

"Well, you picked a hell of a time to come to San Francisco," Kate said as she looked up from the file.

"People with advanced degrees in computers are now working for minimum wage down at the 7-11."

"I know," he said flatly.

"You would have been better off going to Chicago or Atlanta where the need for expertise is greater," she added.

"Computer techs are a dime a dozen here. Ever since the dot-com boom went bust, work in that industry has been tough."

Ross thought about it then said, "You're probably right, Inspector." He paused for a moment, and politely added, "I'd really like a cup of coffee. It's kind of cold in here, and I did not get any breakfast."

"Do I look like Starbucks to you?" Kate said, but then she pulled herself up short. There was something about Philip Ross that bothered her, but that didn't mean she had to be so harsh. The man had just lost his wife and kids, and if he hadn't had anything to do with the murders, why was she treating him with such disdain?

Kate needed a shot of whiskey in her coffee to take the edge off. She took another sip of her coffee as her eyes rolled up into her head. Regardless of whether he was suffering from shock or not, she had a job to do; to break him down. Even though her instincts were clouded, she didn't dare let her guard down.

"Well, since you are drinking coffee from a Styrofoam cup and I can smell coffee percolating, there must be a coffeemaker close by," he guessed, focusing his gaze on the two-way mirror. "Probably on the other side of that glass with your supervisor and fellow detectives."

Kate and William exchanged a quick look of surprise.

What arrogance, she thought, turning back to Ross.

She had never seen a suspect with such a big pair of brass balls before. But then, maybe she could use them against him. She might even be able to convince him that he was in control by making him a deal.

"And I would also like one of the donuts they're eating as well."

Kate took a sip of her coffee and nodded. "I'll make a deal with you, Philip. You don't mind if I call you Philip, do you?"

"No, as long as you don't mind me calling you Kate," he replied.

"I'm Inspector Dawson," she said.

Ross grinned. "Okay, Inspector, what's your deal?"

"You answer a few more of my questions, and I'll see that my partner comes up with a whole breakfast for you."

"Deal."

Kate glanced at William over her shoulder and shrugged. He nodded, and then wrote the word "breakfast" in big letters in his notebook. William walked back to the door and held up his sign for Mikhail and Jorge to read.

She turned back to Ross. "Where were you Tuesday night?"

"On Tuesday nights I attend a men's Bible study group at the First Pentecostal Church of God," he said, with a practiced tone. "This past Tuesday was no exception. We started our fellowship around seven p.m. and broke up about eleven-fifteen p.m. That's when I went home and went to bed. Ask any one of the guys in my group, and they'll tell you I was there with them the entire evening."

"Yes, we've already checked out your alibi," she replied. "The men at the meeting confirmed you were there."

"Good," he remarked. "I wouldn't want you to get the wrong idea about me."

Kate shrugged, looking down at his folder. "There's one thing I don't understand. When you got home from your meeting, you didn't notice anything strange at your house?"

"No, nothing at all."

"Walk me through your actions when you got back to the house."

Ross shrugged. "I parked the car in the garage and went in through the side near the kitchen. Wendy had left me a plate of food from dinner, wrapped in tin foil, in the toaster oven. But since I wasn't feeling particularly hungry, I turned off the oven, and placed the leftovers in the fridge."

"Did she often leave you a late-night snack?"

"Yes, especially on Tuesday nights when I went directly from work to the men's Bible study group." She jotted a note down in the file. "Continue."

"Well, there's not much more to say."

"Did you sit down and watch television? Read the newspaper? Look at your email from the day?"

"I went to bed," he said. "It was late. I was dead tired. And all I wanted to do is get a good night's rest."

"You didn't bother to look in on your children?"

"No."

"And you didn't think it was strange that your wife wasn't in bed waiting for you?"

Ross shook his head. "No. She often crawls into bed with one of the children if they're sick or having trouble sleeping."

Kate sipped her coffee. "What was your relationship with your wife?"

"My wife and I were married for ten years, and we had five beautiful children. She was a very good woman," Ross replied, as if he had been reading from a prepared script. "She was a good wife and a good mother. We were high school sweethearts and got married right after college. I suppose she was my best friend."

"You don't seem to be too broken up about her death or the deaths of your children," she said. "When I first saw you yesterday morning, you were sitting calmly with your friend."

"Mitchell. John Mitchell," he volunteered.

"Most men would be out of their minds with grief. They would be demanding to make sense out of the senselessness of the tragedy. But look at you, you are . . . calm and not the least bit upset by what happened."

Philip smiled, but there was no amusement in his eyes. "We do not believe that death is the end. When a person's soul is called back to God and returns to paradise that is ultimate joy. There is no sorrow in death. We don't permit tears or expressions of grief. We believe in celebrating those who have died, not grieving for them. They have gone to be with the Father in a place where there are no more tears."

"No tears," Kate repeated. "So then, you're not upset about the death of your wife or children?"

"No," he replied. "I'm not upset."

Bullshit, Kate said to herself.

"Inspector, I am happy they were called back to God and spared all the suffering and misery that the world has to offer."

"You are a very religious man."

"Yes, but not religious in the way you mean it," Ross corrected her. "Everyone is religious in one way or another. They believe God and follow required obedience to a particular set of laws and rules. The Jews have the Old Testament and The Ten Commandments, the Muslims have the Koran, Buddhists have the teachings of Buddha to follow, and so on. Even those who don't believe in God still have laws and structures they follow. They're all necessary for the common good."

"Are you saying that your beliefs run contrary to those that are necessary to create and maintain an ordered society?" she asked, a little more than curious.

"No, not at all," he responded, his hands firmly planted on his thighs. "I'm just saying that most people settle for a self-righteous compromise where they judge their worthiness by comparison with other people and are satisfied with their own performance as long as are there are others 'out there' who are worse than they are. It's sort of like the speed limit. We are good Christians as long as we drive fifty-five miles an hour in a fifty-five-mile-an-hour zone, but we are bad people, condemned to hell, if we drive one mile above that speed limit. That's what I call 'second-hand Christianity.' As long as we follow all of the rules, we'll earn enough 'merit badges' to impress God and be saved."

"You lost me at that last turn," Kate confessed.

Philip Ross nodded his head. "God's love for us isn't predicated upon whether we drive the speed limit or not, or earn enough merit badges. He wants us to obey His commandments, but our salvation is built upon Christ. We have all sinned and fallen short of the glory of God. But God showed His great love for us by sending His only son, Jesus, to die upon the cross and redeem us as sinners with His sacred blood. As long as we believe in Him, we are saved."

Kate studied his face for a long moment, then looked back at his file. "That sounds like one of those quaint little fairy tales we tell our children to get them to clean their room or eat their vegetables."

"The Bible is not a fairy tale," he said with deep conviction. "It is the living and breathing testament of the Lord God Almighty."

"Okay, okay, let's just say you're right," she said, raising her hands to stop him from saying anything more. "Is God so insecure that He has to keep putting us through these agonizing tests to prove that we still love Him?"

"God's test is whether we act on His word or not."

Kate shrugged and looked up from Ross's file.

He hadn't answered her question, and she was growing weary of the interrogation. "Do you know the story of Abraham and Isaac?"

"Of course," Ross said confidently.

"Doesn't God instruct Abraham to take his only son Isaac to the top of some mountain and sacrifice him there as a burnt offering?" She stared straight into his dead-pan eyes.

Ross considered her question. "Yes, but God was testing Abraham. He never intended for Abraham to cut Isaac's throat and place his body on the altar and burn him there."

"I've got to be honest with you, Philip. I'd be pissed off with God if he played a nasty trick like that on me."

"God works in mysterious ways."

"Did you come up with that all by your lonesome?"

"No," he replied, with a smirk. "I seemed to have picked it up along the way."

Kate's features hardened. "You know, I've got a low tolerance for bullshit, and I've just about reached my limit with you. Now, you'd better start talking straight with me, or I'm going to fuckin' bury you in one of the deepest, darkest cells I've got and make sure you've got plenty of time to work it out with your god."

"I don't know what you're talking about," he stated, not the least bit ruffled.

"You know damn well what I'm talking about!" she exclaimed, slamming her fist down on the table. "Stop pretending you weren't there! I've got a mountain of forensic evidence that says otherwise!"

"I'm not lying to you."

"Do I need to trot my witness out here who can place you at the scene of the crime," she bluffed.

At that very instant, William Clark answered a knock at the interrogation room door and said to Ross, "Looks like your kid's meal is here." Clark opened the door wide to take the fast-food bag from Jawara. Behind him, in the background, a short man dressed in an expensive, handtailored William Fioravanti suit was arguing with Roberts.

The short man was very loud and obnoxious.

Ross heard the voice and leaned forward in his chair to have a look. Suddenly, he felt shock jolt through his body. When he had recovered, he fumbled for the right words, and came up short. "No, no, I already told you," he stammered. "I-I wasn't there. I-I didn't have anything to do with it. I was at church, in a Bible-study group. Just ask anyone of the men in my group."

Kate noticed the sudden change in him. "Philip, I'd like to believe you, but I've got two real problems with your story: One, the disposition of your wife's body at the crime scene, and two, the 911 call," she said, standing up and walking over to the door. She nudged Clark out of the way and peaked around the corner. She saw the short man and nodded her understanding.

To Clark she said, "Close that door, and don't let anyone in."

"Are you out of your mind?" William asked her.

"It might seem that way," she replied.

"I've already explained that I wasn't there," Ross pleaded with her. "Just ask anybody, and they'll tell you."

Kate returned to the interrogation table and leaned over her suspect. "Something out there scares you, doesn't it?"

"No," he lied.

"For forty-five minutes I've been waiting for you to show me that you're still human, like break out into a sweat or shed a single tear over the death of your wife and children," she said, face to face with Ross. "But then, a short man in an expensive suit arrives with your breakfast, and you suddenly fall to pieces. What gives? What kind of power does this man hold over you?"

"Just maybe I like kids' meals."

She rolled her eyes and sighed, folding her arms protectively across her chest. "C'mon, Philip, level with me."

"I can't."

"You can't? Or you won't?"

"Inspector," Ross said quietly. "You might as well put a gun to my head and pull the trigger. I'm a dead man no matter how you cut it. There's no way they'll let me live once I've been in police custody."

Kate Dawson was confused. *What just happened to the arrogant and self-assured Philip Ross?* She looked down at him and watched his face turn pale like a white linen shroud. His breathing was shallow, uneven. His hands were trembling. She could see that Philip Ross was terrified. But then again, she couldn't help but think this was all part of a well-rehearsed act to get him off.

"Tell me what you're afraid of," she demanded.

"It's a death sentence," he whispered. "I'm as good as dead, Inspector, once they take me out of this building."

"They wouldn't dare harm you, Philip."

"They're not who you think they are," he replied, slurring his words. "They're going to think I betrayed their trust, no matter what I say or do. They're going to drive me out into the country far beyond the city limits, force me to dig my own grave, and then kill me right on the spot."

"I thought you weren't afraid of death, or was that all bullshit?"

"You don't understand," Ross sighed, the words under his breath. "They won't just kill me. They'll beat me to death, and in my last few moments of life, they'll rip my soul out of my body and tear it to shreds."

"You talk as if they're the mafia."

"Oh, they're far worse than the mafia," he corrected her. "They represent the will of God, and they can act with impunity under the guise of the church. John reminds us that no man gets to the Father without first going through the Son."

Kate shot Ross a sideways glance. His rhetoric was beginning to break down and sound more like a mashup of fifth-grade Sunday school lessons and Summer Bible camp verses than the actual truth. She didn't know whether to trust his account of high-level assassins in the Pentecostal Church or chalk up his ravings to a man suffering some serious guilt over the death of his wife and children. She looked back at him, full of confusion and doubt, and then saw that look children often make when they have been caught red-handed with their hands in the cookie jar.

"You had better start talking straight with me," Kate said. "What is this all about?"

"The end of times," Ross said, glancing up at her, "is finally upon us. The forces of light and the forces of darkness are marshalling their army right now, as we speak, and the start of the war to end all wars is imminent. My guess is that it will begin sometime in the next seventy-two hours."

"Are you talking about a terrorist strike?"

"No, not exactly."

"Then tell me who's behind this," she demanded.

Ross's eyes had bugged out of his head. "They're all behind this!" he exclaimed, but those were the last words he spoke.

"That's enough! Not another word," the short man said, shouting at them from across the room. He pushed through Clark and the detectives at the door and got between Kate and her suspect. His diminutive stance made him seem like the young King David standing next to the formidable Goliath with Kate's stature. There was no greater humiliation for a cop than to be dismissed without a word. He stared at her with unblinking eyes, then turned away without as much as a backwards glance.

"Inspector Dawson, I'm afraid that I'm going to have to pull the plug on this interview—," the Lieutenant started to say, but was cut off in mid-sentence.

"This interrogation is over," the suit said as he produced a document and held the piece of paper up in the air like some occult talisman that gave him great power and authority. He looked past William and the other detectives at Kate. He then put the paper in her hand. "I am serving you this Writ of Habeas Corpus on behalf of my client, Philip Ross."

Kate scanned the document for her suspect's name, and when she found it, she read the attorney's name, George A. Friedman. She was aware of his reputation.

"My client was denied due process," Friedman continued, "and was unlawfully detained without sufficient cause or evidence. Clearly, his rights were violated by you and your partner when you pushed him through your booking office without allowing him the right to appear before a judge. You further compounded the problem by denying him his Miranda Rights, specifically his right to an attorney and his right to have an attorney present during questioning—"

Kate put a hand out to try to back him down.

"Mr. Friedman, we were merely having a conversation, not a formal interrogation. But I am now convinced that I have sufficient evidence to hold your client as an accessory-after-the-fact in a multiple homicide."

Friedman stared at Kate, surprised by her defiant tone. "If that's true," he said, at last, sounding conciliatory, "then you'll have plenty of opportunities to present your evidence before the court when he is officially arraigned. Until that time, Mr. Ross is remanded into my custody as an officer of the court. Please get him on his feet and arrange to have his personal belongings released."

He turned and marched the length of the interrogation room floor and stood at the door, glancing at his expensive watch and tapping his foot, waiting for his orders to be carried out.

George A. Friedman, Esquire, was used to getting his own way. Though diminutive in height and stature, he was a ruthless member of the California Bar Association and successful at what he did. For fun, he would often invite rival attorneys for lunch and dine on their remains after he had devoured them in court, because he could. Few attorneys knew the law as he did, and few attorneys wanted to face him in court. He handled high-profile cases. His clients were the rich and famous of the San Francisco Bay area or those close to them. He was best known in the press for not only representing the poor Latina housekeeper that brought down one of the biggest celebrities in the world but also for litigating the paternity of her lovechild with the former governor.

Friedman chose his cases based upon how much money and publicity he would receive. He never worked pro bono, and that's what struck Kate as being odd. As far as she could tell, the Ross family didn't have any money, other than a broken-down split-level in Noe Valley, and Philip Ross was not a high-profile celebrity. He was nobody from Sioux Falls, South Dakota.

Kate was curious. She watched as the Lieutenant and the other members of Homicide treated him like a celebrity when all she felt was contempt. She leaned over the interrogation table and reached down to help her suspect to his feet.

"Inspector," Ross whispered, "Don't let them take me."

"I can't legally stop them," she said.

"That's enough! Not another word," Friedman shouted. He took Ross by the arm and steered him toward the door. He walked by the detectives with the look of a biggame hunter who bagged his prize and was trumpeting his victory to the natives. Ross did not react at all; he walked along in a trance, with his head lowered like a dead man walking.

In the outer office, Friedman's enforcers took charge.

They looked like two gorillas in black Armani suits as each one of them grabbed an arm and fast-stepped Ross down the corridor. Friedman remained behind long enough to collect his briefcase and top coat before he scurried on his short, little legs after them.

Kate looked from face to face and at Ross's retreating back as he was led away. "Wait, wait," she said, pleading her case to each one of them. "Ross told me he's in tremendous danger. We've got to stop them."

"Are you out of your freakin' mind?" asked Lieutenant Roberts, fixing her with a cold stare. "We just dodged a bullet."

"Don't you know who that was?" William questioned. "With one snap of his finger, we could have been back on the street pounding a beat—"

"—or worse. Standing in the unemployment line," Mikhail completed his sentence.

"And what about our suspect?" Kate demanded, the reality of his fate dawning on her. "He said that they were going to kill him—literally beat him to death. What if he was telling the truth?"

"Better him than me," Mikhail said.

"Get your head out of your ass, Inspector," ordered the Lieutenant. "A man like Friedman doesn't become a man like Friedman by killing his clients or representing people who would kill his clients. He's too far above that sort of thing. More than likely, Ross was just seeing how far he could jerk your chain."

Kate shook her head. "No, you're wrong. If you had seen that look of terror in his face, you'd know he was telling the truth."

"Forget it, Dawson. It's not your concern."

Lieutenant Roberts took a deep breath then turned and started to walk calmly from the interrogation room. He acted as if he had heard all that he wanted to hear from his detective. It was one thing to question the authenticity of a writ signed by a lower court judge and discuss reasonable options, but it was quite another thing piss off one of the most powerful men in the state with accusations of murder.

He understood, more than most, the unmarked line that should never be crossed. Roberts was a pragmatist.

Kate caught up with her boss as he walked back into the Homicide Bureau and pulled him to the side. "C'mon, Lieutenant, please listen to reason," she said, out of breath.

"Philip Ross is a nobody. He doesn't have any money; he doesn't have any unique skills. In fact, other than a brokendown house, he doesn't have a pot to piss in. So why would a high-powered attorney, like Friedman, or whoever hired Friedman, give a shit about him? Unless Ross is important for what he knows. Maybe he and his wife saw something they weren't supposed to see or witnessed some event that now places him directly in the crosshairs."

"What are we talking about?" Roberts asked her.

"Murder? Robbery? Theft? Some drug deal gone bad? What?"

"I don't know, sir," she confessed, "but I think it was something serious enough to have cost him the lives of his wife and children."

"So, then, you don't think he did it?"

"I don't know," she replied, climbing out on the proverbial limb. "I think Ross may have been forced to watch each of his children and, then finally, his wife put to death in order to protect some grand secret. They're all dead because he refused to talk. But now that they've run out of people to kill, Ross is their number-one target. They can't exactly get at him while he's in police custody. So they hire a big-name attorney to break him loose, and then they serve him up on a silver platter."

Roberts looked at her sharply. "Who are 'they'?"

"I don't know, sir. But if we can find out what Ross knows, then we should have a pretty good idea who wants him dead."

Roberts shrugged. "That may sound reasonable, Inspector," he commended her. The Lieutenant looked tired, drained, and older than his fifty-one years. "There's just one problem: Friedman. If he finds out we're after his client, it won't be pretty. He'll see us all lose our badges."

"That's a chance I'll take, Lieutenant," Kate persisted, like a boxer trying to wear down his opponent with a combination of jabs and punches. "You don't have to be involved. In fact, it's probably better off that you don't know anything more about what I'm doing. That way, you've got plausible deniability."

"You know, Dawson, most of the time, you're a real pain in the ass," he said, looking her squarely in the face. He didn't smile or grin or change his expression in any way, but there was something in his voice that reassured her. "But every so often, I see a glimpse of someone who's a good detective. Don't fuck this up."

Kate nodded her head. "Just be ready to send in the cavalry when I call," she said.

CHAPTER FOUR

Twenty minutes later, Friedman's limousine pulled away from the curb in front of the Hall of Justice.

Kate and Jorge followed in his late model Ford pickup truck. They hung back on Bryant Street, a safe distance, giving the limo a long lead but still keeping it in sight.

Kate reasoned that it was always better to lose a lead in traffic than to have the driver make the tail. Besides, she had a good idea where they were going, and she confirmed her suspicions when the limousine made the right at 16th Street.

They caught up just past the Bart Plaza and followed within a car's length for about six blocks, past the Roxie Theater. Kate cautioned Jorge about getting too close, and he backed off to where they were once again a block behind. The limo made a left before Dolores Street; a winding street that ran north to south through the Mission District. They passed signs for the high school and the park, slowing down a block or two before Liberty Street, the Lincoln Town car made a sharp right turn and pulled into a parking spot that barely fit its length.

Jorge slowed as they drove by the limo. Kate ducked down in the passenger's seat, struggling to glimpse the reflection from the car's mirror, and watched as the limo driver parked, shutting down the engine. He got out of the limousine and opened the side door for Friedman, his two gorillas, and Philip Ross. She lost sight of the entourage as they entered the side door of a nondescript building.

"Go down to the end of the block, hang a right at Liberty, and then another right at Dolores," she said, climbing back into the seat. "We'll come around on them from the front."

"No *problemo*," Jorge replied, following her T instructions.

Two blocks down on the right, they found the limousine parked across two metered parking spots on the right-hand side of a building, one which had been renovated to give it a more modern appearance. Its harsh brick and mortar exterior was tempered by wood-clapboard siding applied for cosmetic reasons in the last couple of months. They continued past and came upon a storefront, with the name *First Pentecostal Church of God* painted in white letters in the store window. Below, in red letters, it read, *End Time Ministries*. An attractive man with long brown hair and a day-old beard, looking like a modern-day prophet, stood in the open door of the church greeting passersby and handing out bulletins.

They parked a few cars down on the right, and both Kate and Jorge settled in for the long wait.

The First Pentecostal Church of God looked like the product of a bygone era when newly-formed churches started out in storefronts until they became vested with property and a proper church building. Located in the Mission District, it was about four blocks away from the much more famous Mission Dolores, the eponymous former mission that gave its name to the neighborhood. This, the fifty-fourth church that had received a charter from its community action group, stood as a symbol for anyone who had a few dollars and dream.

The church was more of a compound with several homes and the old storefront knitted together to form a modern-day fortress, not unlike the Kennedy Compound in Hyannis Port, Massachusetts.

The Sanctuary was built into the old storefront and contained bench-board setting for about two hundred parishioners, an altar, a pulpit, and a modern audio-visual system. Smaller rooms dedicated to prayer and fellowship were located just off the Sanctuary, with connecting doors to other buildings in the compound.

The Main House, largest of the three, was behind the storefront and served as the living and dining quarters of the church's leader and entire staff. The two smaller houses were gutted and functioned as open space to house the kitchen, pantry, utility rooms, library, game room, television room, as well as assorted bedrooms and offices. An old wine cellar was converted into a room for cold storage. Several secret doors and back staircases, identified only in the original blueprints but forgotten with age, gave the compound a sense of intrigue. Similar to a French chateau during the height of the German occupation in World War II.

Kate didn't like stakeouts, and after twenty minutes of staring at the church compound, she became restless. She looked over at her partner, and wasn't surprised he had fallen asleep, since he was up with the baby three or four times a night. That would have drained most men of the energy they needed to stay conscious every day, let alone policemen under the daily stress of their jobs. She didn't have the heart to wake him, and she decided to let him sleep longer.

She got out of the truck to stretch her legs and surveyed the other buildings on the block. They were a mixture of retail and residential, much like the days before the mayor and city-council embraced gentrification with the Mission District becoming a haven for yuppies. She liked the diversity. It gave the neighborhood character. The area was supposed to be a melting pot of cultures, where artists, musicians, actors, dancers, and writers created a gritty Little Bohemia.

Forget the chain restaurants and megastores, Kate preferred the cultured food, sizzling nightspots, quirky political bookstores, and galleries that made the Mission District unique to the entire world.

By the time Kate circled back to Jorge's latemodel Ford pick-up truck, he was starting to stir. She leaned into the driver's side door and craned her neck to look out the back window at the church storefront. The Jesus-look-alike was still standing there in the front door, talking to people and handing them church bulletins as they walked by.

"It's been over an hour," she reported, checking her watch. "I'd like to know what's going on in there."

"*Si, claro*," he replied.

"Why don't we shake things up a bit?" Kate asked with a devious smile.

Jorge shrugged. "*Bueno*, whatever you have in mind."

She studied her partner for a long moment and then said, "Lose the shirt and tie, get rid of the belt, and untuck the undershirt out of your pants. Let it hang out, maybe even a little uneven. And muss up that hair."

"*¿Qué coño?*" He did not sound happy.

"You're going on your first undercover assignment."

Kate considered her words and then added, "Look, Friedman and his gorillas got a good look at me, the Lieutenant, and probably William. I doubt if he even noticed that you were there. But on the off-chance he did, the sunuvabitch would never suspect the itinerant Latino who just happened to wander in off the street to take a piss as the cop he met a few hours earlier."

Jorge had loosened his tie and was starting to unbutton his Turnbull & Asser dress shirt. "Itinerant Latino," he repeated, with disdain.

"Sorry, it's the best I could come up with on such short notice."

"That makes it worse."

Kate helped him out of his shirt and then tousled several locks free of his sculptured hair to make him appear unkempt and sloppy. She reached down, took a handful of dirt from the street and worked it into the lines on his face.

"What about my shoes and socks?" he growled at his partner. "Maybe I should go barefoot?"

"No, that would be obvious." Then she thought about it again. "Your shoes are polished. See what you can do about scuffing them up some before you loop back around."

Jorge looked at himself in the car mirror and played with his hair to make it look even more unkempt. "*Bueno*," he said, admiring himself. "What is the plan?"

Kate took a deep breath and let it out slowly. She was nervous, but she tried to hide her true feelings. "See the Jesus freak in the storefront door?" she said, glancing over her right shoulder. "I think that's the same guy that was sitting with Ross yesterday morning. I think his name is John Mitchell. He's involved in all of this, but I don't know how much."

Jorge shrugged his shoulders.

"I'm going to get him talking, so he doesn't notice you or say anything to you when you come by and ask to use the bathroom. I'm hoping he waves you through, but if he doesn't, be prepared to put on this big act that you really need to take a leak and you're not going to take no for an answer. Threaten to piss on him. That should work."

"And then, once I'm through the door?"

"Find whatever you can. Open doors, look in closets, shake the place down. You won't have a whole lot of time in there. So move fast, and be ready to run in case they spot you."

"Like a jackrabbit," he added.

"Whatever you do, don't get caught," she warned, looking Jorge square in the eyes. "Your disguise is good, damned good for what we could do on such short notice, but it won't stand up to scrutiny. If they catch you, don't play the hero. Just give it up, and we'll take our chances with the Lieutenant. Okay?"

"*Bueno*," he replied.

"Now, give me about fifteen minutes, and we'll hit them hard."

Jorge nodded and then headed north on Dolores for a leisurely walk around the block. Kate turned away, without a backward glance at her partner, and focused on her target ahead.

The ruggedly handsome man standing in the doorway of the First Pentecostal Church of God looked like the long-haired, blue-eyed man that so many western artists had depicted of Jesus. This didn't bother Kate, she had seen plenty of men with long hair and beards over the years. She lived in San Francisco where the Summer of Love never ended, and hundreds of men with long hair and beards still lived in the Haight-Ashbury neighborhood. However, the attraction she felt toward this Jesus look-alike did bother her.

This man stood tall, over six-feet-four, well built, with long brown hair, a day-or-two-old beard, and piercing blue eyes. He looked angelic and saintly, but rugged, like he should be up north in Washington or Oregon chopping trees. The incongruity of the prophet and the lumberjack created a mystique—at least in her mind. His manner of dress also challenged the way she looked at him. He should have worn a red-and-black flannel shirt, blue coveralls, and heavy work boots. But instead, he wore dress jeans that were pressed with a tidy crease, a button-down Oxford shirt, and penny-loafers. He did not look at all like John Monroe. Rather, he was a manly man that stirred something deep within she thought was long dead.

Kate walked up to him on the street and took one of the church bulletins from his hand. She betrayed none of those feelings, nothing; her face was as hard as an ancient ceremonial mask.

"Dear sister, have you found Jesus?" he asked, greeting her with a warm handshake and smile.

"I didn't know He was missing," she replied.

"Ha, ha," he laughed. "That's such an old joke."

"Really? It never made me laugh."

He smiled at Kate; his deep blue eyes sparkling.

"You wear your cynicism like a mask, Inspector, but I can see right through it," he said. "Ecclesiastes teaches us to laugh often and be joyful in all things."

"I don't think we've met," she said, trying to cover her surprise.

"Maybe not formally," he replied, "but I know who you are."

She looked long and hard at him, then looked away. Her fleeting curiosity had been satisfied, and Kate knew if she kept staring at him she would be undone. His blue eyes unsettled her. They were wide and knowing, and they swept over her face like search lights, looking right through her.

"Then you must be John Mitchell," Kate said.

"That's right, but most of my friends call me Mitch."

"What's your involvement with the First Pentecostal Church of God, Mr. Mitchell?" she asked.

He flipped his hair to one side, and then said "hello" to another female passerby and handed her a church bulletin.

"I guess you could say I help out around the place," he replied. "Eighteen months ago, I was injured in a logging accident up north. Three other people were killed, but I survived. So, when I got out of the hospital, I promised God to devote my life to serving Him. I've been here ever since and can't imagine doing anything else with my life."

"I envy you, in a way," she said honestly.

"Sometimes it takes people an entire lifetime to figure out what gives their life meaning."

"Do you believe in God, Inspector?"

Kate shrugged. "I stopped believing in God when I learned there was no Santa Claus or Easter Bunny."

"He still believes in you."

"Then it's really a one-sided relationship," she concluded.

"You know, I don't think you'd feel that way if the Holy Spirit touched your life," Mitchell said, his face glowing with compassion and the love of God. "You should join the church, get involved, and be a part of something larger than yourself. I'd be happy to guide you."

Kate sighed and turned away from him, as if she'd get a third-degree sunburn if she continued staring at his face. "I go to mass at Christmas and Easter. That's about what I figure I owe Him."

He reached out with a big, rugged hand and gently turned her face back to him. "Kate," he said, softly, almost a whisper, "God loves you and wants to fill your empty vessel with love. He will cleanse your soul and purge you of all of your sins and doubt. There is no greater love than His."

"Why is this so important to you?" she asked.

"Do you get so many brownie points for each passerby you bring in?"

"Your reclamation—"

Kate cut him off, holding up a hand like a cop stopping traffic. "I don't need your help or God's help."

Mitchell ignored her. "All of us have sinned and fallen short of the Kingdom of God," he said. "The message of Romans 3:23 tells us that there is not one person on earth who is perfect. All of us have sinned, and yet many of my brothers and sisters who attend services here still seek God's help and salvation in their lives."

"Let me ask you," she said, arms folding across her chest. "How much of a churchgoer was Jesus?"

But before John could reply to her question, an iterant Latino approached him, leaning over to whisper in his ear. "*¿Puedo usar el baño? Tengo que tomar pis,*" Jorge said, then repeated his message again in English, "Can I use the bathroom? I need to take a piss."

"*Casa de Dios es su casa,*" Mitchell replied clumsily and pointed him through the door and to the left.

Kate and Jorge exchanged glances. Her partner followed the path that had been outlined for him and disappeared into the storefront church.

"You speak Spanish," Kate observed, paying him a compliment.

"*Un poquito,*" he replied, holding his thumb about an inch away from his forefinger as a small measurement of what he spoke. "A little bit."

"Well, that's more than me," she lied.

"Really? I would have expected someone in law enforcement, like yourself, to know several languages."

"No, not really," she shrugged, trying to buy her partner time. "I never had a tongue for language, but then I understand some of the members of your church speak in tongues. How strange is that?"

John Mitchell was unruffled. "Yes, that's right. Some members do speak in dead languages that have not been heard on this planet for thousands of years, but then, it's not a strange occurrence. The Book of Acts records two other occasions in which the Holy Spirit caused people to speak in tongues. Then in his letter to the church at Corinth, the apostle Paul gave instructions about speaking in tongues."

"Mr. Mitchell, you've very knowledgeable about the Bible," Kate complimented him a second time. "Have you given any thought to my question? How many times did Jesus attend church?"

"Christ came to earth to die upon the cross to save us from our sins," he said. "He also came here to teach us how to live out our lives. If we are to proclaim Jesus as our Lord and Savior, shouldn't we also want to live our lives the way He lived His life? I know I do—"

Kate cut him short. "You're not answering my question."

Mitchell closed his eyes for a moment, as if to summon a suitable answer to mind. He struggled for a moment, then smiled thinly. "Of all the lessons Jesus taught us, prayer would have to be the one I consider most valuable. Without prayer there would not be any way for us to speak to God—"

"Twice," she said, interrupting him. "The Bible only talks about two occasions when Jesus attended the temple:

Once, when He was twelve years old, His parents found Him in the temple questioning His teachers, and the second time was when Jesus cleansed the temple of its money changers."

He listened and nodded and smiled.

"During the rest of His life on earth, Jesus spent His time among the people, walking and talking," she continued. "He didn't waste His time on the pious churchgoers who went to temple to be seen by others. He walked among the sinners in the street. And *that's* a job I know something about."

"Bravo," Mitchell said enthusiastically, clapping his hands. "Now, I'm the one, Sister Katherine, who should be complimenting you."

"Katherine was a saint," she said. "I'm just Kate—to my friends."

"Just Kate, it's a pleasure to meet you," he replied sincerely.

At that moment, Friedman pushed his way through the storefront door and stood between Kate and Mitchell. He took out a handkerchief and mopped his brow. The afternoon sun was hot, and Friedman's pasty features looked like they hadn't seen the light of day for years. "Inspector Dawson, twice in one day," he said sourly. "If we meet a third time today, I'll suspect you were following me, and I'll swear out a formal complaint."

"Mr. Friedman, what a coincidence . . ." Kate did not look surprised or apologetic, just gazed at him coolly.

"I believe you've lost something," he added, snapping his fingers.

Flanked by Friedman's two associates, Jorge was brought out of the church and turned loose on the sidewalk.

The only thing hurt on him was his pride. Jorge raked the hair back from his eyes and shrugged his shoulders.

"Didn't I warn you not to drink all that coffee," she pretended to scold him.

"*Si, bueno*," he replied, doing his best to keep up the image of the iterant Latino.

"You just never know where you'll find a restroom," she said.

Friedman looked sharply at her. "Your business is done here, Inspector. I don't expect to see you or your partner back here again for any reason. And if, by chance, someone loses a dog or reports a car that is double-parked, I'll expect to see two other detectives respond to the call, and not the two of you. Am I making myself clear?"

"Crystal," she replied.

Friedman wiped his forehead again, and then he pushed his way back through the door. He was followed closely by his two associates, their large hulking bodies barely fitting through the storefront entrance.

John shifted uncomfortably. He'd been duped. "I hope we'll see one another again," he said finally to Kate.

"Count on it," she replied.

Her partner stood there, licking his wounds.

Kate decided it was time for them to get the show on the road. Nodding at Jorge, he returned her nod, and the two walked toward his truck.

"What did you find out?"

"*Un poquito*," he replied, still in character.

"Did you find Ross?" Her tone was anxious and curious.

"*Si*, he was being held in a room by those two *pendejoes*," Jorge said, describing Friedman's associates as "stupid morons," as he climbed into the driver's side door of his truck. "I might have gotten away if I hadn't run into Friedman himself."

Kate opened the passenger's side door and slid in next to him. "Ramirez, you did real good," she said, smiling.

"I'm proud of you."

"*Gracias*," he replied, with a modest nod of his head.

"On our way back to the precinct, let's make a stop at the Building Inspector's office and see if we can't put our hands on the original architectural plans for that compound and hope they're still on file."

"And Ross?"

"I think we've bought him another twenty-four hours," Kate replied with a deep exhale. "Friedman wouldn't dare do anything to him right now, not as long as he knows that we're watching him."

Back at the San Francisco Police Department headquarters, Kate sat at her desk, hunched over the computer terminal in the darkened, deserted detective room of the Homicide Bureau. Detailed drawings and architectural plans of the four buildings were spread across her desk, but as most of them were more than thirty years old, she didn't have a single plan that represented the church compound today. She hunted and pecked at the letters on her keyboard. She typed in: *John Mitchell, white male, forty, 70 Dolores Street, San Francisco*, then hit enter and waited for the computer to return its results.

The wait was long, but then she knew she would have to temper her expectations for a quick response against those of a computer system ten years out-of-date. The computer's flashing icon started processing information. It moved through the files in the SFPD data banks for John Mitchell, and then it reported NSEF—which was shorthand for "no such entry found."

"Great," Kate sighed. She wasn't surprised, but had hoped for a parking ticket at the very least. That would have given her some kind of trail to follow, but as it was, the computer said he did not exist.

She cleared the screen and opened two separate windows: One was for the National Sex Offender Registry, and the other was for the FBI's National Crime Information Database. She typed in her clearance code for each window, entered as much information about John Mitchell as she had then hit enter on her keyboard. The computer screen sat silent for a moment or two then began to spit out names, dates and information. There were twenty-seven John Mitchells in the National Sex Offender Registry, but not a single one of them matched her guy. When she turned to the window for the FBI's crime database, there were a couple of dozen entries for John Mitchell, but not a single one matched him either.

Anxious, Kate turned to the internet and typed his name into the search engine. The computer thought about her request for a moment, then it printed out several million entries for the name John Mitchell on her computer screen, including references for the former attorney general, some for a professor of computer science at Stanford, and a few for a hockey player for the Colorado Avalanche. She started over again and tried cross-referencing his name against logging and logging accidents in the Pacific Northwest, but the result was always the same. There was no such person as John Mitchell, or at least not the man that she knew. He must be using another name, but she was uncertain as to why he would have lied to her.

Kate took a deep breath and settled back in her chair, lost in thought. After some time, she sat forward and once again hunched over her keyboard, typed a few keys and punched the enter button—3,580,000 entries came up for End Time Ministries. She started with the first entry:

"End Time Ministries is a splinter group from the American Pentecostal Christian Church that maintains a close vigil on world politics and the connection between today's news and the ancient prophecies recorded in the Bible. Believers, also known as End Timers, think we have entered the period known as 'The Final 7 Years' and anticipate events heralding the Antichrist, the Great Tribulation, the Mark of the Beast, and a final world war that will take the lives of more than five billion people in its wake. After the tribulation, Jesus Christ is expected to return to the earth and reveal Himself to the faithful. The Second Coming of Jesus Christ is the most anticipated event of the Christian Church . . ."

She read one website after another, and in the course of three hours, she had worked her way through hundreds of sites. Most of her research revealed that the End Time Ministries was a collection of smaller groups spread throughout the United States and Canada, like individual cells of a much larger organism. They all made the end of the world the focal point of their theology, comparing current events in the world with those prophesied in the books Daniel and Revelation in the Bible. Emphasis on prophecy and the exposition of eschatological theories is what set them apart from other similarly themed groups. Within its groups, Kate saw division. Some members disagreed with others on the Millennium and the rule of Christ for a thousand years while Satan was bound in the bottomless pit.

Others argued about the Rapture and whether true believers would experience any of the Great Tribulation. Most of their disagreements, she felt, were petty ones.

As she completed her reading, Kate noticed that she had scribbled down a dozen words and phrases that kept repeating themselves over and over again: *religious cult, army of God, mysterious deaths, mind control, promised land, end time, self-styled prophet, home schooling, Lake City, God's wrath, deprogramming*, and *mass suicide* were mentioned in nearly every one of the articles she read. The name Charles Hampton Kenilworth recurred, and she suspected that he was a major player, but she didn't know how or why a former dot-com millionaire was involved with a religious cult.

In the final article, Kate read through tired eyes about a California state legislator who had written a book chronicling her thirteen-year ordeal as a member of the cult church group: *"State Senator Gabriela Santiago of Sacramento, California, spent several years as a member of the End Time Ministries. Her new book reveals how she was lured as an idealistic teenager into the group with a form of 'thought control' by its Svengali-like leader, and then she fought for thirteen years to break free . . ."* Kate checked the date on the article—almost two years ago. She wondered how Santiago had faired with her book. She Googled the State Senator and found that the woman was still in office.

"Ain't you got nothing better to do than come in here searching through the personals on Craigslist for true love?" Mikhail asked.

Kate smiled but never took her eyes off the screen. "I ain't looking for true love," she replied, thinking of her earlier encounter with John, "but if he's out there, I'm gonna find him."

Mikhail dropped into a chair next to her. "Ramirez told William and me about your gutsy move today. Way to go, Kate. I wish I had been there to see the look in that fat fuck's face."

"You mean Friedman?"

"Yeah. I'd like to lock his ass up and listen to him squeal as some brother turns his flabby white ass into his bitch."

"We bought Ross a day or two, maybe," she said, looking away from the screen. "I wish I knew who was behind it all."

Mikhail craned his neck and peered at the information on Kate's computer screen. "Jesus Christ! End Time Ministries. Senator Gabriela Santiago. You're in there deep, my friend." He looked at her with pity shaking his head. "Talk about real Looney Toons. You might as well be re-opening the case into the thirty-nine Heaven's Gate members who offed themselves when they figured out the alien spacecraft inside the Halle Bopp comet passed them by."

"What do you know about Santiago?"

"She was all over the news a couple of years ago," he said with an easy shrug. "Claimed she was abducted by some religious fanatics who planned to bring about the end of the world. Nobody took her seriously. But she did parlay her fifteen minutes of fame into a state senate seat."

"I don't remember any of that," Kate confessed.

"Well, it wasn't a huge story back then. More like one of those Ripley's Believe-it-or-Nots, I tend to remember."

Kate shrugged leaning back in her chair to rub her eyes. She had been working for three hours straight.

"Why don't you let me buy you a drink?" Mikhail urged her.

Kate shook her head no. "I'll take a rain check. I'm tired. I want to go home and get some rest."

She gathered the detailed drawings and architectural plans into her arms, and hurried down the stairs. Mikhail followed her. They reached the lobby and pushed through the outer door together.

"Anything I can say to change your mind?" he asked, taking Kate by the arm.

"No thanks. But I appreciate the offer," she replied, climbing into her car.

Kate drove toward South Beach, taking the long route along Bryant to Beale Street instead of jumping on the Eisenhower Expressway to the Embarcadero. A light rain was falling when she pulled onto Delancey Street and stopped in front of her building. She rolled to a stop at the curb and killed the engine. The only sound was the rain tapping lightly on the roof as she gathered the architectural plans into her arms.

She scurried across the sidewalk and climbed the steps to the third floor of her apartment building. Kate had already decided that she needed some special help to bring the detailed drawings together into a single plan that represented the church compound of today, and that special help was Lenny Provolone.

As a program director at Northrop-Grumman, he controlled one of the most powerful surveillance satellites in the world. NEMESIS, short for National Emergency Management Electronic Surveillance Intelligence Systems, had been conceived as the ultimate tool for assisting FEMA track victims of man-made and natural disasters and connect them with supplies and recovery resources. She had seen it in use on the night when her partner Frank Miller was killed and relied on its technology to track down the serial killer John Monroe. The satellite had proven its worth to the SFPD, and she needed her friend's help again.

Kate approached Lenny Provolone's apartment and knocked on the front door. "Lenny, this is Kate," she said, after rapping on the door a couple of times. "I need to ask you a favor."

"Hi," he said, cracking the door open. "Am I catching you at a bad time?"

"No."

"I wanted to talk to you about a favor . . ."

"Come on in." He opened the door wide and stepped away, leaving a clear pathway into the kitchen and front sitting room.

Kate walked into his apartment and glanced around. The first thing she noticed was Lenny wearing the same dingy gray t-shirt and briefs he had been wearing a couple of days earlier. The second was the smell of day-old urine that had collected in his toilet, but had not been flushed all week long. It was no wonder why she thought Lenny's apartment smelled worse than the public toilets down on Skid Row. Those were flushed from time to time. Things were the same as they had been the last time she was there—except the garbage in Lenny's kitchen was gathered into several large trash bags lined neatly in a row. She picked up fast-food bags on the kitchen floor and shoved them into the last full trash bag. *That's it, no more. Gotta stop cleaning up after him.*

"Lenny, you should think about getting a maid," Kate suggested. "This place may be more than you can handle."

"Maids cost money, and every maid who has ever seen this apartment has run off into the night screaming."

"Sorry to hear that."

"It's the story of my life," he sighed, still feeling sorry for himself.

"Well, then, I'll get right to the point," she said, rolling out her collection of detailed drawings and architectural plans on her friend's dining room table. Kate arranged them in order of importance, with the storefront closer to her and the rest of the buildings occupying places left, center, and right on the table. "I'm working on an important case right now where my suspect is held up in this compound. I can't make another move without knowing more about what's inside. And since most of these plans are thirty or more years out of date, I'm blind as to the exact layout of the compound."

Lenny adjusted his thick horned-rim glasses and leaned over the table. He looked from one diagram to the next tracing his fingers over the architectural plans. He coughed lightly, his hand going to his throat, as if the old documents were making him congested. "Kate, it is serendipitous that you should come here this evening," he observed. "I was going to stop by your place later on tonight and ask you a favor."

The storm was intensifying outside, rain coming down hard, thunder rumbling, and lightning crackling with frequency. The apartment lights flickered on and off again.

"Is that right?" she asked, looking all around, distracted by the weather.

"Next weekend is WesterCon," he reported.

"What's that? An event for people into Westerns?"

"No, I said Wester-Con, not Western-Con," he corrected her. "It's a science fiction convention."

Kate wagged her finger at Lenny. "I'm not sharing a room with you. You can just get that notion right out of your head."

Lenny's shoulders slumped, disappointed. "Oh, okay, if that's how you feel," he replied. "Would you at least come and pretend to be my girlfriend? I want to make Rebecca jealous."

"I don't see how that's going to help," she said.

"Lenny, this woman has moved on with her life. Shouldn't you be doing the same thing?"

"Kate, that may be how things work in your circles, but that's not how they work in mine."

Kate narrowed her eyes, thinking. Outside of some sixth grade hijinks on the school playground, this is how things worked in the real world. She knew from her own dating experience that if a person rejected her it was time to move on. Trying to make the person jealous was just pointless, a waste of energy. She wasn't sure how much of this bullshit she was going to be able to put up with, but for the time being, she was willing to see it through.

"Okay, have it your own way, Lenny, but don't say I didn't warn you."

"I picked up a costume for you to wear," he said cheerfully.

"You know, I'm not really the kind of person who goes for wearing costumes," she replied. "Not even at Halloween."

"But you've got such a nice body for a woman your age."

Kate shrugged. "What does it look like?"

Lenny walked over to the closet near the front door, and pulled out a garment bag. He unzipped it and exposed a copper brassiere, red silk loincloth, copper plates, and a pair of pixie-shaped leather boots.

"I went to a lot of trouble to find you an official reproduction of the Slave Girl costume that Princess Leia wears in *Return of the Jedi*," he said with a great deal of pride, handing Kate a bundle of the items, "but I think you'll find it's the best quality and will fit you. There are a couple of other adornments, including a hair fastener, a snake arm-wrap and two bracelets, which I've got here."

She held the metal bikini in front of her, and for an instant, modeled the skimpy costume in the hallway mirror.

Then she thought better of it. "Are you crazy? What the hell were you thinking? I'd rather die than wear something like this."

"But it's such an iconic costume," he said, sputtering.

"For a twenty-year-old, maybe."

"But I think it could still work for you."

"I'm not going to wear a costume, particularly not that one," Kate said with finality, handing the item back to her friend. "Even if you're too stupid to realize it, I have to draw the line somewhere."

There was another sudden flash of light. Kate went to window in Lenny's front room and looked out at the street from behind the blinds. The clouds were rolling, swollen, purple, and angry. The storm was gearing up. Lightning flashed, snapping the top branches off a tree across the apartment complex. The severed limbs fell across the road to block traffic.

"One helluva storm brewing out there," she said.

Lenny glared at her, his lower lip turned up into a pout. "Will you at least wear a fan-*ish* t-shirt I bought you?"

"Sure, Lenny, what is it?"

Hastily, Lenny returned the garment bag with the Princess Leia Slave Girl outfit to the front closet and pulled down a t-shirt from an upper shelf. He then held it about shoulder-height air for Kate to see. It was a black t-shirt with the bright yellow image of a modified broomhandled Mauser and the words "Han Shot First." He seemed to be very pleased with himself.

Kate took the t-shirt from him and modeled it in front of the mirror. It looked about right, and black was her color.

She made a mental note to wash it as soon as she got home to cleanse any telltale odors. "What does it mean?" she asked, pointing to the words.

"'Han shot first' is a phrase used by *Star Wars* fans to refer to a controversial change made by George Lucas to a scene in *Star Wars Episode IV: A New Hope*," Lenny explained. "In the scene, Han Solo is confronted by the bounty hunter Greedo at the *Mos Eisley* Cantina. The 1997 altered version depicts Greedo firing a shot at Han Solo shortly before Han responds in kind. In the original 1977 version, Han stealthily readies his own blaster beneath the table and shoots first. Lucas altered the scene for the purposes of political correctness. He didn't want kids to think Han Solo was a bad person because he shot first."

Kate rubbed a hand across her face, confused. "This stuff really matters to you, doesn't it?"

"Yeah," he said, deadly serious. "We spend hours and hours debating things like this all of the time."

"Well, since it's that important to you, I'll wear the t-shirt—but no costume."

"Thanks, Kate."

"I still don't think it's going to make much of a difference," she said, knowing.

Lightning flared close outside followed a heartbeat later by thunder. The apartment lights juiced bright white for a second, then dimmed to semi-darkness then returned to normal.

She walked back to the window and looked out.

Traffic was jammed up around the fallen limbs, muffled honking coming through the sealed glass. There was a hint of smoke where the lightning had struck.

"What time should I be there?" Kate asked, over her shoulder.

"Convention registration opens at nine a.m. for general admission badges," he reported, as if reading the Amtrak train schedule for the San Francisco to Los Angeles mainline run, "but most things won't get started until ten."

"Saturday, ten a.m. it is."

She patted Lenny on the back and then led her friend to the dining room table. She reached down and rearranged the collection of detailed drawings and architectural plans, shuffling them around until they were right back to their starting point. "I need your help in looking beyond these plans to know what's inside that compound. I need the help of your satellite, NEMESIS."

Lenny took off his glasses and held them up to the light, checking for smudges. He then rubbed them on his dingy gray undershirt. He adjusted the glasses on his face, and leaned over the plans. After a moment, he said, "Do you have the coordinates for this compound? Latitude? Longitude?"

Kate shook her head. "Will an address do?" Lenny looked up from the plans and smiled.

"I'm so used to dealing in geographic coordinates, I forget people rely on addresses to get them around."

Kate wrote the address down on the first set of diagrams, then stopped when she heard a steady rat-ta-tat at the window. She walked over to the blinds and pealed them back to see large hailstones bouncing all over the apartment complex. They were the size of golf balls, coming down hard.

"Hail," she said, feeling an irrepressible cold shudder, as if someone had stepped on her grave. "Here? In San Francisco?"

"I suppose it's not that uncommon," he conjectured, ever the nerdy scientist.

While she continued to stare out the window, Lenny came up behind her and put his hand on her shoulder. She was focused on the unusual hailstorm, but the moment his touch registered, she jumped. Kate felt like she was going to come out of her skin.

"Jesus Christ! Are you jumpy," he said.

Kate turned away from him, her arms folded across her breasts, hugging herself for warmth. Her body felt strangely cold with a chill that went right down to her bones.

"Sorry, it's not you," she replied, rubbing her arms with the palms of her hands. "I happened upon something on the Internet about the earth being pounded by hailstones, and it's given me the chills."

"Don't worry about it. Those end-of-the-world predictions aren't based on scientific fact," Lenny reassured her. "Hail forms in strong thunderstorm clouds, particularly those with intense updrafts and high liquid content. Mix that with a cloud layer below freezing, and you're bound to have a hailstorm."

"In San Francisco?"

"Sure," he replied. "I think the last one was in 2011 or 2012."

Kate nodded her head and smiled a well-practiced smile at him. She knew he was trying to make her feel better, but the cold feeling stayed with her.

Hours later, when she climbed in her twin bed and pulled the covers over her head, Kate was still shivering. The chill would remain with her throughout the night and into the early morning hours.

CHAPTER FIVE

A few blocks away from the church compound, Thaddeus Morales walked into the bathroom of his small home and turned on the faucet to let water flow into his bathtub. He played with the hot and cold water tabs and adjusted the temperature to be hot but not scalding. He sat down on the edge of the tub and looked at his watch.

Thaddeus had less than an hour to live. He was not afraid to admit to himself he was having second thoughts about his decision, but he dared not share those thoughts with his wife, Luisa. No matter what he said, she would have insisted that he go through with it. They both gave their lives to God, and nothing was more important to the world than what they were doing.

In a way, he felt already dead and sought comfort from that knowledge. He reasoned there was nothing more liberating than knowing that his life had come down to just a handful of actions, and the final disposition of his soul was secure. Those last few actions are what troubled him.

Thaddeus filled the tub to an imaginary line where there was just enough water to submerge a child's body without causing an overflow and turned the faucet off. He closed the door to the bathroom to keep the steam in and joined his wife in the front room of the house. Luisa was sitting on the sofa with the Bible spread out on her lap.

For a moment or two, he was silent, standing in the center of the living room, arms folded in front of him, looking at the photographs of his three children.

Five-year-old Alejandro, three-year-old Austin, and Anna just fourteen months. There were few pieces of furniture in the room other than a large easy chair and an old sofa that sat on wooden blocks. No television, no stereo or sound system, no computer; no evidence that the Morales family was connected to the outside world. And other than the family photos, the room lacked any personal touches that would have made the neighbors think the house was a home.

"Are you having any second thoughts, Thad?" Luisa asked, not looking up from her Bible.

"Yeah—I mean no," he replied with a lie, the sudden look of terror washing over his face when he realized what he had said. Thaddeus walked over to the front door, and listened. The hail had stopped, and now only rain was coming down hard. He pulled down the blinds to block out the rat-ta-tapping. He repeated the action at the two front windows, then he stood looking out from behind one blind. He looked up and down the street to make sure that no one was there in the rain, and when he was satisfied, he put the blind down. "You know that it's forbidden. We shouldn't even be talking about it."

"Remember the lesson from Ecclesiastes, my husband," she said, reading from the good book. "'There is a time to plant and a time to uproot what is planted.' Well, now is the time to uproot what was planted."

"I know, I know," he said, trying to keep her voice down,

worried that someone may be listening. "I'm just not sure I can do this."

"You must!" Luisa insisted, glaring at him. "You know what's at stake here."

"But they're our children. We gave birth to them; we raised them; we wiped their noses when they were sick and bandaged their knees when they were scraped.

"We have given our lives to caring for them," Thaddeus said, pushing back the tears not allowed.

"Exactly! And now, as their loving parents and guardians, we are tasked by God to return them home to His loving embrace."

Thaddeus turned away from her, confused.

"Do you want to watch them suffer, Thad?" she asked, holding the Bible to her chest. "Face starvation?"

Sickness? Festering sores that never heal? And eventual death and damnation? You know what the scripture says: There will be no hiding place for anyone. No escape. This night, we have the power to spare them all of the horrors they would face during the Tribulation."

"I want another way," he said.

"There is the way of the Lord," Luisa reminded him.

Thaddeus gave no indication of having heard her. He stared at his wife, searching her face for a sign, some symbol of a last-minute reprieve that never came. After a moment of silence, he gathered himself together and headed to the nursery. He knew what he had to do.

He pulled back the covers of his daughter's bed and lifted her, sound asleep, into his arms. She was lightweight and easy to manage. He carried her lovingly down the corridor to the bathroom and opened the door. Sitting on the edge of the tub, he leaned over and kissed her on the forehead. For an instant, Anna stirred in his arms and muttered a few incomprehensible words to him, but she promptly fell back to sleep.

After he hugged and kissed her one final time, Thaddeus placed his daughter's body into the water and held her down until she stopped kicking and splashing. He waited a few moments to make certain she was dead, then lifted her body from the tub and toweled Anna dry. He returned her body to the nursery and headed to the boy's room. One after the other, Thaddeus took both of his sons into the bathroom and drowned them in the shallow water of the tub. Austin went quietly, without much of a struggle, but five-year-old Alejandro fought his father to the last breath as the instinct to live triggered a violent thrashing that took every ounce of Thaddeus's strength to manage. In the end, it was all the same.

With each body tucked into bed for its eternal slumber, Thaddeus returned to the bathroom and refilled the tub. He had already said his goodbyes to Luisa, and with the children now dead, there was one last task to accomplish.

His life had come down to one final action.

He removed his clothing and folded the items neatly on top of the clothes hamper. He also set his watch on top.

With his flat razor in hand, Thaddeus Morales stepped into the warmth of the bath water and sat down. He summoned happier thoughts to mind, remembering that Easter Sunday when he first met his wife and then the days when each of his children was born. The memories mitigated the sharp pain he felt while slitting both wrists. He paid particular attention to making certain that he opened the artery on each side and didn't cut the tendon instead. Thaddeus didn't want to spend the last few minutes of his life in a great deal of agony. He preferred the calm and peaceful approach.

Thaddeus laid back in the hot water, with his wrists at his

side. The water felt warm and comforting, much like a mother's womb. He closed his eyes and thought of his mother. Memories of her mingled with hallucinations of his dead children and his wife, Luisa, as he floated further and further away. The water turned pink and then dark red as he bled out.

Within fifteen minutes, Thaddeus Morales was dead.

His wife Luisa sat in the front room of their house, reading the family Bible for the rest of the night and into the wee hours of the morning. She could hear the storm as it continued spitting intermittent rain and hail, blowing winds colder than any the San Francisco Bay area had experienced in twenty years. She sat on the sofa and did not move, other than to turn the page. She never said a word or uttered a sound of any kind as the rain continued to come down.

Then, around three a.m., as the storm continued to rage, she stood up, walked over to the house phone, and dialed 911.

An operator responded, "911. What is the nature of your emergency?"

"I'd like to report a suicide," Luisa replied.

"Suicide?"

"Yes, it's my husband . . . He took the lives of our three children."

Kate lay shivering under the blankets when her cell phone's distinctive ringtone roused her to consciousness.

Four a.m. The voice on the other end of the line summoned to her to the scene of another homicide.

She drank down a hot cup of coffee while struggling in her small apartment bathroom to pencil in some eyeliner, brush some color into her face, and put on lipstick. Kate pulled on a heavy, cable-knit sweater to keep her warm and tugged a brush through the tangles of her hair. She had just enough time to brush her teeth and pull on a London Fog classic belted trench-coat and scarf. She was out the door fifteen minutes later, driving to yet another typical suburban street in the Noe Valley.

Lightning laced through the night sky in all directions, and thunder rumbled like a series of cannon blasts off in the distance. If she didn't know better, Kate would have thought a great pirate ship was anchored in the Bay, blasting at targets in the city. The rain pounded down on the slick, wet pavement as sirens sounded from somewhere nearby.

Kate made a right at the intersection near the church compound and slowed to look in the storefront window.

At four-fifty a.m., things were quiet, but she could still see John Mitchell standing there in the front door, talking to people and handing them church bulletins as they walked by.

Kate would not have admitted it to anyone, not even to herself, but she was looking forward to seeing John again.

In the fifteen hours since they met, she had thought about him dozens of times. She was attracted to him, but to more than just his rugged, manly good looks. There was something about him that captivated her, but she could not quite put her finger on it. She let her thoughts range over every word they had exchanged during their brief encounter the day before and savored each one, like a bite of Ghirardelli chocolate, as she continued through the intersection.

She drove two blocks over and one block up past the Mission Dolores Park to Cumberland Street. At the end of the street, several police cars were in front of a small, split level home. Their flashing lights guided her to the scene. She parked up on the grass and stepped out into the rain. Pulling the collar on her trench coat up, she walked toward the house.

Detective Clark ran out to greet her. "Looks like we've got another one of those murder-suicides."

"Yeah, I heard," she replied. "Who called it in?"

"The wife. Luisa Morales."

"She was here?"

"No," replied William, without his notes. "She came home late from a women's Bible study group and discovered the bodies."

"Sounds familiar."

"Come on," he said, starting for the door.

Alone on the rain-swept street, Kate stood for a moment. She looked east in the direction of the church compound and thought about John Mitchell one last time before she went to work. Lightening flashed overhead, and for a second, the house was a bright white; then it dimmed to semi-darkness.

Kate trudged up the front steps and walked through the front door. In the foyer, she removed her soaked trench coat and shook out as much of the rainwater as she could before hanging it on a coat rack to dry. She pushed her way through the patrolmen who were standing around talking and trying to keep warm. She noted the cold interior of the house and worked her hands up and down her arms to generate heat.

She walked past several other uniformed officers and coroner's investigators nodding until she came upon the forensic men who were knee-deep in carpet fibers.

"How's it going, guys?" she asked. "Not bad," one replied, looking up. "Okay," another one answered.

"Hey, Dawson!" Mikhail called, waving.

She waved and smiled as she kept moving through the house.

"*Madre de dios*. We've got another bad one," Jorge informed her.

"Yeah, I understand," Kate said, "but don't say it's the work of a demon. I need you to be entirely focused and observe everything no matter how trivial."

"*Bueno*," he replied. "Where are they?"

"One's in the nursery and the other two are in the bedroom. The father's body is still in the bathroom."

She left the front room of the house behind her and headed to the bathroom. Kate opened the door without knocking, and stuck her head in. The naked body of Thaddeus was stretched out in the bathtub, his slashed wrists floating on the surface of the water. The man looked like he had taken a bath in cherry punch. She noted his clothes were folded neatly on the clothes hamper with a cheap Timex crowning the top of the heap. The medical examiner, Dr. Brogan, straddled the toilet seat, leaning over the tub and examining the body.

"How long?" she asked Brogan. "About six hours."

"Cause?"

"Massive hemorrhage," the medical examiner replied. "He cut the arteries deep in both wrists and let them pump out into the warm bathwater. Probably bled to death in ten or fifteen minutes."

Kate nodded her head in agreement.

"You'll find the children tucked in their beds," Brogan added. "All three were drowned in the bathtub. I'd hazard a guess and say the oldest boy put up a struggle before he died because there are contusions on his head and body that are not evident on the other two children. I'll know more about their last few minutes once I've been able to conduct a formal autopsy."

"So then, let me try to understand this," Kate said, with effort to wrap her mind around the murder-suicide.

"Morales brought them in here, one child at a time, and held their face down in about twelve inches of water and drowned them? Then he carried each child's body back to bed and tucked them in for the night?"

Brogan shrugged. "Yeah, and then climbed in the same warm water and offed himself with a flat razor."

"Thanks, Doc."

Kate turned and walked toward the bedrooms at the back of the house. She made a cursory check on the boys in their bedroom and watched as the forensic and medical teams collected their trace evidence. She then glanced in the nursery and saw the littlest member of the Morales family in a slumber she would never wake from. The police photographer brushed by her and snapped off several pictures of the fourteen-month-old.

When she returned to the front room, Kate was shaken by the bodies of the three children despite attempts to hide her personal feelings. The sight of an innocent child's body cut down in the prime of life reminded Kate of her own daughter's senseless death at the hands of her drug-addled ex-husband.

Her daughter had been the innocent one caught up in the middle of a domestic dispute between her parents. Kate blamed herself for Stephanie's death, particularly when she was killed with Kate's own service pistol. Forging a healthy conscience and a sound character had become part of Kate's lifework and was largely dependent on the extent to which she could begin to forgive herself and still develop concern for the welfare of others. It was a struggle. Kate still had a lot to learn about empathy and forgiveness, the natural capacities that have to be present, and she worked on the process every day. Some days were less effective than others. Mikhail and Jorge watched her struggle.

"Has anyone questioned the wife?" Kate asked.

Roberts looked around for someone to respond to her question, but when it was not forthcoming, he pushed his way through the crowd. "No, it doesn't seem like anyone has talked to her yet," he reported. "Why don't you and Clark take a crack at it? Keep it light and conversational."

Kate shrugged her shoulders. She took a couple of steps toward the kitchen and then signaled William to follow. He was busy jotting something down in his notebook and had to scramble to keep pace with her.

"What can you tell me about the wife?" she posed to him.

"Her maiden name is Martinez. She's an ROTC graduate and did three tours of duty in Afghanistan before resigning as a staff sergeant," William replied, reading from his notes, "to become a stay-at-home mom."

"You're shitting me."

"No. She also has several medals for marksmanship she earned in the Army."

"Morales doesn't sound like your typical shy, retiring Bible-thumper," Kate commented.

In the kitchen, the two detectives found Luisa Morales sitting next to a uniformed officer while she read the Bible. She was thirty-five years old, plain, and had the rugged appearance of a woman who had had a hard life. Her black hair was beginning to gray and was pulled tightly into a bun on the back of her head. Her brown eyes, which looked tired, also revealed that they had not shed a single tear.

"Mrs. Morales, I'm Inspector Dawson, and this is my partner, Inspector Clark," she said, showing the woman her badge. "I'm sorry about your loss, ma'am."

"Thank you," she replied.

"What time did you come home last night?" Kate, looking up from her Bible asked.

"Around midnight."

Kate glanced at William and then back at the woman.

"That seems awfully late, Mrs. Morales. Were you out working?"

"I was at a women's Bible study group," she reported without emotion.

"Until midnight?" William asked, his notebook in hand.

Luisa Morales looked at the two detectives. "I said I returned home around midnight," she insisted. "My Bible study group broke up about eleven-fifteen, but I stayed after to pick up and help put away the leftover food."

Clark inquired, "Is there someone in your group who can vouch for your whereabouts last night between ninethirty and midnight?"

She shrugged lightly. "Sure. Ask any woman in my group, and she'll confirm that I was there."

"Mrs. Morales, could you provide me with a list—"

William started to ask, but he was cut off in mid-sentence.

"What's the name of the church that hosts your Bible study?" Kate asked.

"The First Pentecostal Church of God," she replied, looking directly into Kate's eyes.

"And you were there the whole evening?"

"Yes."

"You didn't notice anything strange when you got home," Kate asked her.

"No, nothing at all."

Kate got right to the point. "Your husband had just murdered your three children and taken his own life, and you didn't notice a thing?"

Luisa Morales rolled her eyes, folding her arms across her chest. "*No*. I got home from Bible study, and the house was quiet for the first time all day. Maybe you don't know what it's like to have three children under the age of six chasing after you morning, noon, and night, 'Mommy this', and 'Mommy that'. It's really exhausting. So here I was, in a quiet house, no kids around, and I decided to take some 'Mommy time' for me."

"At midnight?" Kate added.

"Yes, at midnight."

"Mrs. Morales, I'd like to believe you, but I've got two real problems with your story: First, I can't believe that a mother would come home after being away all night long and not want to check on her children or at least tuck them in; maybe give them a kiss goodnight. And second, I don't understand how you can be so cool and collected when your babies are lying in the other room dead. I'd be out of my mind with grief. They'd have to lock me up."

"I don't care what you believe, Inspector," Luisa said, unruffled by the statement. "I've told you the truth."

The two women glared at each other.

Looking through his notes, William asked, "If you arrived home around midnight, why did it take you so long to call 911?"

"I've already explained to you that I didn't notice anything strange when I first got home," she said, with another sigh.

"When did you first suspect there was a problem?"

"I didn't suspect a thing. At about three a.m., I got up from my seat on the couch and went into the bathroom. That's when I discovered my husband had taken his own life. I'll admit it was a gruesome discovery, but not as bad as finding that the children were dead, also."

"What did you do during those three hours, Mrs. Morales?" William asked.

"I read the Good Book."

"For three hours?"

"Yes, for three hours," Luisa repeated herself.

"Haven't you ever read a book that you just couldn't put down?"

"No, I can't say that I have," William replied as he thumbed through the pages of his notebook, looking for his next question. Kate moved over to him and closed the notebook on his fingers.

"Thanks for your cooperation, Mrs. Morales," she said. "We'll be in touch with you if we have any additional questions."

Detectives Dawson and Clark left the kitchen of the small split-level house and walked back to the front room.

William looked upset as they moved through the house.

They walked past several uniformed officers and waved.

They then walked past the forensic men and nodded. And finally, they passed the coroner's investigators.

"I wasn't finished questioning her," William whispered to her, heated.

"She's not going to tell us anything more, Clark. She's had this story of hers rehearsed for months now. She probably knows it backwards and forwards, and she is just making fools out of us."

"You don't know that," he persisted.

"The first rule of interrogation, Clark, is to know the answer before you ask the question. This lady knows the answers to all of our questions, and she isn't about to say anything that's wrong or make a major mistake. We've got to figure out another way to get her to talk to us."

She and William entered the living room and came in on a conversation Mikhail was having with Lieutenant Roberts and Jorge near the front door.

"That's right around the time I was a patrol cop with the Baltimore City Police Department. So anyway, my partner and I get the call. We drive down to the Marriott near the Inner Harbor, and we arrest this guy on suspicion of drowning his three children, one-by-one, in the bathtub of his hotel room," Mikhail continued telling his story. "He didn't put up a struggle. He confessed to drowning them. Everybody says he was a wonderful father. His next-door neighbor says he was very polite. So, what happened? He went off his nut one day and murdered his three kids. Maybe that's what this is all about? Two random incidents where the parents just lose it one day and off their kids."

"These weren't random incidents, Jawara," Kate interjected. "They're both connected in some way to that church, the End Time Ministries."

"Damnit to Hell!" Roberts cursed.

William and Mikhail looked at Kate. She caught their glances. "I've been doing my own research, and I found that this church believes they are living in the end times. They seem to think that Biblical prophecy is playing itself out in world events, and they are working to bring about the end of the world with actions of their own."

"*Cuando el diablo no tiene que hacer con el rabo mata moscas,*" Jorge said under his breath, looking at Kate.

"So this is all about a bunch of cultists?" asked Roberts "I'm not entirely sure, Lieutenant, but their church leader maintains some degree of mind control over his members," she said, poised, cool, in complete command of herself. "That Morales woman didn't shed a single tear over the loss of her children when any normal woman would be hysterical. There is a possibility she was hypnotized or scared enough of the leader that she accepted everything as normal. What kind of man has that kind of control?"

"Mind control?" asked William, while thumbing through his notes.

"We talkin' about little green spacemen?" inquired Mikhail, with a smirk.

"No, I'm not talking about some irresistible force that aliens in the movies use to take over people's minds," she replied. "It's more like a gun. The leader points an imaginary gun at the member's head and says, 'If you don't do what I tell you to do, you're going to go to hell.' He relies on his own force of will and the fear of great personal loss to force them to obey. And when you're in so deep into what you've been told is the 'one true church', the last thing you want to do is leave, because leaving the group means leaving God and His salvation."

Lieutenant Roberts turned to his senior detective.

"Clark, does any of this match up with what you found?"

"That's difficult to say, Lieutenant," he replied, notebook in hand. "I found nine apparent murder-suicides spread throughout the San Francisco Bay area in the last month. The majority of them involved a parental figure, usually the mother, taking the lives of two or more children before committing suicide. However, I didn't crossreference the cases with any religious groups."

"Make that a priority," Roberts ordered. "I'd like to see if we have just two isolated incidents or if we have a real pattern here."

"Thanks, Lieutenant," Kate said.

Roberts turned back to her. "Don't thank me yet," he said gruffly, like a man who had missed his morning cup of coffee. "Use whatever resources you need, including the public library, to track down information on this cult group. But for Pete's sake, don't go anywhere near that compound.

Ross is now the DA's headache, not ours."

"Yes, sir," she said, in compliance.

"I think we've got something, Lieutenant," said one of the forensic technicians, approaching the group.

"It's an iPad," the other replied, producing a blackened hunk of metal.

Kate and her fellow detectives had stopped talking and were now starring at the odd but familiar shape in the technician's hand. It was clearly an Apple iPad, but it looked like it had been burned to a crisp in a fire.

"What the hell happened to it?" Roberts barked.

"Fire," the first technician observed.

"Charbroiled likely in a barbeque pit," the other conjectured.

"Where did you find it?" Kate asked.

"In the laundry room," replied the first technician.

"Under the dirty clothes," the other added.

"Okay, I'll take whatever lead I can get," he said.

"Get it down to the lab and see what information you can recover. Put a rush job on it. "This may be the first break we've gotten."

Everyone was excited by the discovery, except Kate. As far as she was concerned, whoever was behind all of this was far too clever and disciplined to have left any evidence behind. She knew she was dealing with a dangerous psychopath who would stop at nothing to see his agenda unfold.

CHAPTER SIX

On Saturday afternoon, Kate strolled along the Embarcadero and watched the sailboats leave the Marina at South Beach and sail out into the bay; their tiny little masts bobbing up and down on the water. She took in a deep breath, tasted salt from the ocean air on her tongue, and smelled that aromatic sea. She loved living by the water's edge, and she felt renewed by that connection between land and sea. Smiling, she felt tempted to take off her shoes and feel the sand of the beach between her toes, but it was windy and cold. She settled for a hot coffee at the marketplace.

Bayside Marketplace was a festival spot that served SoMa's Bayside Village housing complex and the whole South Beach area. Built around the original Bayside Market, which was a small grocery/deli that specialized in vegan and organic foods, the marketplace had expanded to include vendors selling fresh fruits and vegetables, a few trendy outdoor restaurants, several souvenir shops, and live entertainment at the Bayside Marina stage. Some of the best local bands played everything from rock'n'roll and reggae to salsa and pop music; for the more popular groups, there was AT&T Park at the south end of the marketplace.

AT&T Park was also the home field of the San Francisco Giants, and off-season played host to concerts and other sporting events, including football.

"Coffee, extra lite with sugar," Kate ordered politely.

"That surprises me," said a deep voice a few costumers behind her. "I would have expected you to order one of those blended coffees."

With a thin smile, Kate nodded to herself. She recognized the voice as John Mitchell, but she did not turn around right away. Instead, she waited for the barista to fill her order, then turned to pick up a plastic lid and a couple of napkins. She stood with her back to him, but spoke to the barista when it was his turn. "I believe the gentleman will have a cup of regular coffee, black."

"Black coffee?" asked the barista.

"No, I don't drink coffee," Mitchell said, "but I would like the Pretty Passion Iced Tea. Tall."

"Don't drink coffee?" Kate was surprised. "What are you, some kind of mutant?"

"No, I never developed a taste for it." He allowed her the moment.

"Let me guess," she said, with a raised eyebrow, "you're one of those cheerful guys who manages to get up at the crack of dawn with a smile on his face, feeling alert and ready to take on the world without any caffeine?"

John Mitchell shrugged. "Pretty much."

"We're not going to get along," she said with a smirk, heading for the door.

"Hey, wait a minute," he called after her, grabbing his drink off the counter and following her out of the door.

"The last time I spoke with you, I got into trouble with my boss. I'm not sure I should be talking with you now, unless it's on the record," she explained. "Is this a social call, or have you decided to come clean and help me with my investigation?"

"I wanted to see you, Kate."

"Someone might see that as a conflict of interest," she said coolly. Kate thought about it for a moment and then added, "Or maybe they sent you to feed me false information. You know, throw me off the scent." *How did he know I would be here, right now?*

"No one knows that I came down here today."

"Come to think of it, how did you know where to find me?" She had to ask him outright, bluntly, glancing over her shoulder at him. Kate was so busy walking and talking that she missed a slick spot of water until she slipped. She looked like a skater on ice that had hit a rough spot and lost her balance.

Mitchell practically tackled Kate to prevent her from falling or that's how it appeared to bystanders at the marketplace. When he reached out to take her by the arm and steady her, Kate's momentum carried her forward a few steps, and threw him off balance. His hold on her forced her into a downward spiral that spun her around on an axis, slamming her right back into his arms. Her coffee flew in the air when she reached out to grab hold of something to steady herself. She pulled him down on top of her.

For a moment, they laid in each other's arms on the cold concrete pavement as several vendors and fellow shoppers raced to their aid. Kate raised her head and looked around her surroundings, paying particular attention to the beautiful man lying on top of her. When she realized what happened, she laughed out loud to break the tension. John joined her laughing as he struggled to his feet and put his hand out for her.

"Give me your hand," he said, sweeping his long hair out of his face and to one side.

Kate took his hand to steady her and climbed to her feet. "Thank you."

"Are you all right?" John's intense blue eyes met hers.

"Yes, I think so," she replied, brushing herself off, "but it does give new meaning to the expression falling for someone."

He retrieved her empty coffee cup. "I'm afraid there's nothing left of your coffee. Would you like me to get you a refill?"

"No, I think I've had my fill of caffeine for the day. I want to go look for some fruit."

"Sure, why not?"

As they walked over to the fruit table, Kate looked at him several times and smiled to herself. He seemed like a nice guy, and she *was* attracted to him. More than anything, she wanted to take one of his huge, rugged hands into hers and hold it, as if to say to the world, 'This is my boyfriend,' but she thought better of it. She just met him a few days before, and in her mind, there were still plenty of unknowns about this man; not the least of which was his involvement in the murder-suicides she was investigating.

"How *did* you know where to find me?" she asked him again.

Mitchell walked along beside her in silence and sand, "Does it matter? I wanted to see you again."

"I'm glad," she sighed, but was not satisfied with his answer.

"After our conversation the other day, I haven't been able to get you out of my mind," he confessed.

"Nice to know I can still leave that impression on a man."

John nodded his head. "Don't sell yourself short, Kate. You've got a lot to offer."

"Well, you're not too shabby yourself," she said, stopping in front of a table with fruit and looking up into his eyes. "In a city like San Francisco, that's filled with gay or married men, it's always a surprise to meet a single man who's straight. You are single *and* straight, aren't you?"

"Yes," he replied smiling. "I'm guilty on both counts."

Kate picked up a red delicious apple from the table. She threw it playfully in the air and caught it. "Do you like apples?"

"Sure," John replied. "Should I call you Eve?"

"If you let me call you Adam."

"Why not?"

She handed the vendor a dollar and change and shined the apple on her beige cable-knit sweater. When it was as polished as it could be, she took a small bite out of the apple, then held it out to him, just as Eve must have, with a slight smile. Mitchell smiled back with a twinkle in his eyes, and took a healthy-sized bite, the tasty juices running over his lips and down his chin. She reached up with her other hand and wiped them away, naturally.

"I hope this isn't the part in the story when the serpent appears," she said, chewing on her bite of the apple. "I don't like snakes."

Mitchell shook his head. "No, that happened much earlier. I'm afraid to say that this is the sad part in the story when God throws man out of the Garden of Eden for disobeying Him. You see, as soon as they ate the fruit, a change came over Adam and Eve. They became unhappy and fearful of God. He had warned them not to eat from the Tree of Knowledge, but they didn't listen to Him—"

"—and that's the reason things are so screwed up today," she said, finishing the story for him.

"Something like that."

Together, they finished the apple, and Kate disposed of the core in one of the trash receptacles. She dabbed her mouth with a napkin and wiped his face with it, too.

"Why aren't you married?" Kate was attracted to him and thought he was kind, but she wondered what the downside might be.

"Never found the right woman, I guess. What about you? Are you married? Do you have a family?"

"Divorced."

"Really?"

"Yeah. When you're a cop, you put in a lot of long hours. That means working sixteen-hour days and overtime on weekends. It takes a special man to understand that."

"I think I know what you mean," John replied.

"We put in a lot of long hours at the church as well—"

Kate put a finger to his lips. "Let's not talk shop today."

"Okay, so what would you like to do?"

She and Mitchell exchanged glances. She liked how he looked at her. It thrilled her. She could see he was having a good time and didn't want things to end. She knew she had to come up with a good idea. And as she looked to the south end of Bayside Marketplace, there was AT&T Park. "Do you like music?"

"Sure."

"C'mon. I've got an idea."

They walked to the end of the marketplace and crossed the parking lot. She then directed Mitchell to the security gate at AT&T Park and flashed her police badge at the officer on duty. He nodded at her and waved them through. Kate opened the gate wide and walked through, leading the way into the stadium. John followed, watching her as they moved past security. They walked down a long tunnel and emerged on the other side of the stadium. The bright green turf of the infield grass and the thousands of screaming fans caught them both by surprise, but they kept walking until they were standing in a crowd before the stage.

The Moody Blues, a classic rock group originating in the 1960s, from the city of Birmingham, England, appeared on the raised stage at AT&T Park. At the front of the stage, Justin

Hayward was singing at the microphone and playing his guitar while his fellow guitarist, John Lodge, stood next to him, strumming on his bass guitar. In the back, the drummer, Graeme Edge, pounded away on the drums while Alan Hewitt played the keyboard. They enjoyed renewed success as aging baby-boomers continued to demand their music in venues like AT&T Park. They looked older, grayer, and flabbier than their golden years in the 1960s, but they still played classic rock music that appealed to their broad range of fans.

"All right! The Moody Blues!" Kate was so excited.

"I love this group!"

"I've never heard of them before," Mitchell confessed.

"Never heard of them?" she asked, shaking her head.

"Where on earth have you been living? A cave? The Moody Blues have been one of the top rock groups for over forty years."

"Sorry, I just never heard of this group before."

"I grew up listening to their music." For an instant, Kate was lost in memories from long ago. "My parents were hippies who met during the Summer of Love. They lived in Haight-Ashbury in 1967; that's where I was born. They had this small turntable in the front room, and I remember how my dad used to play The Doors, and The Beatles, and The Moody Blues over and over again on that turntable.

This music takes me back."

"Sounds like you had a blessed childhood." He had to speak a little louder to be heard over the music.

"Yeah, I guess it was okay when they weren't fighting." She stopped talking when she heard the orchestral lead-in music for the next song, then whispered, "This is my favorite song."

John nodded and turned to focus on the stage.

Justin Hayward sang, strumming his guitar, singing "Nights in White Satin."

Kate closed her eyes, listening to Justin's haunting lyrics, moving her body in unison with the music. She moved her upper torso back and forth and felt her hips swaying. She let her arms go. They were moving over her head in rhythm to the music. The lyrics formed an image in her mind of a great bed covered in satin on one of the darkest of nights, and she felt herself falling backwards onto the bed, into the arms of her lover. Her body moved backwards, pushing into John, up against his chest. She felt the grip of his rugged hands come down and take her arms, but she continued to sway back and forth to the rhythm and cadence of the music, never letting up. She rubbed against him and felt him responding to her moves.

As the music began to wind down to its orchestral conclusion, Kate felt desire wash over her, stopped dancing and faced him, slipping from his grip. She looked up into his eyes, took his head into her hands and kissed him deeply.

John reached for her and gathered her into his arms. She melted into them, kissing him with all her soul.

He placed his right hand under the back of her neck and kissed her back, his tongue meeting hers and dancing around her mouth. Their bodies pressed hard together. His left hand reached and touched her cheek, lovingly stroking her jaw line. He felt her hips exploring his, and he reciprocated.

When her lips dropped away from his, she reached up and kissed his ear, whispering, "C'mon. Let's go—back to my place."

He kissed her back and said in a whisper, "I can't. I want to, Kate, but I can't."

She kissed him one last time, more of a polite kiss, and backed away, eyes turned down. Kate smiled thinly and straightened herself up. "Leave it to me to get carried away by a song," she said, nervously.

He reached out to take her hand, but she moved away from him. "It's not you, Kate. It's me. I took an oath of chastity, and I mean to keep it until I'm married to the woman I love."

"Please, don't say anymore," she said, putting her hands up in the air like a traffic cop.

An awkward silence passed between them as they listened to the next couple of songs and clapped politely after each one. They did not say a word to each other.

Then, in an effort to cut through the unease, John asked, "What does the song 'Nights in White Satin' mean?"

"The song is about unrequited love," she replied, refusing to look at him. "The loneliness and heartbreak of not having the one you want, which intensifies at night when you're alone."

"Beautiful song."

"Justin Hayward wrote it when he was just nineteen."

"Which one is he?" Mitchell asked.

With her hands on his shoulders, Kate turned him back to the stage and pointed. "He's the cute one with microphone and guitar."

"Talented guy?"

"He and John Lodge wrote most of the songs they recorded," she explained, pointing to the bass guitarist.

Mitchell reached up and grabbed her hand. "Kate, you probably don't want to hear this, but I've got to say it any way," he announced, holding her hand to his heart. "I like you. I like you a lot. You're smart. You're pretty, and you've got a lot of things going for you."

"You're just not attracted to me," she said with a shrug.

"I didn't say that. I *am* attracted to you! I'm just not at a place in my life where I'm willing to compromise my moral and spiritual values to have a sexual relationship with you."

"Do you know how old fashioned that sounds?"

"Well, I guess I'm just an old-fashioned kind of guy, but that doesn't mean we can't have a meaningful relationship."

Kate stroked his cheek softly. "Tell you what, John, let's just table this discussion about abstinence for right now and try to enjoy the rest of our day together."

"Sounds good to me."

"Have you ever had a Mudslinger's freestyle vegan before?" she asked, her mood lightening.

"No, and I'm not even sure what that is."

"Well, c'mon. You're in for a real treat."

Kate bought him an ice cream cone at Bayside Market, and they sat on a park bench looking out by water's edge. The sailboats turned and were riding the cold breeze in from the bay. She could feel the last rays of the sun on her back as it dissolved into the Pacific.

"What's he like?" she asked, licking her ice cream.

"Who?" He held out his cone for her to hold as he pulled his hair back from his face and secured it with a band, then took it back.

"Your pastor."

John smiled. "I thought we weren't talking shop today."

"Sorry."

"He's one of the most dynamic men I've ever met. Confident and charismatic, he has a vision for the church. I feel blessed to know him."

"I'd like to hear him preach sometime," Kate lied.

She really wanted to see him locked up behind bars for the damage he's done to those two families, but she wasn't about to say that to her new friend.

"We have an open house for new members every fourth Sunday. That's a week from tomorrow. Why don't you plan on coming?"

"We'll see . . . I don't want to promise anything."

The hope shown through as ice cream appeared on his day-old beard.

Kate laughed when she saw his face and leaned over with a napkin. "Come over here, silly."

"What's the matter? Have I got something on my face?"

"Yes." Fighting to contain her laughter, she dabbed the napkin around his mouth, like a mother cleaning up after her infant.

"Hey! I was just saving that until later!" He could not help laughing at himself.

Kate leaned over and kissed him. He kissed her back, and they held each other on the park bench. The sun was set, and the day was coming to a close. It had been a glorious day, one Kate would not soon forget.

"I don't mean to seem rude, but it's getting late for me," she said, continuing to hold him as long as she could. "I should be getting home."

John nodded. "Maybe we can do this again sometime soon?"

"Yeah, that would be nice."

Mitchell gave her one final kiss, a passionate one, and walked away. When he reached the parking lot, he turned, waved at her, then climbed into his car and drove away. Kate continued to sit on the park bench until well after the street lights flickered on.

At one-fifteen in the morning, the phone rang, and then it rang again. Kate rolled over to the edge of her bed next to her night-stand and picked up it up. The words she heard cut through the fog like a beacon at water's edge and caused her to sit up.

"Yeah," she answered, then paused to get a street address. "Okay, I'll be there in about twenty-five minutes."

She hung up, weary.

Kate sat with her legs dangling off the edge of the bed,

thinking. She didn't have anything to drink in the last couple of nights, but Kate felt hung-over. She went to bed on both nights, thinking of her date with John Mitchell, and those thoughts had filled her in a way that alcohol never did. But now she was sobering up. The news was bad, and she wondered how she would handle it once she had reached the crime scene.

Kate managed to haul herself upright and get out the door in about ten minutes. Stepping on the gas of her BMW, she raced out of her apartment complex, picked up speed on Highway 101 just south of Broadway, then cut north and west across the city. When she could see the distinctive orange-colored rooftops of the Presidio, she moved into the right lane and made the turn off for the Palace of Fine Arts.

At the entrance, Kate pulled up next to the Lieutenant's late-model sedan. She recognized a few other vehicles that belonged to members of the SFPD as she walked toward the Palace. Several police cars, their red lights flashing, were parked along Lyon Street to discourage any curiosity seekers, but they still managed to gain access through the neighborhood off Baker Street. She looked up at the beautiful dome and saw the interior rotunda bathed in a white light, reflecting out onto the nearby lagoon. She walked along the path through the Colonnades and passed the fountain spewing forth water.

The Palace of Fine Arts, located in the Marina District, was built for the 1915 Panama-Pacific Exposition to showcase works of local artists. Ten palaces were constructed for the Exposition, but only the Palace survived demolition after the event was over because it was so beloved by the people of San Francisco. Overlooking a large lagoon, the monumental structure was a tribute to the classical structures throughout Europe. Australian eucalyptus trees lined the eastern shore of the lagoon where swans, ducks, geese, turtles, and frogs had taken up residence.

One hundred years after its construction, the Palace remained a popular attraction for tourists and locals as a favorite location for weddings and engagement photographs.

It had also become known as a notorious spot for dumping bodies. As she reached the south end, Kate found Lieutenant Roberts, William, several uniformed officers, and a few of the crime-scene boys gathered around a body.

They parted as she approached to give her plenty of room.

She crouched down, looking, and could hardly believe it.

Philip Ross lay on the ground naked and dead. He was beaten, with contusions from his head to his toes. His arms and legs were broken, and the cartilage around each of his joints was smashed beyond comprehension. His face was barely recognizable, as if flattened like a Jack-o'-lantern on the day after Halloween.

"There's no evidence of a struggle," William said, walking the grounds.

"No, I don't think it was done here," said Roberts.

William shone a flashlight on the body. "Looks like he was hit with a blunt instrument," he observed.

"Something like a baseball bat," the Lieutenant said.

"An aluminum baseball bat," William interjected.

"Aluminum bats are better than wooden bats because they don't break. They're favored by the mob. Even if this wasn't a mob hit, it's meant to look like one."

Roberts looked at Kate. "Are you all right?"

"Jesus Christ," she said, her face pale against the dark of night, "we should have done more to protect him."

"There wasn't much more we could have done, Kate," her fellow detective said.

"Clark's right. We pulled out all of the stops on this one," said Lieutenant Roberts, as he scratched the stubble of his day-old beard. "Ross was scheduled for his arraignment hearing this morning in district court, and I know the DA was prepared to offer him protective custody."

"That doesn't do him much good now, does it?" she asked venomously.

Roberts shrugged his shoulders. "Don't worry, Inspector, we'll get whoever did this to him."

"I think we know who did it to him." Kate's defiance was tangible as she glared at her superior.

"The only thing we know for certain is that our number-one suspect in a murder-suicide is dead."

Roberts was desperate for some answers, but reasoning with Kate at that moment was bound to be onesided.

She had already mentally arrested, tried, and convicted Friedman of Ross's murder, and she wasn't ready to listen any more theories. "Right now, there is no evidence that links Friedman to this crime scene."

"Well, don't you think it's a little odd that the last person we saw Ross with was Friedman?" Kate put her hands on her hips and leaned to her right.

"That's merely circumstantial," Roberts said.

"Sometimes circumstantial is all you've got to go on—"

"We're not going to turn this into a witch hunt!" he shouted at her.

William again glanced back through his notes.

"Lieutenant, what I don't understand is why Friedman or one of his associates would dump the body here. Why not dig a hole out in the desert and be done with it?"

"He's sending us a message to back off our investigation." Kate remained firm in her stance, cutting her eyes at William and then back at Roberts to make her point.

Lieutenant Roberts brought the discussion to a close.

"The only message that's clear is that we don't have enough

evidence against Friedman or anyone else to make a case. We've got victims piling up down at the morgue, including this one, and we're not any closer to solving this case."

"Right, Lieutenant," said William, falling in line.

"Don't cops ever make mistakes?" she asked.

Roberts was silent, brooding, his arms folded across his chest. He had not taken his eyes from her face since the moment she posed the question, and he was not about to give her the satisfaction of an answer. The police lieutenant was solid as a rock and towered above her like a great alabaster statue of Zeus or Apollo, his visage proud and arrogant and unyielding.

Kate looked at her boss and nodded. "Or they don't *admit* it when they've made a mistake?"

"What would *you* have done differently?" He wanted to catch her in flaw.

"We should have had 24/7 surveillance on that compound, Damnit!"

"I did."

"You did?" Kate looked puzzled. "But you didn't say anything to me about it."

"No, I didn't. It was my decision to make, *not yours*," he said, with a who-the-hell-are-you tone of voice. "I followed something called standard police procedure, something you don't give a shit about, and notified the District Attorney's office after Ross was released into Friedman's custody. He's had men posted there around the clock since last Thursday."

"But you let me and Ramirez go down there."

"Sure, I did. How else was I going to let Friedman know that he was being watched by the police department?"

"Then you used me?"

"Don't look so surprised, Dawson. That's what police officers do. We use our assets. A detective depends on three major tools available to him: instrumentation, information, and interrogation," he said, counting the three tools off with his fingers. "What did you think this was all about? Picking up little clues and figuring out Colonel Mustard had killed the Lord of the Manor with a lead pipe in the study?"

"No, of course not," she disagreed. "But I had hoped it would be about collaboration and communication."

"Well, get your head out of your ass, and find me something so we can nail this prick," demanded Roberts, glaring her squarely in the face, then turned and stalked away heading for the parking lot and his car.

Kate awoke with a headache, like someone was pounding on her head with a jackhammer all night, and with a tongue that had been licking up its dust and debris. She could cope with a hangover, she had had them before, but the hatred she felt for herself ground her down like the jackhammer. She still felt there was more she could have done to prevent Ross's death, and she spent the rest of the night tossing and turning with that on her mind.

By the time she got down to police headquarters, the morning review of open cases had been going on for over an hour. She walked into the conference room and headed for the cantina. She poured herself a steaming cup of coffee and added two sugars and a shot of milk. Kate picked up a couple of donuts and slid into an empty chair at the conference table. A handful of photocopied materials sat in front of her. One of the homicide detectives she didn't like was talking to the group.

"You look like shit," said William with a whisper.

"I've seen shit that looked better," Mikhail added.

"You guys are such a laugh riot," she said under her breath.

"Nice of you to join us, Inspector," Roberts said, checking his watch. "When I set a meeting for nine o'clock, I expect all my people to be ready to go at eight fifty-nine, and not just strolling in at ten o'clock."

"Sorry, Lieutenant, I got tied up in traffic," Kate lied.

"There was a serious accident at Bryant and Beale streets."

She downed a couple of Advil and sat back in her chair at the table, listening.

"So as I was saying, Lieutenant, the ex-husband confessed after we shook him down a little," the detective said. "He won't be giving us any more trouble, and we've turned everything over to the DA's office."

"Great. Good job, Balardi," Roberts said. "Corcoran, Farris, where are you guys on your case?"

"Crime scene is clean. No weapons, no prints, no witnesses," Farris reported.

"But we are reaching out to known associates and neighbors," Corcoran added. "We're hoping the victim may have said something to someone before she ran down that bullet to the head."

The Lieutenant nodded. "Okay, keep on it, and see what you can do about getting me an update by Friday."

"Yes, sir," they replied in unison.

"All right, what about you, Clark? What did your research turn up on the murder-suicides?"

William opened his notebook and thumbed to the right page. "Of the nine apparent murder-suicides spread throughout the San Francisco Bay area in the last month, five of the families were religious. Four had ties to the First Pentecostal Church of God or the End Times Ministries."

"With the two recent ones, that would make a total of six," Jorge did the math.

"You see, that's what I was trying to tell you," Kate said, leaning forward in her chair and thumping on the table. "Their leader must have enough control over their lives that all he has to do is give them an order and they carry it out. Hypnosis? Drugs? Scare tactics? Whatever means he's using, it's about a religious vision and the end of the world.

"Sorry, I'm just not buying it," Mikhail said, throwing his pencil down on the stack of photocopied materials. "People aren't that gullible."

"Why don't you try asking one of Jim Jones's followers?" Kate challenged him. "He managed to convince over nine hundred of them to drink Kool-Aid that was spiked with cyanide. He had every one believing they weren't committing suicide but rather stepping onto 'another plane of existence.'"

Mikhail countered, "You are forgetting they were facing death by gunshot if they didn't comply. Plus today, people are better informed through the web and cable news networks."

"Tell that to the followers of David Koresh or Warren Jeffs or Joseph Di Mambro or even Osama Bin Laden," she countered, standing firm in her debate. "For every well-educated and well-informed person out there, there's a dozen or more people who are sick, lonely, isolated, broken, or disaffected and are willing to exchange their obedience for friendship and acceptance into a group. Match those poor lost souls with someone who is charming and charismatic but demands loyalty, and you've got a powder keg ready to explode."

"But why order his followers to murder their own children?" Mikhail asked, still not buying it.

"*Si, bueno,*" Jorge added.

"Mikhail is right," William said looking up from his notes. "I've investigated each of these murder-suicides, and I still don't know the *why*. How does the death of these innocents fit into a larger plan?"

Grasping at straws, Kate said, "Biblical prophecy. The leader is egotistical. He has the power to bring about the end of the world or some bullshit like that."

"What are you saying?" asked William.

"That somebody's about to seriously fuck with this city."

"What the hell is that supposed to mean?" Roberts demanded, sitting up in his chair at the end of the table. He turned his gaze to Kate and fixed her in place with a glare.

"I mean, I know we're all dummies here, Dawson, so give us a little taste of your brilliance. What are we talking here? A suitcase nuke? An airborne pathogen? A cyber-attack on the city's infrastructure? What?"

Kate shook her head. "Look, I'm not sure, all I know—"

"Oh, she's not sure," said Balardi, with tongue in cheek. "Well, I'm stunned. I've got to go lie down in the Lieutenant's office."

Corcoran, Farris, and one other homicide detective who shared Balardi's disdain for Kate laughed and added their voices to his in mocking her. She fought the urge to strike back. She knew they blamed her for Frank Miller's death.

She turned to face Balardi straight on, "You got something to say to me, Balardi, quit being such a pussy, and come out and say it."

"You're bad news, lady. You got Miller killed, and you let this department get dragged through the mud because you were fucking the chief suspect. I'm not gonna let you drag us down any further with this new obsession of yours."

Jorge saw his partner go rigid. She was like the springs on a clock, ready to strike out at Balardi. Her hands curled into hard fists. Jorge put a hand on her forearm, ready to pull his partner back down should she decide to strike.

Kate swallowed hard. "Miller was my partner and my friend," she said, fighting to control the anger in her voice. "I would have traded my life for his."

"That's easy for you to say, sitting here safe around this table. But the truth of the matter is, you didn't," Balardi said, taunting her.

"You let him get killed in a fuckin' toilet in a sex club while you were downstairs boffing the chief suspect on the dance floor."

"You know damn well that's not how it happened!" she exploded, springing to her feet, fists up and ready, while Jorge and Mikhail pulled her back down to the table.

Balardi was on his feet. "You want to hit me.

C'mon, hit me. Show me what kind of man you are."

"That's enough, Balardi, Dawson," Roberts said, standing up, his commanding presence casting a shadow over the two combatants. "This isn't a boy's boarding school, and this is not how we solve our differences. You want to fight about something, go down to the gym and put on boxing gloves, and settle it man to man. But when you're in this room, you're going to act civilly toward one another. I don't give a rat's ass whether you like each another or not, but you damn well better work together, or I'm going to start busting heads. Is that understood?"

"Yes, sir," Kate said finding her chair.

"Okay, Lieutenant, if that's how you want it," Balardi agreed, shaking his head as he sat back down.

Roberts sat back down in his seat and glanced at his agenda. "Okay, we're moving onto the next agenda item . . . Clark, you had a report from forensics."

"Sir, I wasn't finished," Kate interrupted.

"You've said enough for one day," the Lieutenant replied, leaning across the conference table until his face was close to hers. She remembered their last few meetings and shrank from him. "You want to pursue this line of inquiry? That's fine. But do yourself a favor and get some proof that substantiates your claims."

"I've got an interview set up with—" she started to say.

"I don't care. Just do it."

"Yes, sir."

"Well, Clark, we're still waiting," Roberts said impatiently.

"Sir, the forensics team found a damaged iPad hidden in the Morales household," he stuttered, going through his notes. "Someone tried to charbroil it over the backyard grill. Forensics was able to recover one file. It was a text file of some type, but it's encoded. The only thing that's recognizable is a series of numbers: 121.535889-36.845083. But we don't know what it means."

"Maybe it's a Bible chapter and verse?" Balardi joked, as he stared at Kate.

She looked at him for a fleeting moment, engaging his eyes, then looked away. "It looks like an IP address." *Asshole.*

"That was our initial thought, too," Clark said, reading over his notes. "Internet Protocol addresses are represented in dot-decimal notation, four decimal numbers, each ranging from 0 to 255, separated by dots. For example: 172.16.254.1. Each part represents a group of eight bits, which is known as an octet, of the address. But the problem is there are too many numbers."

"Security code?" Jorge suggested. "Maybe, but to what?"

"What about a numbered Swiss account?" Mikhail offered.

"Or a safety deposit box number?" Kate asked.

"All of these are excellent suggestions, and one may be the answer, but without something more specific to go on, we're just pissing in the wind," William said.

The Lieutenant asked, "Was there anything else, Clark?"

"No, that was all, sir."

"All right, let's break it up then," Roberts said, climbing to his feet. "You've all got your assignments, so let's just get 'em done."

Kate didn't have to hear any more. She felt a red-hot rage burning inside her toward Balardi and his buddies.

Over the years, she'd grown accustomed to their sneers and sexist comments, and she dismissed their jokes as a bore. She didn't need to be reminded of Miller's death. She carried that guilt around with her every day and fought the demons in her sleep every night.

Kate gathered up the materials on the table into her arms and walked toward the conference room door. She pushed by Balardi, Corcoran, and Farris, anger smoldering within her, ready to be stoked into a blaze of fury.

"Don't miss your eleven o'clock, Katherine," Farris said, trying his best to imitate the Lieutenant's gruff voice.

"Dr. Glass wouldn't like it very much, and neither would Internal Affairs."

"You need a good shrink," Balardi said, with a smirk, "to get that huge ego of yours shrunken back to size."

Kate betrayed nothing; her face was stone. She went through the door without a backward glance.

Kate walked into Dr. Glass's office, precisely at 11 a.m., and shut the door. She moved past his couch and sat down on standard office chair. The chair had a straight back with no padding, forcing her to sit up straight, like she had a disciplinary meeting with the principal. She folded her arms across her chest and looked over at Dr. Glass, who was bent over, reading the contents of a folder on his desk. He was wearing one of his familiar Hawaiian shirts—yellow hibiscus surrounded by beautiful floral designs in green and burnt orange. She thought he looked better suited for a day at the beach than probing the depths of the human psyche.

He glanced up from his desk over the top of his wire-rim

glasses and met her blood-shot eyes. "You look like you've been up all night," Glass observed with concern.

"Are you still experiencing problems with sleep?"

"No, doctor, I've been sleeping just fine." She planted her feet. "I got called to a crime scene just after one, and by the time I got home, it was tough to settle back down."

"Do you think your lack of sleep may have contributed in some way to the disagreement you had with your fellow detective an hour ago?"

Kate shrugged her shoulders. "I guess scuttlebutt travels fast."

"Lieutenant Roberts called me and expressed his concern for you," Glass corrected the record. "Everyone is concerned about you. They're worried that the stress of the last few months has caused certain less desirable behavioral traits to bubble up to the surface."

"Behavioral traits?" she repeated the two-word phrase as a question.

"Yes, behavioral traits, like insubordination or impulsivity or anger management problems," he replied, listing them out on his fingers. "When we're feeling good about ourselves, these traits are controlled and self-regulated by our mental processes. However, when we are suffering from stress-related symptoms or we're experiencing posttraumatic stress disorder, it's hard for us to keep all of our negative traits under control. A person who's feeling on the top of the world is less likely to get into a fight compared to someone who's feeling down and out."

"I don't have anger management problems," Kate said, biting down hard and grinding her teeth. "I don't have any problems. I feel great!"

"Kate, listen to me," Glass said hands together like a penitent man. "My job here is to help you deal with your feelings and to ameliorate any problems you may have in functioning in your everyday life."

"I deal with my feelings plenty." *Anger management? Shit, he has no idea.*

Dr. Glass looked at her with pity. "You are looking a little rough around the edges."

"I told you. I didn't get enough sleep last night."

"Why don't you let me make you a cup of tea? Chamomile tea does wonders with insomnia. There's an active ingredient, known as bisabolol. It will help you with anxiety and panic attacks."

Kate shook her head. "No, thank you."

"How would you characterize your relationships with your co-workers?" He shrugged his shoulders.

"Clark, Ramirez, and Jawara are my closest friends—my only friends."

"What about Lieutenant Roberts? How would you characterize your relationship with your boss?"

"Okay, I guess," Kate responded, choosing her words carefully. "At times, he rides me hard, but I know that he's trying to get me to be the best cop I can be. When he trusts my work, it's a compliment. I suppose, when it comes to bosses, I could have done a whole lot worse."

"What about Matt Balardi? Jeff Corcoran? Jim Farris? And the others in your department?"

Kate grinned. "We're never going to be friends."

"And why do you suppose that is?"

"They blame me for Miller's death. It's more than that. I'm starting to realize I have more enemies than I thought."

"Everybody has more enemies than they think," Glass concluded.

The doctor picked up her folder and leaned back in his leather chair as he thumbed through the pages. He paused and read it through in its entirety. He then rifled through the balance of the pages, as if he was looking for something.

Glass was silent and focused as he reviewed the contents of the folder. He paused for an instant to check the time before he resumed his hunt.

"Are you sure I can't offer you some tea?"

"No thanks, doc," she repeated.

"Your daughter Stephanie was killed with your service pistol during a domestic dispute with your exhusband, and you spent two years on administrative leave," he said, working from the notes in her file.

Kate was on her feet, heading for the door. "No offense, Dr. Glass, but there are things that are off limits here. I don't need a shrink to figure out what my problems are."

"Are you running away from tough emotions and throwing yourself into your work?" Glass made a point of catching her eye and holding it. "Do you think you're all that unique, Inspector? I've seen this with hundreds of other cops over the last thirty years. They blow a case, lose a partner, or worse, shoot someone who's innocent, and they shut down. They channel what they're feeling into their work, and they're working eighteen-hour days on a collision course with a major breakdown or suicide. Don't pretend that you don't know what I'm talking about."

"I hope it was a good read," Kate said.

"So now, you've lost someone else you loved—your partner—and your relationship with a man has fallen apart, what do you do? From your file, my conjecture is you lean on your crutches again. Work. Drinking. Protecting people."

"I took an oath to serve and protect."

"But who are you really protecting?"

CHAPTER SEVEN

Kate drove the eighty-eight-mile trip from San Francisco to Sacramento; loved the open road and felt a rush driving along Interstate 80 with the moon-roof open and the windows down. She could feel the warmth of the sun on her face and the cool breeze blowing through her hair.

She put the accelerator down and raced through the sleepy bedroom communities of Albany, Richmond, and Tara Hills.

She blew by the Phillips 66 refinery and the Mare Island Naval Complex without shifting gears and tore down the straight-away between the great Windmill Farm and the University of California at Davis. She then veered left to pick up 275 and took the turnoff for Tower Bridge Gateway, the main artery leading into Capitol Mall.

When Kate was nearing the outskirts of Sacramento, she realized she spent most of the drive living in the moment. She didn't think about the murders or John Mitchell since she left San Francisco. She could have driven all the way to Lake Tahoe, but as she clanked across Tower Bridge Gateway, she was reminded why she had driven to Sacramento.

She pulled into the K-Street Parking Garage and parked on

the roof of the complex, then hurried along the tree-lined path to the Capitol and scrambled up the stairs, briefcase in hand.

The Senator's intern was waiting for her at the top of the steps. Once Kate had shown her police ID to a woman scarcely out of her teens, she was led to the Senator's office.

"Thanks for agreeing to see me on such short notice," Kate said, her hand extended for the Senator to shake.

Gabriela Santiago shook her hand. "You said it was an urgent matter," she replied. "I suppose I wouldn't be seen as a good 'law and order' legislator if I turned away a member of the San Francisco police department. Please take a seat."

As the intern closed the office door, Kate sat down in a comfortable leather chair and looked at the Senator.

Gabriela Santiago was an attractive woman, forty-five years old, and two years into her second term. The beautiful Latina was dressed elegantly in a three-piece, navy-blue Versace suit with a white ruffled Valentino blouse and Louis Vuitton shoes. But below the surface, Kate suspected Santiago carried a great deal of baggage from her thirteenyear ordeal as a captive of a religious cult. She read about the Senator's divorce from her husband James Adamson in the tabloids and knew about her daughter's death from pneumonia when she was still a member of the church. It was hard for Kate not to feel a kinship towards her, considering they had both been divorced and suffered the loss of a child, but she needed to maintain her objectivity.

"In the last ten days, I've investigated two crime scenes in which a parental figure took the lives of his or her own children and then killed themselves as a part of an apparent murder-suicide," Kate said, choosing her words carefully, almost stiffly, as she spoke. "In both cases, there was a connection traced back to the End Times Ministries."

"Could I see the files, Inspector?" asked Santiago.

Kate already had them out of her briefcase. She sat forward in her chair and passed the folders across the desk.

"Help yourself. I would prefer for this information doesn't leave the room."

"No problem," said Santiago.

The first thing the Senator removed from the manila-colored folder was the black-and-white crime scene photograph of the five Ross children lined up in a row under the oak tree. She looked through them and thumbed through the photographs from the second crime scene. The images were cold and stark, yet glossy and glaring. The more Gabriela looked at them, the paler her face grew. Few people are prepared to look at crime-scene photographs, and even fewer when it involved violence against a child.

She closed both folders on her desk and stood up. She was noticeably shaking as she crossed the room to her small kitchenette and took a stiff drink of bourbon.

"And so it begins . . ." she said, under her breath.

Kate heard her and was puzzled. "This means something to you, doesn't it?"

"Maybe . . . I'm not certain," replied Santiago, then she was silent for a long time, until coming out of her daydream. She straightened the folds in her jacket in an effort to deflect attention from her face, then downed another drink.

"May I offer you something?"

"No thanks," Kate replied.

Gabriela pulled herself together and returned to her seat behind the desk. "So you were telling me you traced both of the murder-suicides back to the End Times Ministries."

"Yes, and I was hoping you could tell me something about the cult."

"Well, when people hear the word 'cult,' they conjure up a certain image in their mind," she said, with a thin smile.

"They think of Jim Jones and the suicides that happened in Jonestown, Guyana, or they think of Marshall Applewhite and his thirty-eight followers who killed themselves when their spaceship failed to materialize. 'Cult' has become synonymous with religious groups whose beliefs are abnormal. That wasn't the case when I joined the End Times Ministries, or at least not in the beginning."

"Why don't you tell me about it?"

Santiago sat back in her chair, her eyes distant.

"Back then, we were just a bunch of young college and high school-aged kids who liked to sing, hang out, and read the scriptures," she replied, with a hint of nostalgia. "None of us fit into the typical groups at school. We weren't cool enough to be part of the 'in' crowd, and we certainly weren't brainy enough to be accepted as nerds. We weren't jocks or druggies. We didn't even have a particular affiliation with any church. We were just different."

Kate nodded, understanding.

"I suppose what set us apart from all of the others was our love of the Lord and our desire to be part of something bigger than ourselves," continued Santiago. "I was raised Catholic, but didn't find anything meaningful in the Mass, just a lot of genuflecting and bowing to men in black robes. My best friend Angie was raised in a Lutheran Church, but she complained that the Lord's message was being drowned out by all the talk of money and fundraising. Really, it was the same thing for all of us. We were looking to find spiritual direction for our lives, and we found each other. That's when our group started to go to this one Baptist Church that opened its chapel doors to us every night and gave us a place to meet."

"Was that where you met your husband?" Kate was taking mental notes.

Santiago looked at her sharply. "You know about James? Well, we had known each other in high school, but we didn't date until after I had seen him a few times at church. He was very handsome and charismatic, and soon became our group's leader."

"I'm sorry for asking all these questions, Senator. I know these are painful memories."

"It takes me back to a place I thought was behind me." Santiago nodded as if agreeing with Kate, drew in a deep breath, then continued telling her story. "So, where was I? Yes, the beginning. Our group had found a home at the Baptist Church and a leader and we were all very happy. We got together four or five times a week, and we spent a lot of time singing Christian songs, reading and discussing the Bible, and praying together. Then one night—and I can remember this like it happened yesterday—James came into our group all hyped up about a preacher he had heard on the radio, and he played us an audio-cassette tape he recorded. The preacher's name was George Meador. I didn't understand a whole lot of it at first. In fact, a lot of what he said made me feel uncomfortable, but I kept listening because I wanted to know more about his message."

"George Meador?" Kate interrupted her, reaching into her briefcase for a yellow notepad and pen. "Reverend Meador was the founder of End Times Ministries," Santiago reported. "He started out humbly enough in Sioux Falls, South Dakota, with a handful of young people who were anxious to learn the gospel of Jesus. They met in living rooms, garages, and various meeting places. But it wasn't until he moved his ministry to Indiana and then Lake City, Florida, that his message went viral. Everybody in the country suddenly knew his revelation about the end times."

"You talk about him in the past tense."

Gabriela Santiago nodded her head. "George Meador died in 2010, but not before creating a network of churches and ministries throughout the United States and Canada, known collectively as the End Times Ministries."

"What was this revelation of his?" Kate asked, without looking up, her hand taking notes.

"Meador believed we were living in the end times, and we were rapidly approaching the time of the Great Tribulation, the rise of the Anti-Christ, and the final Battle of Armageddon," she explained. "I was skeptical because none of this sounded right to me. I had heard about Biblical prophecy, but it was always something that was years away, certainly not in my lifetime. But we kept listening to his broadcasts and trading the cassette tapes back and forth. We probably knew his message better than he did. When he started talking about building an army for God to preach the gospel to every living person on earth, the message resonated with us. We were looking for direction for our lives, and he gave it to us. So shortly after, James and I got married, and our group moved to Lake City, joining hundreds of other young people like ourselves who loved the Lord and wanted to make a difference in the world."

Kate put her notebook down and looked up at Santiago. "In one of your interviews, you stated that was one of the worst mistakes you made in your life."

The Senator sighed as tears were pooling in the corners of her wide brown eyes. "When you're eighteen years old and in love, you think there's nothing on earth that can harm you." A single tear ran down her cheek. "But then you learn about the fragility of life. My best friend, Angie, was the first among our group to get married and pregnant. She died giving birth to her baby in a bathtub because the church didn't believe in medical services. Our faith alone was what should have seen us through any difficulties. If a mother or a baby died in childbirth, it was part of God's will. So when my own daughter took ill and died of pneumonia, I was told there was nothing that could be done to save her life. It was part of a much larger plan. Antibiotics would have cured her." Gabriela Santiago buried her face in her hands and forced back the tears.

Kate was tempted to take the Senator into her arms and comfort her. She knew all too well about the fragility of life and about the loss of a daughter, but then thought better of it. Kate had come to Sacramento on police business and needed to maintain her objectivity. She pulled tissues from her briefcase and handed them to Gabriela.

"Oh, thank you. I'm okay," the Senator replied. She shook her long brown hair out and dabbed her face with the tissue. "I wasn't permitted to shed tears when my daughter Rosalie died. That was another one of the church's rules. And now, I cry whenever I think about her."

Kate nodded her head. "I understand the church controlled many aspects of your life."

"I suppose that's true, but no more than what we allowed them. George Meador didn't think it was appropriate for women to paint themselves up like harlots, so we gave up lip gloss, eyeliner, mascara, even rouge. Animals were considered instruments of Satan; none of us owned a dog or a cat or even a hamster. We didn't wear Nike sneakers or Izod polo shirts. None of us had digital watches or cell phones. We lived a simple life-style. He had his reasons for everything, and none of us thought that much about it."

"But you left them after thirteen years?"

"I did," she confessed, the features in her beautiful Latina face turned to stone. "Towards the end, Meador was convinced that there was an invisible war taking place between the forces of light and darkness. I believed in the power of Satan and his demons, but I had trouble believing that they were waging a guerilla war against true believers, like James, my friends, and me. I challenged Reverend Meador. I called him out right in the middle of a sermon, and he promptly quoted to me chapter and verse to support his case. He was right. His words opened my eyes, but it also caused some of the more radical factions in the church to take matters into their own hands."

Kate laughed. "Invisible war? Radical factions? Are you kidding me? Now you sound like my friend who's into science fiction."

Senator Santiago didn't think it was a laughing matter. She admonished Kate with a frown. "This is no fantasy, Inspector; no careless product of wild imagination. There is a war going on, whether you believe in it or not. Satan is waging spiritual warfare against the weak, the weak-minded, and the ill-informed. That discouragement and doubt you feel each day are part of his subtle attacks against you. That feeling of helplessness and fatigue and apathy are all arrows in Satan's quiver. The only defense we have against the everyday schemes of the evil one is the armor of God that Paul wrote about to the Ephesians. When we take up the shield of faith, the helmet of salvation, and the sword of the Spirit, we are prepared for spiritual battle. We are protected from those who would seek to do us harm."

Kate stared at her. She had never heard such a farfetched story in all her life, and she wanted to attribute the fanciful tale to something playing on the big screen at the local Cineplex instead of the ramblings of a state senator. *Spiritual warfare? Final battle? Armor of God? What would Lenny think? Or for that matter, what the Senator's constituents must have thought when she got going on the subject of the end times.* At least, how Santiago told it, there were no spaceships or light-sabers.

"So then, what you're saying is that you left the church because you didn't want any part of what this radical faction had planned?"

"Yes, that's true, but there were many other reasons why I left, not the least of which was watching my daughter die.

"You see, as long as George Meador ran the End Times Ministries, we had a clear vision of what our mission on earth was. We were to bring the word of God to every soul on the planet in preparation for the end times. But when he had his first heart attack, certain factions within the church questioned his leadership and vision. They became impatient with his peaceful methods and wanted to shake things up. They planned guerilla attacks against targets they believed were in the hands of Satan and his minions, like abortion clinics, half-way houses for drug offenders, welfare offices, and gay men's bathhouses. I didn't want to be part of any of that, and I begged James to escape with me. I was the only one who got out."

"And here I thought churches just held bake sales and flea markets," Kate quipped, shaking her head in disbelief.

"They also have the power to start wars," the Senator said unequivocally, "and I fear that's the direction the End Times Ministries has taken. I think they're plotting to touch off the final war. Meador's successor has said as much in one of his recent sermons."

Kate looked back at her notes. "When I was doing my Internet research, the name Charles Hampton Kenilworth kept reoccurring, but I couldn't figure out how or why a former dot-com millionaire was involved. He became Meador's successor, didn't he?" Kate wanted confirmation.

"That's right." Santiago was starting to see Kate in a different light. "When George Meador died in 2010, the End Times Ministries was left without a spiritual leader and a clear direction for its future. Preachers from the various church groups throughout the United States and Canada squabbled amongst themselves, each vying for the top spot, but no one person had a clear majority. That's when Kenilworth emerged from the pack with a clear vision forward. He told the church leadership, in no uncertain terms, that the only way they were going to win their war against Satan was to bring the battle right to him. Most conservative members disagreed with this confrontational approach, while the radical factions saw Kenilworth as a kindred spirit. The disagreement between members led to a schism that split the church into two halves: one that continues to be fractured and divided today over its mission, and the other committed to Kenilworth's vision of catalyzing the end times."

Gabriela saw the look of confusion on Kate's face.

"Senator," Kate said, trying to sound as diplomatic as possible, "that's a whole lot for a lay person like me to swallow down in one gulp."

"Simply put," Santiago tried to dumb-it-down, "there is a time of great upheaval coming. The world will be engulfed in war, famine, and pestilence. The war will start in the Middle East, but it will touch all nations as the forces of good and evil battle for control. At first, the forces of evil will win and unleash a great pestilence, which will destroy all plant and animal life and make the rest of us sick with plague. With limited resources, famine and starvation will sweep across the globe. No one will be spared the horrors that follow, until one leader emerges to unite all those who are left alive under his totalitarian rule. The few faithful who remain will fight his rule in a last battle that will bring humanity to the brink of extinction."

"I think I get the picture," Kate confessed, her head whirling.

"It's a pretty grim one, but Christ returns to earth and destroys evil once and for all."

"That's an ending I wouldn't mind seeing, but that still doesn't explain what the End Times Ministries hopes to achieve."

"They want to precipitate the end of the world," the Senator said. "So, I'd imagine they'd start by targeting a major city, like San Francisco, with a suitcase nuke or a cyber-attack against its power grid and then blame it all on Iran or ISIS or the Muslim brotherhood. With relations already at a breaking point between the United States and the Middle Eastern countries, it wouldn't take much for a war to break out with them. I mean, just think about how much damage Osama Bin Laden accomplished by crashing two planes in the World Trade Center and another in the Pentagon on September 11th. He nearly brought the world's biggest superpower to its knees and ignited two wars in the Middle East. What do you think would happen if it appeared our enemies had destroyed a major American city?"

Kate closed her eyes and shook her head. "It's too frightening to think about."

"Nearly a million people live in the San Francisco Bay area. That's a lot of lives that would be lost, but nowhere near the hundreds of millions of lives lost in a global war."

"What did you mean before when you said 'and so it begins'?" Kate asked, with a worried glance.

Santiago looked at the detective and kept her emotion out of her response, but not her lack of conviction. "We always knew there would be a time when the end of the world was imminent, when the time of the Great Tribulation was upon us," she said evenly.

"We always knew that we'd have to decide as parents whether we were going to allow our children to face starvation, sickness, diseases, and death, or spare them by sending them onto God. James and I discussed this many times, but we never came to a resolution. I don't know if I would have had the courage to 'free' my daughter. But it sounds like the

End Timers have been told that the end is near, and they now have to make the toughest decision of their lives."

"So, you're saying the clock is ticking?" Kate asked, already sensing the answer.

"It's five minutes to midnight," Santiago replied, then she said no more.

The image of the Doomsday Clock set at five minutes to midnight stayed in Kate's mind throughout her drive back to San Francisco. She thought about everything the Senator told her and tried to temper the fanciful against what she knew was true and real. Kate would have been the first one to confess that she didn't know a lot about the Bible, and she certainly didn't buy into most of the stuff related to Biblical prophecy, but she did know there was a group of fanatics out there who were determined to move the hands of the clock closer to midnight, and it was her duty to stop them.

By the time she got back to San Francisco, the winter sun was going down over the Pacific Ocean. Kate thought about a nice cold beer and an order of chicken wings, but instead of stopping at McGinty's Public House, she went home and to bed early—sober. She slept well, considering the image of the Doomsday clock. When the call came in at 4 a.m., summoning her to a crime scene at the University of San Francisco, she rolled out of bed feeling good and in control. Any other morning, she would have been hung over.

She made fast time on Fulton Street and rolled through the light on Masonic and then left on Golden Gate Avenue without taking her foot off the accelerator.

Just past Roselyn Terrace, Kate slowed and made the left into the University of San Francisco. Pulling up on Campus Drive, she could see a half dozen police cars, red lights flashing, spreading out along the main thoroughfare, plus campus security vehicles parked outside Campion and Cowell Halls.

The stunning glass and steel architecture of the Richard A. Gleeson Library stood out as the geographic center of campus, but she was heading to the brand new science building that opened in 2014. From what she heard, the Center for Science and Innovation transformed the way science was taught at the University of San Francisco.

With the addition of more research laboratories and innovative research projects, USF was no longer a private liberal arts college, but a Research institution that rivaled Berkeley and UCLA.

She drove past the old Harney Science Center and parked in the lot near the renovated Kalmanovitz Hall. A campus cop directed her to the loading dock of the new CSI building and into a maelstrom of activity that looked like a scene from a science fiction movie.

With a sigh of exasperation, Kate emerged from the shadows of the sprawling campus into the twilight zone.

Bright lights flooded the area, transforming the darkness into an odd reality that was neither day nor night. Two HAZMAT trucks with license plates issued by the federal government flanked the loading dock on both sides and created a barrier to keep out the curious. A huge blue plastic tarp was erected from one end of the loading dock to the other and was secured to the concrete with several layers of a white reflective tape. In the middle of the dock, a makeshift opening was cut into the blue tarp, and a clear plastic tunnel, connected to the opening, stretched out about fifty feet to a decontamination chamber in the middle of the driveway. The plastic tunnel and the decontamination chamber looked like they were made of Saran Wrap.

Members of a HAZMAT team worked to secure the seams of the makeshift structures with a heavy-duty tape.

Several men wearing yellow HAZMAT suits, with full masks covering their heads and breathing apparatus strapped to their backs, walked down the narrow plastic tunnel to the loading dock while several others waited their turn in the decontamination chamber to be scrubbed down.

Another yellow-suited man sprayed the first two with a gray foamy substance that liquefied and turned into soap bubbles.

He scrubbed over their suits then cleansed them with water from a high-powered hose, like the ones used by the fire department. The first two in yellow suits zipped open the plastic door cover and exited the makeshift chamber while the third remained inside to complete the decontamination procedure.

Near the entrance/exit, a man sat on a folding chair while another helped him secure his wrists, ankles, faceplate, hood, and waist with the white reflective tape. The tape wound around the joints several times to prevent any exposure. On his feet, he wore heavy steel-toed work boots covered by a yellow bootie, also taped to the suit and the boots. His voice sounded robotic as he spoke to the other man through a two-way radio receiver embedded in the mouthpiece of the suit. Each time another one of them emerged from the clear plastic door of the decontamination chamber, the next man who was suited up entered and made his way to the loading dock.

Kate advanced carefully wondering what major hazardous material they were dealing with. *Chemical? Biological? Nuclear?* While Kate watched the precision of the operation, she could not help but feel anxious.

The men in the yellow HAZMAT suits did not appear to be afraid. They drilled scenarios like this one for years and managed to work beyond their fears. The thought didn't relieve her anxiety, for Kate's worst fears seemed to be coming true.

"I wouldn't get too close, Miss," said a campus policeman.

"It's Inspector," Kate replied, holding her badge out.

"Inspector Dawson. I'm with the San Francisco Police Department."

With aged, arthritic hands, the campus policeman struggled to take hold of the badge and keep it from shaking while he squinted at the name and photograph. He was a middle-aged man in his late sixties who was working the only job an ex-cop could find for a couple of hours a week's employment. He looked like he had been a virile, handsome man before the effects of aging and retirement had taken its toll. Now he could barely manage to keep his hands from shaking.

He handed the badge back to Kate and smiled.

"Sorry, I mistook you for one of the government stiffs, Inspector," he said. "I was a patrol cop for the Santa Barbara Police Department for thirty-five years before I took early retirement and moved up here to live with my daughter. Been working here a couple nights a week for the last twelve years. Not much police work. I'm a glorified night watchman."

"I'm pleased to meet you, Officer. . . ?" she said, stretching her hand out in friendship and taking his hand in hers. He seemed like a kindly soul who reminded her of Frank Miller.

"Peck. Bob Peck," he replied, smiling a big toothy grin, revealing all his lost teeth.

"What's going on here, Officer Peck?" Kate asked, speaking to the old guy as if he were still a real cop at a crime scene. "I got a call forty-five minutes ago about two campus policemen being gunned down, and I come upon this scene from *Star Wars*."

The old man groaned. "There are two campus cops down. They were killed during a robbery about an hour and a half ago."

"Robbery? What was stolen?"

"About four kilograms or nine pounds of enriched pluto-nium," he reported.

"Plutonium? Are you sure?" Kate was aghast.

"Yeah. C'mon, I'll show you," he said, with a wink.

The old campus policeman led Kate into the Security Operations Center. The room was a cramped maze of television monitors and computer consoles thirty-five feet across and twenty feet wide. Its interior was uncomfortably close for Kate as she stepped between the narrow aisles. She tried to imagine what working conditions were like during the day when three or four campus cops were on duty monitoring the panty raids and beer bashes on campus. The center was tight. The main instrument panel was a glowing Christmas tree with red, green, and yellow lights blinking on-and-off. At eye level, there were eight different television monitors; one had a televised image of the loading dock at the back of the Center for Science and Innovation building, while the other monitors were changing, selecting other parts of campus to display. Off to one side, there was a small kitchenette with coffee and donuts, and Kate fought the urge to pour herself a cup and dip into the box for glazed donut.

"This is our main operations center where we monitor everything that's happening on the campus," Peck explained, showing off the expensive monitoring equipment.

"Very impressive," she remarked, taking it all in.

"I forget. What was the reason we came up here?" asked the old campus policeman, a frown on his face betraying his own frustration.

Kate shrugged her shoulders. "You were going to show me something?"

"Yes, now I remember," he replied, walking over to one of the monitors. "My mind isn't as sharp as it used to be, but at least I remember my name most days. Other than being regular, you can't ask for much more than that at my age."

"You're doing great, Officer Peck," she humored him.

The old man sat down in a chair in front of one of the television monitors and pushed green and red buttons on a DVR. The image on the screen was replaced by a montage of other images moving backwards at a fast pace. Bob played the digitally recorded images backwards. He slowed the recording down until it reached the starting point.

With a backward glance over his shoulder, he said, "Inspector, this is what happened earlier this evening."

Kate leaned over his shoulder and watched the flickering images on the monitor giving new meaning to reality television. On the monitor, she watched as a green and white front-loading sanitation truck with the letters 'WM' for Waste Management stenciled on its side pulled into the loading dock. Two automated forks reached out for the large dumpster and lifted the waste container over the truck. Once it had reached its apex, the container was flipped upside down and the waste emptied into the vehicle's hopper. Powerful hydraulic motors revved up and compacted the waste into the rear of the truck. Then two forks flipped the dumpster upright. But instead of returning the waste container to its original position, the automated forks held the dumpster out in front of the garbage truck. The truck backed up a few paces then charged forward, squealing its tires, blasting through the loading dock door.

"Could you hold the frame right there, Officer Peck?" Kate asked, looking closely to read the license number, but the image was too blurry.

"Sure," the old man replied, pausing it. "Why is there no sound?" she inquired.

"This isn't like a movie you'd watch on television," he explained. "Security cameras record images but don't have the capabilities to record sound with accuracy."

"I knew that." Kate was somewhat befuddled. "I guess I was just having a senior moment."

"Please don't apologize, Inspector. I have them all the time."

Kate smiled at his joke and asked him to continue.

When the digital recording resumed, two large men wearing gorilla masks and dressed in gray sanitation suits jumped out of the garbage truck carrying MAC-10 machine pistols. They dragged a third man out of the cab and marched him along between them. He was wearing a campus policeman's uniform, but his face was obscured beneath a burlap bag pulled over his head. The two gorillas trained their automatic weapons on the back of the hooded man's head. They fast-stepped him through the loading dock and pushed him through the darkened storage area.

One of the security cameras lost them in the dark, but another one picked them up as they approached the central containment vault.

"Could you freeze the frame again, Officer Peck?"

She looked closely.

"Whatever you like, Inspector," he said pausing it.

"What are we looking at?" Kate inquired, pointing at what appeared to be a bank vault.

"This is the containment vault where the plutonium was stored. The walls around the vault are several feet thick and are shielded against high levels of radiation.

Security personnel are housed in this control room, and they maintain authority over the six different safeguards it takes to get into the vault. Standard equipment within the vault includes a linear accelerator, a digital imaging detector, and program-mable remote handling equipment."

Kate nodded to herself, as if he confirmed something she expected to be true. "What kind of safeguards?" She squinted to try and make out any distinct or obvious images.

"The usual," he responded. "Keys and key cards, code numbers, and palm print identification."

"Please continue with the recording."

Outside the central containment vault, one gorilla barked out orders that neither Kate nor Peck could hear, but the meaning was clear, while the other placed C-4 charges at key points around the vault door and the control room.

The two gorillas forced the hooded man to his knees, primed their MAC-10 machine pistols, and pointed the barrels of their automatic weapons at his head. The campus cops had to make a choice: surrender and save the man's life or ignore their fellow security guard and protect the safety of the vault.

Kate folded her arms across her chest as she watched the recording and thought about what choice she would have made. There was a long pause, and during the passage of time, the two men continued to bark orders at the control room door. When they were ready to execute their hostage, the door opened, and two campus policemen walked out with their hands in the air. They dropped to their knees when they had reached the open floor. The hostage removed his burlap hood, took one of the MAC-10s, and shot each campus cop at point blank range right in the head. Kate raised her fist to her mouth and bit down hard to keep from screaming. The two gorillas shook the body of each campus policeman down, removing a set of keys and a key card from each one of them. They brought a small, battery-powered hand-saw down on the first campus cop's wrist, sawing through the uniform, flesh and bone.

Kate turned her eyes away. They turned to the other campus cop, while the third man trained his MAC-10 on the security camera and blasted away at it. There was a blinding flash, and then static. "Shit!" Kate screamed.

"Sorry you had to see that last part, Inspector," Bob said, looking into her eyes. "My guess is they used the palm prints right off the men's severed hands and broke right into the containment vault, then used the keys and key cards to access the storage area and took whatever they wanted from the plutonium reserves."

"Fuckin' animals."

"What department did you say you were with?"

"Homicide," said Kate.

"I dare say you've seen plenty of bodies in your time."

"After the crime, not during it. I don't suppose you could rewind that recording back to the spot when the garbage truck first appears and insert me in the picture. I'd give them a real taste of justice. Right between the eyes."

Bob looked at her disapprovingly, as if beginning to suspect the raw emotions that burned deep down inside Kate. "Simmer down, Inspector. It won't help either of those two men to go flying off the handle on some half-assed notion of vengeance. Build your case first, and then put them behind bars."

"I hear you." And she did, but if given the chance, she would blow them all away.

"C'mon, I'll walk you back down to the loading dock area," Peck said, taking her by the arm and escorting her out of the Operations Center.

By the time they returned to the science building, Kate found the usual crime-scene frenzy in the driveway behind the loading dock, but this one was bigger, considering the multi-jurisdictional aspects of the crime. In addition to the crime-scene boys, forensics, people from the ME's office, and uniformed policemen, there were men in yellow HAZMAT suits, military types, a handful of campus cops, and suits from Homeland Security and the FBI. William, Mikhail, Jorge, Lieutenant Roberts, and a couple of guys from the Chief's office were each engaged in their own private conversations. It struck Kate as farcical, maybe a little overkill, that they needed so many people to catch three guys in a stolen garbage truck, but then of course she knew a great deal more about the crime scene than she was ready to reveal.

Kate extended her hand to the old campus policeman.

"Officer Peck, thanks for all of your assistance. I couldn't have had a better guide."

"You remember what I told you," he replied, shaking her hand.

"I will," she said with a thin smile.

Kate watched him trudge away, until he was lost in the crowd.

At the edge of the perimeter, Kate stepped under the yellow caution tape, walked up to one of the uniformed officers, and flashed her badge. He was so busy building the barricade he signaled her on without looking. She walked past the coroner's investigators, who were offloading a gurney from their truck, nodded, and then came upon two men from forensics who were pouring plaster in a shoe print.

"How's it going, boys?" she asked, crouching down next to them.

"Not bad," one replied, looking up at her. "I'd be doing a lot better without all this shit from the feds."

"Yeah," the other one answered. "Homeland Security can fuckin' go home."

Kate shrugged. "Sorry I asked."

"Hey, Dawson!" Mikhail called, running over to her side.

"What's going on, Jawara?"

He swallowed down a couple of deep breaths and reported, "We found the sanitation truck. It was abandoned a few blocks away from here. Same one that was reported stolen yesterday by Waste Management."

"You didn't go near it, did you?" Kate asked, the sound of panic in her voice.

"No, the damn feds wouldn't let us," Mikhail replied, still sucking air. "They flashed their badges at us and claimed the truck was being impounded as a matter of national security. Can you believe it? A fuckin' garbage truck! I really hate those guys."

Kate breathed a sigh of relief. "Those guys may have just saved your life."

"Bullshit," the African-American swore.

"I'm telling you the truth," she said, glancing around to see that no one was listening to their conversation. When she was satisfied they were alone, she took his arm and whispered, "That sanitation truck was used in the theft of plutonium, so you could say, it's a very hot truck."

"Christ," Mikhail said, pissed off. "I sure hope it doesn't mean my dick's going to fall off in a few months due to radiation poisoning."

"I really doubt it, Jawara. It takes acute exposure over an extended period of time for plutonium to be lethal," Kate said, recalling some very rudimentary knowledge gleaned in a community college science class.

"You had better be right."

For a moment, Kate paused, wrestling with thoughts that were jumping back and forth between her long-andshort term memories. Her fears and desires and her brooding fascination with John Mitchell and the religious cult were all tied together somehow with this robbery. Long before she realized it, she had the answer, and it stared her right in the face. She shook her head and almost smiled. "Those criminals must have had a real death wish. They weren't wearing any protective clothing, and I'm sure they got more than a lethal dose. Wait a minute. What the hell! Maybe they knew they were going to die anyway and were willing to sacrifice themselves for a bigger cause. I think this theft of the plutonium is tied directly to the End Times Ministries."

Mikhail shook his head. "No, I don't believe it."

"You got a better group of suspects? They want to bring about the end of the world, and now they have the materials to build an atomic bomb."

"I'm telling you, I don't believe it."

"Don't believe it then, but it's true," William said, adding his own two cents as he walked into the middle of their conversation. "They've got a real mess inside that lab; a real hot zone. I sure wouldn't want to be one of the men chosen to clean it up. They're going to be scrubbing away in that area for months. If it were my decision, I'd roll a couple of dump trucks in here and seal the whole thing off with concrete for one hundred years."

"Was it plutonium?" Mikhail asked.

"Yes, Plutonium-239 to be exact," replied William, reaching for his notes. "They took just enough to build themselves a dirty little bomb."

"What the hell was that doing here in the first place?" his partner demanded.

"The University of San Francisco is no longer just a private liberal arts college, but a Research Institution, according to the Carnegie Classification," William reported, reading from his notes. "That means the school now engages in extensive research and receives $40 million or more annually in federal research grants. Those grants fund a variety of military and industrial projects that may employ hazardous materials."

"You didn't answer his question," Kate said, shaking her head. "What was the plutonium doing here?"

"I was just getting to that," he said, scrambling to read through his notes. William may well have had an eidetic memory and remembered every detail of his life, but he had an awful system for remembering details of other people's lives and events that were cross-wired with his own. At times, his notes acted more like a crutch than a genuine resource. "The two scientists who built the Mars Rover at NASA's Jet Propulsion Laboratory have been working in conjunction with Lawrence Livermore National Laboratory and researchers at USF on an electric car that is powered by tiny plutonium pellets. I'm told that one pellet can run a mid-sized car for more than a year."

"I didn't know that USF was doing that kind of research," Kate said.

"Blame it on the economic crisis," William said with a shrug. "In the last ten years, most colleges and universities have had to contend with shrinking endowments and tough budget choices as a result. Even Harvard University saw a major decline in its $37 billion endowment and had to increase tuition costs, reduce academic programs, and sell off some of its private-equity holdings. So given a choice between closing their doors and partnering with the federal government on risky, high-return projects, colleges and universities have been fighting each other for those federal research grants."

"But why plutonium of all things?" Mikhail asked.

"Why not? Would you have been more accepting if they had been researching a super-flu virus that got out of hand? Besides, universities have always been the testing grounds for new advances in science and technology," William continued, sounding more like a textbook than a homicide detective. "Plutonium was synthesized in 1940 by a team of researchers in a lab at the University at California, Berkeley."

Kate and Mikhail exchanged glances.

"William is our very own Bill Nye the Science Guy," Kate said.

"Just how much plutonium was stolen?" Jorge asked, as he walked up and joined his fellow detectives in the huddle.

"Four kilograms or about nine pounds," William reported.

Jorge was concerned. "Any immediate danger to the public?"

"It depends on the amount of exposure," William replied, and then he had to consult his notes. "Acute or longer-term exposure carries a danger of serious health risks, radiation sickness, genetic damage, cancer, and death."

"I seem to recall Ralph Nader saying that a pound of plutonium dust spread into the atmosphere would be enough to kill eight billion people," Kate added.

"There are only seven billion people on the planet," Mikhail said.

"Million, Kate. Not a billion," William corrected her.

"The toxicity of plutonium is roughly equivalent with that of nerve gas. So it would be enough to kill six- to eight-million people if released into the air."

"Well, that's it then," Roberts growled—tense and irritable as he approached his team of detectives—but he made every effort to hide those feelings behind a gruff exterior. "The FBI just pulled the plug on our investigation."

"Can they do that?" Kate asked.

"They represent the federal government," he replied.

"They can do anything they damn-well please."

"Jurisdictional mandate," William said, but no one was listening.

Roberts decided it was time to get the show on the road. "Let's get all of our people packed up. We're moving out."

CHAPTER EIGHT

Lietenant Roberts sat at his desk, his head resting on his arm, listening to the press conference on the radio in his office. He was unshaved, and from the dark circles under each eye, he looked like he had been up all night. Roberts glared at Kate from his glass-enclosed sanctuary when she entered the Homicide Bureau, carrying a briefcase, heading towards his office. The look on the Lieutenant's face said it all: Don't fuck with me today.

On the radio, the Media Relations Officer at the University of San Francisco stated, "We are pleased to report that officials at the university responded immediately to the threat and followed the standard safety protocols established by the Department of Energy and the Nuclear Regulatory Commission for situations involving the accidental loss or the deliberate theft of nuclear materials.

The Federal Bureau of Investigation was informed immediately of the theft.

"Earlier this morning, Campus Provost McKinney and Chancellor Williams met with the Regional Director of the FBI and assured her of their desire to cooperate with the investigation. Federal law provides stiff fines and criminal penalties for any attempts to steal nuclear material. I want to remind everyone that the investigation is still ongoing, and it will focus on understanding the causes and the corrective actions to make sure this does not happen again."

"That's enough!" said Roberts, reaching up and turning off his radio. "I've heard enough of this crap for one day. What do you want?"

"I got the authoritative proof you wanted." Kate set her brief-case down on one of his office chairs and pulled out a yellow legal pad. She sat down and crossed her legs with the legal pad in her lap.

"You've got five minutes," he said Kate lifted the top sheet and folded it under the legal pad. "Yesterday, I met with Senator Gabriela Santiago at her office in Sacramento, and we talked about her thirteen-years as a member of the End Times Ministries. I showed her the crime scene photos that were all-too familiar to her."

"Are you telling me that whack job is your authoritative proof?"

"Whack job? Is that supposed to be funny?" Kate didn't see the humor. "This woman's a state senator. She was elected twice into office. She published a book about her time in the cult. It was on the top of best sellers list for thirteen weeks, and she's been on the lecture circuit."

Roberts scowled. "Spare me the résumé, and tell me what she said."

"The murder-suicides are part of the preparation the cultists are making for the end times," Kate replied. "They are trying to spare their children from all the horrors that are associated with the end of the world by sending them on to God."

"End of the world?"

"Yes, sir."

"And you believe her?"

"I don't buy into all this mumbo-jumbo about the end times," Kate confessed. "But the point is, *they* do. Their leader is self-absorbed in his power, and he believes he can precipitate the end of the world."

"Do you know how crazy that sounds?"

Kate shrugged. "Yes, I do. But no crazier than targeting abortion clinics or welfare offices with Anthrax or bombing a federal building in Oklahoma City or crashing planes into the World Trade Center and the Pentagon. Sometimes it takes one madman with a vision, and he can make it seem like the world is ending."

The Lieutenant scratched the stubble of beard that was growing on his face, thinking. "All right, Inspector, let's say you're right. What happens next?"

"I'm not sure." Kate never thought she'd be asked that question. She had spent so much time building her case against the religious cult that the thought didn't occur to her.

"But it's a good bet they'll use the plutonium to build themselves an atomic bomb."

"And then what?" Roberts asked, playing devil's advocate. "Destroy a major city? Blow up a treasured landmark? Crash a region's power grid? How does the use of an atomic bomb bring about the end of the world?"

"I don't know. I don't know."

Lieutenant Roberts shot a look at Kate then let his eyes drop to a report on his desk. "Well, I hate to burst your bubble, Kate, but your cultist friends didn't have anything to do with that theft of the plutonium. An Islamist militant group, known as the Crimson Jihad, has taken all the credit."

Kate leaned forward in her chair and looked over the report. "I don't believe it."

"Well, believe it," he said. "The government elevated the national terror alert to "high" this morning after the Crimson Jihad made their announcement. FBI officials claim the group is preparing to launch an attack on a major US city with a suitcase nuke, and they are actively looking for a thirty-eight-year-old Pakistani man, named Mohammed Sher Mohammad Khan, with alleged ties to this group."

"They could be wrong."

"Yeah, and they could be also be right. Given the two scenarios, which one do you think is more likely?"

Kate's head was whirling. She didn't know what to believe any more, and she wondered if she ever did. *What had John Monroe taught me about Ockham's razor? All things being equal, the simplest explanation for some phenomenon was likely to be the correct answer. Well, maybe Roberts was right . . . and had been all along.*

She gathered up her yellow legal pad and placed it inside her briefcase. Then as she turned to go, Kate saw her dark reflection in the glass door.

"Good work, Inspector," the Lieutenant commended her. "But I think if you keep digging, you are going to find I was right."

She walked out of the office door without a backward glance.

When the radio dispatch came in, Jorge was choking down a triple cheeseburger with grilled onions and an order of French fries while leaning against the crumpled fender of his Ford pick-up in the parking lot of a burger joint. He reached through the window of the driver's side door and turned the volume up. The dispatcher was calling on any vehicle in the vicinity of the California Academy of Sciences to respond to a possible 10-23 (breaking-andentering).

That was less than a block and a half away from their location, and he wanted in on the action. He crumpled up the grease-paper wrapping of the burger and tossed it into the back of his truck. He honked the horn a couple of times, and Kate came running out.

Jorge spoke into the radio's microphone: "This is 20 William 15, responding to the possible 10-23 at the California Academy of Sciences. We're about a block and a half out and will advise."

"That's a 10-4, 20 William 15," the dispatcher replied.

"What's happening?" Kate asked, reaching for the passenger side door.

"*Vámonos*," Jorge said as he climbed into the truck and started the engine. "There's a break-in taking place at the museum."

"What's the big deal? Let some squad car handle it," she said, settling into her seat.

"*Coño*, I got a feeling these are the *Pendejoes* we're after."

Jorge shifted into first gear and floored the gas pedal. The truck jumped forward from the parking lot onto the highway and bolted down the street like a thoroughbred race horse that hadn't been raced in a while. He wove through traffic, cutting in and out of the line of cars, passing on the left and right, doing anything it took to get ahead of the other vehicles on the road. Kate wiped the sweat dripping down her forehead. She pulled her Beretta .9-millimeter, semi-automatic pistol from its holster, slipped out the magazine, then put it back in, and worked the slide.

KA-CHINK.

The California Academy of Sciences Museum in Golden Gate Park was coming up fast on the right-hand side of the road. Jorge downshifted his truck and moved into the right lane to turn right. One of the largest museums in the world with over four-hundred-thousand-square-feet of floor space, the

California Academy of Sciences was home to an enclosed rain forest, aquarium, planetarium, and natural history museum. It included standing exhibits devoted to dinosaurs, insects, the Atom and Army Ordnance, and its latest project, a full-scale reproduction of the Great Library of Alexandria. Rebuilt in 2008, after the original museum was damaged in the 1989 Loma Prieta earthquake, the museum was a treat to everyone touring its facilities.

Kate thought she saw three men as they roared by the entrance. She and her partner pulled into the parking lot and jumped out of the truck with their guns drawn. They saw flashlights working their way to the back of the museum. Kate signaled Jorge to circle around to the loading dock while she went through the front door.

Gun in hand, Kate stayed in the shadows, crouching behind the turnstile at the front door adjacent to the exhibit celebrating the Great Library of Alexandria. She crouched for a long while until her eyes became accustomed to the darkness. She figured the men who had broken into the museum were not yet aware of her presence, but it was a matter of minutes before the whole place was surrounded by cops. As long as she was there first, she was determined to make the collar herself. She didn't dare consider that Jorge was right and that they were the same ones who had stolen the plutonium from the university. Instead, Kate focused all her attention on the hunt, a dangerous game she perfected during her time on the force. She heard whispered voices and movement ahead in the grand exhibit to her right, and she felt certain she would find the perpetrators inside.

She slowly came out of the shadows, slid down on her hands and knees, and edged herself along the ticket counter. She moved towards the library exhibit, using the empty market stands constructed out of cardboard to the illusion of a marketplace as her cover, then climbed the steps and paused behind a pillar at the entrance. The exhibit looked deserted, despite the voices. She walked through the lobby, down a corridor, and into the central gallery.

The gallery seemed long, dark, and ominous until she searched its length with ambient light from her iPhone. She was struck by what she saw. The cardboard and plaster-of-Paris walls of the gallery were covered in ornate murals and pictographic, sidewall writings that were reflected in the makeshift pool and fountain at the center of the marble floor. Pillars and columns carved from sandstone or some other inexpensive material were spaced at even intervals along the perimeter of the room. The end columns, on the left and right, supported a cardboard balcony, which had attractive frieze work. Beneath each cornice, the frieze work continued in provocative shapes, distorted by her light source. Many statues and busts of the Greek and Roman gods, molded in cheap gypsum or molding plaster, adorned the alabaster pedestals. Dominating the other statues was a large statue of Alexander the Great dressed like a Pharaoh with crook, flail, and headgear as the centerpiece of the main gallery.

Kate let out a deep sigh, looking up at the image of the man-god, and shook her head. She had seen photographs on fliers throughout the city, but none of the pictures could capture the true majesty of seeing it in person.

Kate clicked off her light. She had no time to stop and admire Alexander. The men were still at large, but she sensed they were just ahead of her, and she needed to keep moving ahead to catch them.

She completed her circuit of the main gallery, moving down a narrow corridor that connected to the next section of the exhibit. As she worked her way through the numerous halls and rooms, she heard whispers and movement ahead.

She held her twelve-shot Beretta tightly in hand, with her index finger resting on the trigger guard, ready to engage.

Her adrenalin was pumping like a narcotic coursing through the veins of a speed junkie. Her calm exterior belied the truth of a woman living on the edge.

Kate heard something behind her, took a deep breath, and held it in her lungs. She whirled around into a crouch and pointed her gun at a target, finger on the trigger, ready. She, like one of the Greek statues, watched and waited. Listening closely to the darkness, she heard nothing but the moan of the cool air conditioning as it recycled through the dark chambers. Then she heard it again—a scratching sound. She followed the sound with her gun, tracing the outline of the exhibit at floor level when a lone rat scurried out from under the exhibit, sniffed the air, and scampered back under cover. She rolled her eyes and let the air out of her lungs through clenched teeth.

Kate brought her weapon down and melted back into the shadows.

She crept along the narrow corridor and tiptoed into the next gallery of the museum—still nothing. Her muscles were on fire, and the fight or flight instinct had bubbled over into an acid that coursed through her veins. She was ready for one or the other, but she couldn't bear this high level of tension for much longer.

Tucking herself behind a pillar, Kate paused. She opened her mouth, took in a breath then released the tension. Deftly, she wiped her sweating palms down the side of her trousers, one hand then the other, switching the gun between them. She dropped to her hands and knees, looking into the next gallery for some sign of her quarry, but she found it difficult to see anything in the darkness. She saw odd shapes and patterns, nothing that matched the outline of a man.

Kate tightened and crept forward, foot by foot, moving

between the stone pillars. She heard sound again—the distinctive sound of muffled voices and movement. She stopped moving and listened, trying to decide whether the sound was real or just her imagination. She heard it one more time. *It's real Kate*, she told herself then turned towards the next gallery, tensed, and readied herself to move. Not fifteen feet from her, she saw a light flicker in the darkness. She measured the distance, planned each stride—the trajectory of her final spring—and took one final deep breath. Then, slipping from the shadows like a dark avenger, she got the jump on her prey.

"Hold it right there," she whispered, holding her gun with both hands out in front of her in a combat stance.

The muzzle was targeted on the man's chest.

"Please don't shoot," the man said over his shoulder.

"I'm not with them. I work for the museum. I'm the night watchman."

"Drop your weapon and kick it over to me. Then put your hands over your head," Kate ordered, standing her ground.

"Officer, you've got to believe me," he pleaded.

"Drop your weapon, and put your hands up in the air."

He raised his hands above his head, then stopped mid-way as Jorge staggered like a zombie into view. Kate focused on her partner who was pale and bleeding. The man swiveled around into a crouch, with his weapon drawn, and shot at the two of them.

Kate jumped to the side, tackled her partner to the ground, rolled over, and fired three shots. BLAM! BLAM! BLAM! The three bullets struck the man dead center in the chest. The percussion threw him backwards and down to the floor—the gun tumbling out of his hand.

"Jorge!" Kate screamed. With her gun still trained on the man, she crawled over to her partner's crumpled body and stretched her left hand to feel the carotid artery in his neck. Jorge was alive—just barely. She looked out into the darkness, sighting her Beretta back and forth at imaginary targets. *Okay, so where were the rest of them? I counted at least three, and they must have heard the gunshots.*

She climbed to her feet and struggled to get her partner's body behind cover. She then dropped to one knee, and with her gun trained on the dark void in front of her, she reached for her cell phone. She clicked the "on" switch and dialed 911.

"911, what is the nature of your emergency?" the operator responded.

"Code ten double-zero," she said into the receiver.

"Officer down. California Academy of Sciences museum in Golden Gate Park. Hurry."

"We've got vehicles en-route to your location."

In minutes, the entire complement of police officers in the San Francisco Police Department descended on the California Academy of Sciences. The first officers who arrived at the scene found them, just off the lobby in the Great Library of Alexandria exhibit. Kate was holding vigil over her injured partner, like a well-armed angel of mercy.

Her right arm was stiff, holding the gun out perpendicular to her body, while her left hand cradled his head in her lap.

Kate had already lost one partner, and she was determined not to lose another. Jorge was going to live.

The museum bustled with activity as specialists from each of the departments plied their expertise to the crime scene. Plainclothes detectives took statements from motorists who were driving by and witnessed the break-in, coroners flashed photographs, the scene-of-the-crime boys dusted for evidence, and uniformed policemen kept the curiosity-seekers at bay.

Kate was taking a grilling from Lieutenant Roberts while the other members of the Homicide Bureau—including William, Mikhail, Balardi and Farris—looked on. Roberts was pacing back and forth, his face beet red.

"What the hell were you and Ramirez doing here?"

Kate took a deep breath. She had heard his question clear enough but was pissed off that she had to explain herself in front of the others. *My partner and I had responded to a call. What more was there to say?*

Roberts stopped pacing and half turned towards his detective. "Did you not hear me? I want to know what the hell you and Ramirez were doing here."

"When the call came over the radio about a possible 10-23 at the California Academy of Sciences, we were less than a minute away."

"Didn't it ever occur to you to wait for back up?" Roberts asked.

"Yes, sir. It did. But when we saw their lights from the street and realized they had penetrated so far into the museum, we knew it would be a matter of minutes before they had what they wanted and were on their way."

"Do we have any idea what they took?" the Lieutenant asked, turning to the other members of the Homicide Bureau.

"Parts for an atomic bomb," William reported, looking at his notes.

"Fuck!" Roberts swore. "What the hell was that doing here?"

Kate spoke up, "The museum has a standing exhibit on the Atom and Army Ordnance."

"No, shit?" Mikhail said.

"The parts themselves are harmless, sir, without a power source," William added. "The curator said most of the parts are available on the Internet or at the local Home Depot."

"Lieutenant, the Internet has plenty of sites with blueprints on how to build the bomb," Balardi said, jumping into the conversation. "It wouldn't take much for some brainiac to put all the pieces together."

"I'm really glad you told me that, Balardi. I was beginning to wonder," Roberts said sarcastically.

"Sorry, sir."

Lieutenant Roberts didn't want to hear any more. The fuse to his red-hot anger was burning, and he was moments away from erupting; his face beet red. "Well, why are you all just standing around looking like you got your thumb up your ass? We've got a crime scene to investigate. So, go investigate!"

They all scattered, except Kate. She stood her ground while he paced back and forth in front of her.

"Inspector, I'm very disappointed in you. You keep making the same mistakes, and almost got a man killed tonight," he said, dressing her up one side and then down the other. "There is a reason we follow standard police procedure. It's to prevent cops from being shot in the line of duty."

"I understand, sir," she agreed.

"Pending a full investigation of the shooting, you're on official administrative leave. It's not disciplinary, Dawson, although I think you need a break. You know I have to because of the fatal shooting."

Kate's shoulders slumped fatigue washing over her.

"I know the rules, sir. I'll be by on Thursday or Friday to clear up a few items on my desk."

"Fine," Roberts conceded.

Roberts had something more to say, but he failed to get it out before the paramedics rolled Jorge by in a gurney. He was unconscious but didn't look bad. He had a plastic mask over his face feeding him oxygen and an IV pumping morphine for the pain.

Kate walked over to his side and asked, "Is he going to be okay?"

"Yeah, he'll be fine," a paramedic replied with a reassuring smile. "The bullet hit muscle tissue, nothing vital. He should be up and around in a few weeks, but he's going to have a really sore shoulder."

She walked alongside her partner to the ambulance then followed him in his truck to the hospital.

Several hours later, Kate pulled into the parking spot next to Lenny's Mini Cooper and smiled. The rear hatch was up, and it looked like her eccentric friend was packing the vehicle for a trip. She waved at him, and he stopped loading. Lenny adjusted the NASA baseball cap on his balding head. He then smoothed out the wrinkles in his baggy trousers and smiled at her through his big white bushy beard. She laughed to herself. He looked like Santa Claus, except that he wore a black t-shirt that read *Revenge of the Jedi* and carried a light-saber from *Star Wars*. She'd have to say something about trimming his beard.

"Looks like you're heading out on a trip," she observed, pointing to the things he was loading into his small car.

"No, I've got a Rebel Legion meeting tonight, and I wanted to bring a few props and costumes along with me to the meeting." He stopped moving to give her all his attention.

"*Star Trek*, right?" Kate queried, with a mischievous look.

Lenny shook his head. "No, *Star Wars*. It's a fan-run group. We reproduce the costumes and characters that are part of the Rebel Alliance against the Empire."

"I know that," she replied. "And the character you play is Ben Kenobi."

"We use the term cosplay, short for costume play, because

we're required to wear costumes and accessories authentic to the movies. I still have that Princess Leia slave-girl costume in my closet if you'd like to come join me for some cosplay."

Kate shrugged. "No thanks, Lenny. But listen, you may want to do something about your beard. You look more like Santa Claus than a Jedi."

Lenny looked at his reflection in the car window and frowned. "You're right, this could be a problem. I have a barber trim my beard to the specifications of Alec Guinness's look in *Star Wars*, but I didn't get the chance to get out this week."

"How are you coming along with my project?" Kate had to change the subject.

"I'll have a three-dimensional schematic done by Friday," he replied, still looking at himself in the car window.

"Good. Thank you."

"You haven't forgotten about Saturday, have you?"

She forgot what she promised him and struggled to bring it to mind. Then she remembered. "No, I didn't forget. Ten, right?"

"In the lobby of the Hyatt Regency."

"Right, no problem."

Lenny nodded in satisfaction and resumed his packing. He created a considerable pile of boxes and garment bags in back of his Mini Cooper, and it didn't look like there was enough room for everything. Even if he used the entire back seat of his car, he was going to come up short.

"Listen, Lenny, I know you're busy," she said, watching him struggle to fit the contents of a small U-Haul into his Mini, "but I could use your brilliant mind on a problem from work."

"Sure, what do you need?" he said, somewhat distracted.

"Thanks!" she replied reaching into her briefcase for her yellow notepad. "We recovered a series of numbers from a fire-damaged computer, but we can't decipher the code.

I'm wondering what you make of this number sequence: 121.535889-36.845083."

Lenny took the yellow notepad from her and puzzled over the numbers. "This first number is a longitude," he said. "Yeah, sets of three numbers—degrees, minutes and seconds. The first number has three digits, and the last two are below sixty. These are earth coordinates."

"To where?"

"I don't know," he replied, reaching into his car and pulling a map out of his glove compartment. He unfolded the map on the hood of the Mini and traced longitude and latitude with his fingers. Kate moved next to him to get a better look. "This will not be 100% accurate. I would need access to a good geodetic survey map to get this down to the square mile."

"Could we use my GPS?" she asked.

"Yes, but not to one-hundred-percent accuracy," Lenny said, continuing to work the map. "Wait a second, wait a second, here we go. Those coordinates are about an hour and a half southeast of here in a small town named San Juan Bautista."

"Are you certain?"

"It's my educated best guess. But then, if you didn't want to wait to order a geodetic survey map, you could always put these coordinates into Google and get a fair idea of your location that way."

Kate leaned over and kissed Lenny on the cheek.

"Thanks. Have fun dressing up tonight."

"If I ever get packed." he sighed.

In less than five minutes, Kate was in her apartment on her computer, looking down from a satellite at an image in the map coordinates. She prayed that this was the lead she needed to break the case.

CHAPTER NINE

Kate reached the small historic town of San Juan Bautista a little before two in the afternoon. The heavy fog on Highway 101 slowed her down and turned the hour-and-a-half drive on El Camino Real into three hours. The mist was thick in the vineyards and forest trees along the route, making her break for slower traffic on the curves and the long straightaways. She pressed on ahead, following the coordinates in her GPS system down San Juan Road to 2nd Street. She slowed her speed to twenty-five-miles-an-hour and kept driving until the GPS alerted her she had arrived at her destination. Kate made a U-turn and pulled into the dirt parking lot. The sign read:

EL CAMINO REAL
MISSION SAN JUAN BAUTISTA FOUNDED JUNE 24, 1797

She climbed out of her BMW, looking around. The first thing she saw was the historical marker:

Mission San Juan Bautista

The fifteenth and largest of the Spanish missions, founded in 1797 by the Franciscan order.

The Ohlone Indians, the original residents of the valley, were brought to live at the mission by Spanish soldiers and baptized Catholic by the Franciscan priests.

Over its two-hundred-year history, a soldier barracks, nunnery, hotel, and livery stable were constructed around a large grassy plaza in front.

The farming community of San Juan Bautista grew up around the mission and rapidly expanded during the California Gold Rush to feed hungry miners.

The mission, sitting adjacent to the famed San Andreas Fault, suffered damage from several earthquakes but never entirely destroyed.

She stopped reading the plaque and scratched her head. *Why did the coordinates lead me here?* The old mission and several other buildings looked like they were deserted. The setting reminded Kate of the ghost towns from the Old West. Other than one other car that was parked on the street, she was all alone out there.

Kate was too good a police officer to dismiss the lead out-of-hand, and she took a physical inventory of her surroundings in case she may have missed something critical. She walked to the middle of the grassy plaza, looked, and listened. The plaza was lined on both sides by tall eucalyptus trees with the occasional pepper tree thrown in for good measure. Just beyond the trees, she saw the valley and hills off in the distance. To her immediate left was the Old Spanish mission, its cloisters a long corridor of arches that ran along the southwest side of the adobe building. The mission's bell tower stood high above the trees at the end. On her right, Kate counted three structures nestled in the trees: the saloon, the old Plaza Hotel, and the livery stable. They were knit together by an old wooden sidewalk. Wooden barrels like the settlers used to transport water and other perishable goods were at odd intervals throughout the green and near the structures. An old dirt road made a circuit around the plaza and recalled a time when horse-drawn carriages were the primary mode of transportation. Behind her, on the opposite side of the street, was the whitewashed stone Castro house that once had served as a barracks for Spanish soldiers.

Did I miss anything? Kate stood looking over her surroundings carefully. *What was so important about this location that it warranted a set of coordinates?*

A collection of laughing voices at the old Plaza Hotel, startled Kate, so she watched as three people came out of the entrance and walked over to the livery stable. They were following a walking tour of the grounds, and that was their next stop on the brochure. Kate tried to play down her interest in the threesome by walking over to the mission and picking up a brochure of her own. She had no way of knowing if they were three tourists on vacation or three people pretending to be tourists.

With brochure in hand, Kate pursued her own walking tour and kept one step ahead of the others. She went into the mission and climbed to the top of the bell tower.

When she came back down, she saw the trap door to the cellar and considered going in but thought better of it. She crossed the green to the old saloon and looked inside the silent building. She saw an old billiard table collecting dust, a piano with yellowed keys, and a bar with empty glasses lined up on the counter. Nailed to an inner wall, several "Wanted: Dead or Alive" posters proclaimed rewards for the apprehension of bandits who held up the Wells Fargo Express Wagon. Next, she went to the old Plaza Hotel and looked through the open door into the parlor. The hotel was dark and gloomy, the shades drawn to protect the flowered rug from fading any more. She saw a deserted fireplace with an old clock on the mantle, several pieces of shabby furniture, and an old Victorian sofa. Towards the back, she could see a small organ with a hymnal open on the rack.

Everything seemed perfectly normal, just the way she expected it to be.

As she looked up from her brochure, Kate caught a glimpse of the three people coming out of the livery stable, walking towards their car. She watched them climb into the late-model sedan and drive away. She also witnessed a lone nun crossing the green to the mission when the bell in the tower struck on the half hour. Kate walked into the livery stable and moved among the plastic replicas of horses.

They looked like they belonged on a child's merry-go-round instead of a stable. Each one of them was given a distinctive personality of their own. She sat on the reproduction of the wooden carriage and continued thinking. *What did I miss? Why am I here?*

Kate paused to digest all the information, then went over it again, one more time. She walked out of the livery, turned the corner, and surveyed the scene. The wooden buildings leaned against each other like weary old men, and the sidewalk was a sway-back stretch of rotted planking. She spotted the saloon and walked towards it.

Even though there was a closed sign in the window, Kate looked through the glass and wondered if any of the dusty bottles behind the bar had alcohol. She wanted a stiff shot of bourbon. She leaned back against the storefront and shook her head.

CRASH!

Window glass exploded around her, and she hadn't made a single move. Kate dove for the cover of a wooden barrel, landing belly-down on the wooden deck, which was supposed to be a sidewalk, and covered her head in defense.

The front of the saloon popped twice and splintered, sending sharp slivers of wood flying, like shrapnel through the air.

Kate rolled to one side and risked a glance at the storefront.

Two bullet holes now occupied the space where, moments before, she had been standing.

She tucked herself into a crouch and ran towards the livery stable, using the wooden barrels as cover. As a fourth bullet ricocheted off the planking near her feet, she leaped behind the pair of eucalyptus trees in front of the old Plaza Hotel. She didn't bother glancing over her shoulder because there was no reason to confirm what she already suspected.

Someone with a high-powered rifle, equipped with a silencer, was shooting at her. Panting and perspiring heavily, the inspector crouched in the cover of the trees and waited to catch her breath. She then pulled her Beretta from its holster and worked the slide to chamber a bullet. With her gun now primed for action, Kate surveyed the grounds and determined that the shooter was in the bell tower because it would afford him the best view to a kill. She edged out from behind the tree, and another bullet went whizzing by her ear. BLAM! BLAM! BLAM! She fired back, hugging the safety of the tree.

Then she waited a few seconds for return fire, and when that did not come, she fired three more shots at the bell tower. BLAM! BLAM! BLAM! Kate took off running, using the cover of the trees to shield her escape, bullets from the shooter's rifle nipping at her heals. She moved through the shadows at a fast pace, taking in deep, measured breaths as she ran. The muscles in her body burned from the adrenalin rush, like she had been running for hours, and her legs wanted to quit. But she forced herself along to the end of the wooden sidewalk, and the livery stable beyond. She threw herself through the front door, tucked herself into a roll, and came up with her gun ready.

She barricaded herself behind the old Conestoga wagon and breathed deeply, gulping down the air. Kate saw her car just a few steps from the livery door, parked perpendicular to the street, with the driver's side door exposed to the shooter's deadly line of fire. She could unlock the door and start the car with her key fob, but that still meant a lot of ground to cover, even if she went to the passenger's side door. There had to be another way, and once she had caught her breath, she searched to the back of the livery for options. The rear door had been welded shut in order to prevent vandals from destroying any of the exhibits or historical artifacts. Access to the windows was well out of her reach, and she didn't see any convenient building blocks or ladders to reach them. In fact, she came to the stark realization that the only way in and out of the livery stable was through the front door.

For an instant, Kate thought she may have wounded the shooter because his response time to her second three shots was much slower. She listened to hear anything unusual in the ambient sounds, like heavy breathing, but the grassy plaza was teeming far too much with the sounds of birds and wind blowing through the trees to hear anything. She waited a few moments longer, drinking in his surroundings, then started to breathe again. She knew the shooter was still out there, and he wasn't giving anything away.

Pressing herself against the dark recesses of the livery door, she waited, with all her senses focused on her car parked out front. Her mind worked furiously, trying to run several scenarios through her head, but their outcomes were all the same: her lying dead on street inches from her car door. Kate turned slightly and risked a hurried glance at the shooter. He was still up there and wasn't likely to be leaving at any particular time. Time, the word "time" triggered a thought. She remembered the nun who had crossed the green plaza and the bells that had rung on the half hour. Kate looked down at her watch and realized the bells were about to ring. Perhaps they would provide the distraction she needed to reach her car.

Drawing a few deep breaths into her lungs, she screwed up her courage and prepared to run to her car.

The bells should toll three times to announce the hour, and in those precious three seconds, she knew exactly what she had to do.

Kate waited for it, counting down the seconds in her head. Then, at the first toll of three, she unlocked the car doors and started her car remotely with a press of her thumb on the key fob. Next, on the second toll, she scrambled out of the livery door, and fired two shots at the bell tower.

BLAM! BLAM! And while the bells were sounding their final toll, she fired a third shot and leaped into her car head first. BLAM! She rolled into the driver's seat and floored the engine. The BMW coupe jumped over the curb and blasted down the street as the shooter's one and only shot hit the windshield and cracked the double-layer of tempered glass. Kate didn't take her foot off the pedal until she was miles away.

Kate Dawson found one of the deputy sheriffs of San Juan Bautista standing out in front of the police station, eating a greasy fajita and flirting with one of the local girls.

He was thirty, overweight, and did not fit his cheap, ill-fitting uniform. He seemed to have plenty of time to eat and make time with girls, but was not in any real hurry to conduct official police business. It took Kate ten minutes to get him to acknowledge her badge and listen to her complaint about the shooting at the Mission, and another ten minutes to get him to reluctantly agree to drive to the scene of the crime.

When they climbed out of his white Chevy Blazer at the historic site, another twenty minutes had passed, and Dawson figured the shooter was long gone.

"So, you say someone was shooting at you?" he said very slowly, as if he was having trouble thinking of each word to say. "This is a pretty quiet town. Not a lot happens here. Hell, we haven't had a murder here, goin' on ten years. Are you sure it wasn't just a couple of kids with their BB guns?"

"No, deputy. I already explained the shooter was well-armed with a high-powered rifle," she replied, marching him over to the Saloon. "It was either an SR-25 or an AR-15."

"Wo-Whee, little lady, you know you rifles," the sheriff said, shaking his head.

Dawson rolled her eyes with astonishment.

Everything that she had ever heard about law enforcement in the Valley was true. In fact, it made her wonder if she had driven through a time warp, while fighting her way through the fog, and ended up back in the 1950s. "Does this look like the kind of hole a BB makes?" she asked, pointing at the two bullet holes in the storefront.

"I reckon it don't," he said, bending over for a look. The sheriff's big beer belly had lapped over his patent leather belt, and the butt crack that peered up over the rear of his trousers made an ugly sentry. Anyone approaching him from behind would have been easily repulsed by the appearance of the hairy visage.

Kate Dawson knew the shots had been made by a high-powered rifle. She took out a small penknife, and made quick work of prying one of the bullets free. She held it up in the air, and looked at it for a moment before handing it over to the sheriff. "Just as I thought. .223 caliber. The shooter was using an AR-15."

"Well, I'll be danged."

"He used the tower as his perch," Kate surmised, looking up at the mission's bell tower high above the trees.

She paced off the distance, walking an imaginary line between the Saloon and the Mission across the grassy plaza, dragging the chubby sheriff along with her. She then climbed the stairs to the tower, huffing and puffing as she circled around the narrow wooden steps all the way to the top. The five flights of stairs seemed longer because of their odd shape and construction. Slowly, he lumbered along behind her, reduced to crawling on his hands and knees on the final circuit.

At the top, she helped the sheriff struggle to gain his footing on the wooden floor. His face was crimson like he had been boiling in a pot with lobsters, and he was dripping with sweat. He breathed heavily, gulping down deep breaths of air, and started coughing his lungs up. In an effort to ease his discomfort, Dawson patted his sweaty back, and rubbed his arms up and down until he was calm.

"From up here, he had a perfect view of the square."

She stood at the edge of the tower, forming the shape of a rifle with her two hands. The homicide detective closed her left eye, and pretended to squeeze off several rounds at imaginary targets below while looking out of her right eye.

"If you say so, Inspector," said the sheriff, mopping his brow.

Suddenly, she stopped playing sniper, and looked down at the wooden floor of the tower. There were splotches of red paint at odd intervals. As Dawson got down on her hands and knees, she realized it wasn't paint but blood. *Well, maybe I managed to wound him after all!* She removed her pocket knife, as well as two gloves and baggie, from her pocket. With the Sheriff as a witness, she scraped off several slivers of wood with the blood sample as evidence.

"So, how about it, Inspector, can we head back down?"

She nodded her head. "Let me ask you something, Sheriff. Have you seen any strangers out here in the last week or so? Anything out of the ordinary?" Dawson asked, as she started back down the stairs.

"Well, you see, that's a little hard to say," he replied, following after her. "Most locals don't come out this way anymore, and about the only people who ever come out to the Mission are folks from the city. You know, tourists, and as long as they obey the traffic signs, we don't pay them much mind."

"Has nobody else reported any kind of trouble out here?"

The sheriff thought for a moment, then shook his head. "No, I really can't say that I recall any trouble." He wiped his brow. "About six months back, we had a film crew come through here that didn't have the necessary permits to shoot. They were real nice folks. Very polite. Once we told them they needed a permit, they came by the sheriff's office and paid for it in case."

"They were shooting a movie out here?"

"A documentary. You know, one of those Hollywood true stories. About the Hitchcock film."

"Hitchcock film?"

The sheriff nodded his head. "Parts of the movie *Vertigo* were filmed right here in 1957. A little before my time."

"Is that right?" she said, with her eyebrows raised.

"Yes-siree-Bob, right on this very spot," he replied, his chest pumped up with pride. "Kinda makes you feel real special, don't it?"

"I guess."

"You'd probably like the picture, Inspector. I've seen it twice. It's about a detective from San Francisco who falls in love with a woman who's pretending to be someone she ain't. I had it figured out right from the start."

"I'll bet you did," Dawson said, thinking, suddenly a million miles away.

The sheriff checked his watch, and looked back at the Blazer. He seemed like a man who was going to be late for a dinner date with one of the locals. "We should be getting back, unless there's anything else I can do."

"No, thanks," said Kate.

"Hope I helped you out."

"You did," she said, at last. "You did."

Kate stopped by the medical examiner's office as soon as she hit San Francisco. Dr. Brogan had gone home for the day, as had most of his staff, but the Assistant ME was still there processing a sample. Kate was hoping the news of her administrative leave hadn't filtered down to the ME's night staff because she needed a favor from her old friend.

Rosa Romano was an attractive young woman, thirty years old and two years into her job. They had been friends for several years and had often gone out drinking together with her and a few of the other girls. But since Dr. Romano had started working the second shift at police headquarters, she really hadn't seen that much of her.

"Hey, Kate, what brings you down here? Slumming?" asked Romano, jokingly.

Kate held out a plastic lunch bag with the blood samples. "Rosa, I need this right away," she replied.

"'Right away' takes seventy-two hours."

"I need it," Kate begged, holding out her folded hands and shaking them together, like a penitent man. Kate got down on her knees, looking up at Rosa like a child.

"Okay, okay. Get up. I'll skip a couple of steps for you and run it through the amplification process."

"Can you also run it through CODIS for me?"

"Sure, Kate, no problem."

"Thanks, I appreciate it."

Rosa smiled holding the baggie up to the light and looking at the samples. "You know, I always say you can tell a lot about a person from a sample of their blood."

"Can you tell if they're a good person?" Kate sighed.

"Honey, if I could do that, I'd quit my job as an ME and open a dating service for millionaires."

"I'd be your first client, if I could afford your fee."

"Guy troubles?" Romano asked, her smile fading away.

"I'm not sure if I would use the word trouble," she replied, thoughtful, turning inward. "I met him a week ago. He's good looking, in a rugged sort of way, but has a sensitive side. I mean, we had an awesome first date, if you could call it that, on Saturday. One of the best times I can remember. But there's just something about him I can't put my finger on."

"Is this good looking, rugged, sensitive man single?"

"Oh, yeah."

"Straight?"

"Yeah, in fact, I think he's a forty-year-old virgin," Kate said with a snicker. "He didn't come right out and tell me, but I sort of guessed it by some of the things that he said during our date. I know it sounds weird, with him being a logger, but I believe it."

Rosa closed her eyes as if to imagine Kate's rugged man, and then she smiled.

"Does this perfect man have a brother?" Romano asked.

"I don't know, but I'll ask."

"Well, listen, honey, any time you want to bring me a sample of his blood, we'll find out just how perfect he is for you. Okay?"

"Okay, Rosa. Thanks," Kate replied, as she turned and left the ME's office. She was still feeling shaken from the incidents of the day. Perhaps by tomorrow she'd have a clue to the shooter's identity.

The next morning, John hurried into the Homicide Bureau like he was being followed by the devil himself. He was wearing a SFPD visitor's identification badge clipped to his jacket and carried a bag from Starbucks in his right hand. He stopped at the first desk.

"I'm looking for Inspector Dawson," he said to the officer.

Kate heard her name and looked up. John was the last person in the world she had expected to see in police headquarters.

"She's over there," the officer replied, gesturing with his thumb.

"Thank you."

John walked over to her desk. They looked at each other and smiled. Kate didn't want to admit it, but she was happy to see him. She wanted to throw herself into his arms, missed being in his tender, rugged embrace, but she thought better of it. There was no point in giving them any more reason to hate her.

"I thought I'd buy you breakfast," John said, passing the bag to her. "Coffee, extra lite with sugar?"

"You remembered," she said.

"I've forgotten very little about you, Kate. You've been the only thing on my mind all week long."

Kate removed the coffee then searched through the bag. "I'd be even more impressed if I found a sticky bun in here," she commented.

"I brought an assortment of donuts and pastries." His mischievous grin betrayed him.

"You did good. Thanks," she said, biting into the sticky bun. As she chewed on the tasty morsel, Kate rolled her eyes with pleasure.

"I heard on the news about the shooting at the museum. I hope your partner is all right," John said, sitting down on the edge of the detective's desk. He seemed genuinely concerned.

"He's okay. I stopped by on my way in and saw him. He's doing fine."

"You took a big risk going in there, especially after what happened at the university."

"Don't make a big deal out of it," she said with a dismissive look. "I was doing my job."

"It was brave," he replied, the words sounding trite, almost melodramatic, but delivered with an innocence that made them all the sincerer. He stared at her, like a school boy with a crush on his third grade teacher.

"I can tell you never dated a cop before."

"No, but then I never met anyone like you before."

"That surprises me," she said, taking a sip of her coffee. "Women outnumber the men here by a six-to-one margin. I'm surprised that you don't have women hounding you day and night. I have a friend in the ME's office that would eat you right up."

John nodded his head. "Women do hit on me. But just as soon as they learn I'm a Christian and that I put a high value on my moral beliefs, they drop me like a hot potato. I've had more than a hundred first dates in this last year alone, but few second ones. I've had women excuse themselves from the dinner table to powder their nose and never come back. I got to the point where it wasn't worth it to keep putting myself out there, but you haven't run from me yet."

"Well, I'm sorry you've had to deal with that, John. I don't know what's happened to common courtesy anymore. People used to be a whole lot nicer to each other. But I guess it's their loss."

"I like you, Kate. I wouldn't want to have anything to happen to you."

Looking deep into John's baby blue eyes, she thought she could see into his soul. "I like you, too, but I can take care of myself."

"I'm sure you can," he said, reaching into the bag and taking out a powdered donut. John took a healthy bite, and powdered sugar exploded across his face. He kept eating unaware; he looked like a guy who had fallen head-first into a tin of baby powder.

"Oh, you're a mess," Kate said, laughing. She reached into the bag and pulled out the napkins.

"What's the matter? Have I got something on my face?"

"Yes," she said, fighting to contain her laughter.

She wiped the powder from his nose then dabbed the napkin around his mouth and beard. She wanted to kiss him on the lips, but she dared not risk the scandal in her office.

"I seem to be accident prone when I'm around you," he said, laughing at himself.

Kate reassured him, "Don't worry, I've got your back."

"I know. That's kind of what I wanted to talk to you about."

"Sounds serious. I better have a stiff drink of my coffee first," she joked, drinking down a big gulp.

John did his best to hide the serious look on his face, but he knew she could see right through him. He jumped off the edge of her desk, pacing back and forth like an expectant father. "Do you have any vacation time saved up?"

"I have some leave coming to me," Kate replied, not certain where this was going. "What do you want to do? Whisk me off for a romantic getaway?"

"That would be lovely," he said, with a half-smile, "but I want you to get out of town for a few days."

"I don't understand."

Kate was on guard. She pushed her coffee away and stood up. "What's wrong, John? What's really happening?"

"Something terrible is going to happen," John confessed.

"You're starting to worry me."

"I'm sorry, but you must understand this threat is very real. The day of judgment is upon us all."

Kate sighed. "You know I don't believe in that stuff."

"Believe it," he said, seizing her shoulders and looking at her in the face. "It's going to happen in the next few days."

"John, you know as well as I do that people make predictions all the time," she said, trying to sound reasonable. "That doesn't mean they come true. Do you remember that whole thing about the Mayan calendar a few years ago? People were absolutely convinced the world was going to end on December 21, 2012. So, what happened? A big nothing. What about the Millennium Bug? That was going to wipe out the nation's computer network and all of our bank records. So, what happened? A big nothing. I'm telling you, John, people have been making predictions about the end of the world for hundreds of years, and it still hasn't happened."

"This is real. It is happening," Mitchell said, glaring at her. She tried to turn away, but he held her. "Nobody can stop it now."

"John, what's gotten into you? I've never seen you act like this before. You're really scaring me."

"Kate."

"If you know something, tell me, and we'll put a stop to it."

He let her go and looked down at his quivering hands. "You're in over your head, Kate. You have no idea what kind of people you're dealing with. What they're capable of."

"I may be in over my head," she confessed, "but I'm still going to stop them. Please tell me what you know, and we can stop them together."

"I can't."

John walked away starting back down the row of desks that made up the Homicide Bureau. She hurried after him, nearly catching up at the double doors near the entrance of the department, but he was moving so very fast that he simply outpaced her.

"John, I can protect you."

"Please, Kate," he called over his shoulder continuing to move. "*Please*, get out of town."

"John!" she shouted, but he acted like he had not heard her.

Kate had enough of the chase and stopped walking.

She watched him walk to the end of the corridor then disappear into the elevator. He never looked back.

When Kate returned everyone was staring at her.

Mikhail, Balardi, and a couple of cops tried to catch her eye, but she looked straight ahead and kept walking. She didn't have anything to say. William eased his chair back to stand up, but Kate stared him down. She did not need William asking her a lot of questions for that famous notebook of his.

She walked back to her desk, furious. The last thing Kate wanted to do was call attention to her relationship with John, but she was certain now everyone knew. She crumpled the coffee bag into a ball and hurled it down the long row of desks. It splatted down on one of the empty desks, a mishmash of paper and greasy donuts.

"I hope it wasn't something I said," Rosa Romano joked, as she walked by the empty desk. She scooped up the mess and dropped it in a nearby wastebasket before she continued walking.

"Oh, Rosa, I'm so sorry," Kate said, her face turning several shades of red. "That wasn't aimed at you."

"Yeah, I know. I passed your target in the corridor on my way here."

"So, you saw John?"

"Hmmm, they don't get much better than that, girlfriend," Romano commented, putting a couple of manila folders down on the desk and turning towards the hallway.

"That is, if we're both talking about the same good looking man with the visitor's badge clipped to his jacket."

"Yeah, that's him."

"Well, listen, honey, he can park his size 12 Timberland boots underneath my bed any night of the week," Romano said with a smirk.

"You might be disappointed."

"Oh, you mean that whole forty-year-old-virgin thing. No problem. I haven't met a man yet who couldn't keep his hands off me once I had cured him of his lack of experience."

"Rosa, you are bad."

"Listen, girl, you give John twenty-four hours, and he'll be breaking down your door, pleading for you to give him another chance. Trust me, I know these things."

"I wish it were that simple."

"Well, if he makes it any harder, he'll have me to answer to."

Kate reached over and hugged her friend. She was on the edge of losing it.

"Look, I heard through the grapevine you were placed on administrative leave. Tough break. But if there's anything I can do . . ." Rosa could see Kate was breaking.

"No, but thanks. I wanted to clear up a few things on my desk then go home and relax."

Rosa nodded. "That sounds like a plan."

"So, what did you make of my blood samples?" Kate asked.

"She's dead."

Kate was in no mood to be teased. "Dead? That can't be. I thought I wounded him . . . What her?"

"No, you're not following me," Romano said, with a look that stopped just short of being coy. "According to records I obtained from the Department of Defense, she's been dead for two years."

"What?"

"Yeah, that's right. A ghost was shooting at you."

Rosa picked up one of the manila folders from the desk and read, "Staff Sergeant Luisa Martinez, twenty-nine, of Long Beach, California, was killed in a helicopter accident June 12, 2013.

"She was serving her fifth deployment in Afghanistan's Ghazni Province with Lewis-McChord 2nd Battalion, 75th Ranger Division."

"Impossible. You must have gotten your samples mixed."

"No, Kate, I didn't. Those samples you brought to me belong to Staff Sergeant Luisa Martinez."

"But how?"

Rosa handed Kate the folder and pointed to several items highlighted on the first page. "You need to read between the lines, girlfriend. This chick is a spook. If you read her military jacket, you'll see she was involved in a lot of black-bag stuff. My guess is they faked her death in Afghanistan so she could go undercover."

"Undercover as what?" Kate asked, reading through the report.

"I don't know. But trust me, with a record like hers, if this woman had wanted you dead, you'd be in the morgue," Romano replied, her words sobering. "Those shots she fired at you were meant to scare you off, not to harm you. You may not be as lucky next time."

"One of my suspects is named Luisa," Kate said, thinking out loud. She paused a moment to consider. "Come to think of it, her maiden name was Martinez. You don't think they're the same person?"

"I wouldn't turn my back on her." Rosa handed her a second folder. "You're not going to like this one any better."

"What's this?" she asked, opening to the first page.

"The stiff you capped at the museum is a John Doe," Romano reported. "No wants, no warrants, no nothing. It's like he's been living off the grid most of his life.

You'd think there'd be something on file somewhere. Either this man's never been documented, or his files have been wiped clean."

"Great!" Kate sighed. "Just when I was hoping to get some closure before I went out on leave, you give me two more mysteries. What kind of friend are you?"

Rosa shrugged. "Look on the bright side, girlfriend. Five minutes ago, you were pissed off at your boyfriend, now you're just pissed off. Things look like they're improving."

Kate looked at her, then back at the two folders. She had to admire her friend's cockeyed optimism; a sense that no matter how bad things got, there was always a silver lining. But things *were not* getting any better.

CHAPTER TEN

At ten a.m., inside the grand ballroom at the Hyatt Regency, hundreds of science fiction fans gathered for opening ceremonies. A power failure at the hotel had delayed the festivities until Saturday morning. Lenny and his friends crowded into the room to cheer the guests on.

Kate had not arrived yet.

Richard Bradford, the master of ceremonies, moved to the front of the room and was standing in front of a microphone next to where members of the Con Committee had stretched a wide, red ribbon across a makeshift stage.

Bradford was a celebrated folk singer whose first novel was recently nominated for the John W. Campbell award. He was chosen by the committee as the MC because he was an up-and-coming fan who was comfortable in front of large groups of his peers. He had one last duty to perform for the evening's masquerade party, and he was anxious for things to go off without a hitch. Bradford assembled the guest of honor and some of the other guests on stage behind him to introduce them before WesterCon was officially opened. He asked members of the fan press to line up near the front of the stage with their cameras and recording equipment to capture the event for future posterity.

On cue, the lights dimmed and a crude spotlight illuminated him.

"Ladies and gentlemen and intergalactic species from throughout the cosmos," his voice echoed through the sound system, "I want to welcome you to the 68th WesterCon. We weren't able to launch our annual celebration of all things sci-fi last night, due to a power outage, but I am thrilled the problem has been fixed, and we can start things off right this morning with the introduction of our convention guests, followed by the ceremonial cutting of the ribbon."

The ballroom thundered with applause as spotlights bounced playfully around the stage where Bradford was standing. He tried to get everyone to temper their applause to continue, but fans continued clapping and stomping their feet. They were just getting warmed up. The real noise would come later at the masquerade.

"Thank you. Thank you, so nice to be back here in San Francisco," Bradford shouted into the microphone.

"You know, the last time WesterCon was here was way back in 1979. Think about it. That was over thirty-five years ago. Al Gore hadn't invented the Internet yet. Most of you weren't born, and those of you old enough to admit it were standing in line already, more than a year out, for *The Empire Strikes Back*."

The room broke out into laughter, followed by more applause.

Bradford relished it, especially after the false-starts they had the day before trying to launch the opening ceremonies. He had been coming to science fiction conventions for thirty-five years himself and remembered being a starry-eyed fan at that WesterCon back in 1979. Not long after, he started singing folk music, a music genre tied to science fiction fandom, and established a following among those enjoying the odd fusion of folk and rock-n-roll with sci-fi lyrics. He would still be singing today if he hadn't turned to the real passion in his life, which was writing.

"Tonight, well actually, today, we celebrate our love of science fiction, whether that love takes the form of letters, brush strokes on canvas, celluloid, musical notes, or fabric we've sewn into unique costumes," Bradford continue speaking, first smiling into the cameras for the fan press then looking out over the hall. "I want to thank you all for coming, but more importantly, I want to assure you that . . . I don't have a long speech."

The ballroom broke out into applause once again.

"Now, if I can coax our guests to join me on the stage, I'll make short work of introducing them to you," the master of ceremonies said, smiling and looking off to his right and then to his left. "Our author guest of honor is George R. R. Martin. Our artist guest of honor is Bob Eggleton, our fan guest is former chair Kevin Standlee, and our celebrity guest of honor is the one and only George Takei. Please come up and join me on the stage."

George R. R. Martin, creator of *Game of Thrones*, moved forward first, nodding to the fans and making his way towards the front of the room. He stopped to shake hands with friends then continued walking forward. There was a murmur as Martin's image appeared on all of the monitors on stage, followed by the celebrated author himself. His appearance led to spontaneous applause from the crowd. He was followed to the stage by Bob Eggleton, one of the most celebrated artists of his generation, and Kevin Standlee, a fan who had often been the man running things behind the scenes. Finally, George Takei, Commander Sulu from *Star Trek*, joined the three other guests on stage. He had an infectious smile that made everyone feel right at home.

"I have one more surprise for you," Bradford announced,

leaning into the microphone. "This year's Metal Bikini award-winner, Miss Jacqueline Johnston, please join us on the stage with the other guests."

As Jackie stepped forward, wearing a beautiful replica of the Princess Leia slave-girl outfit, she was overwhelmed by the fan photographers fighting to take her picture. She carried a pair of large scissors to fight off the anxious male fans and their digital cameras. Miss Johnston was a tall, statuesque brunette with gleaming white teeth and sparkling green eyes. She smiled and waved to the crowd like she had just stepped off the Miss Universe stage in Miami Beach. She looked like she could have been crowned at any beauty pageant for her good looks and figure.

The ballroom grew silent when she handed Bradford his half of the scissors. It was a dramatic moment that deserved a drum-roll. Bradford looked on with anticipation as she lowered the scissors to the wide red ribbon to cut it. There was a sudden jolt, like someone had stepped on the brakes of a car and just as quickly released them, as a slight tremor from an earthquake struck the city. The Hyatt swayed back and forth; the lights flickered off, then on, and off again. Everyone in the room gasped or screamed. The monitors around the room blacked out and then moments later displayed the message: PLEASE STAND BY. Several people pushed aside their chairs, running for the exit doors.

Several others searched for exits while others pushed their way through the double doors at the back of the ballroom into the hotel lobby.

Bradford worked his way on stage back to the microphone, but when the sound would not come on, he looked over at the sound crew. They were working the controls, trying to return everything back to normal. He was afraid people would panic and stepped to the edge of the stage.

"Now, that's what I call a real bang for the opening ceremonies," Bradford said in a loud, commanding voice meant to ally all fears.

At first his joke did not register, but as it filtered through the crowd, people began to laugh, eventually filling the hall. As the laughter increased, the ballroom lights came back to life and the crisis seemed like it was over.

Smiling, Bradford moved out among the fans, shook hands, and exchanged pleasantries with people he knew and with others who wanted to bask in his spotlight for a few seconds. The faint aura of edgy politeness settled down as he worked the ballroom. By the time he reached the main doors, Bradford felt things were fine, and he headed to the bar for a stiff drink.

As the herd of people clogged the ballroom exit and the hotel lobby just beyond, Kate pushed her way through the crowd, looking for her friend Lenny. She had been at the registration desk getting her convention badge when the tremor hit, and she considered it an omen of things to come.

She moved against the flow of traffic when she nearly ran right over Lenny in his Obi-Wan Kenobi costume.

"Lenny, is that you?" she asked, doing a momentary double take.

"Ah, the Force is strong with this one," Lenny replied, doing a good vocal imitation of Alec Guinness from *Star Wars*.

"What do you think of my t-shirt?" Kate asked, modeling the black, *Han Shot First* t-shirt.

"Kate, you look fantastic," he said.

"Thank you, kind sir," she said with a curtsy.

Then Kate lowered her voice and whispered, "Have you seen Rebecca?"

Lenny looked around as people continued to exit the ballroom. "Not yet, but I was just thinking it would be a good time to go for a stroll around the convention. I can point out some of the highlights to you."

"I would love it."

"Walk this way," he said, taking her arm like a gentlemen; escorting her out of the chaos of the mass exodus from the ballroom.

Kate and her escort Lenny took the escalator up to the next level and walked into the Hyatt Regency's garden room. The beautiful garden room had been converted into an intergalactic marketplace where merchants were selling a wide variety of merchandise. Spread over the fifty dealer's tables were old and new comic books, toys, action figures, trading cards, jewelry, costumes, t-shirts, Anime merchandise, posters, movie memorabilia, DVDs, Blue-rays, and new and used books. Vendors sat or stood behind the different tables, talking with shoppers, while convention attendees browsed through the books or handled the toys.

Everyone was rearranging their disrupted tables and chattering about the quake.

As the two of them entered the room, Lenny's friends gathered around them, each dressed as a character from *Star Wars*. Kate felt crowded in her personal space.

"Kate, these are my friends from Docking Bay 94," Lenny said, proudly, pointing to each one as he introduced them to her. For each of the asides, he whispered in her ear. "My friend Lincoln is our Chewbacca, he's heavy into furry fandom. John is our Han Solo—yes, I know Harrison Ford was a few pounds lighter and didn't have a mustache, but that's John for you. Vinnie is our token black friend, and he always plays Lando Calrissian. Billy Dee Williams, he ain't, but then he's a helluva nice guy. And this is Harold—since he likes teddy bears, he often dresses up like Wicket the Ewok. The only one that's not here is Sebastian; he's our Darth Vader. He's a talented costumer and make-up artist. He made my Obi-Wan Kenobi costume."

"Why is your group called Docking Bay 94?" Kate asked, looking at the costumed characters, one man to the next.

"Technically, it's not Lenny's group," John explained, stepping forward as the overweight and mustached Han Solo. "Harold and I started the group when we both enlisted in the Rebel Legion. Lenny kind of hangs with us."

Harold lifted his Ewok mask off. "Docking Bay was one of three-hundred-sixty-two docking bays, owned by Mos Eisley, scattered throughout the city on Tatooine. Where the Millennium Falcon waited to rendezvous with Obi-Wan Kenobi."

"Oh," she responded, head spinning.

"So, Lenny tells us you're a real cop," Vinnie said, throwing his Lando Calrissian cape back over his shoulder like a swash-buckling pirate.

"Yes, I am," she replied. "An inspector in homicide."

"Are you armed?" Harold asked, wiping the sweat of his hot costume from his face.

"Yes," Kate answered.

John was close to her, reading her t-shirt and admiring how it fit her curves. "Do you believe that Han Solo shot first?"

"Absolutely!" She lied. She couldn't remember what Lenny had told her.

"Cool," John said, moving away, pulling the modified, broom-handle Mauser from his holster, twirling it like a gunslinger, and returning it to its holster.

"Hey, she's one of us!" Harold declared.

Vinnie slapped Lenny on the back. "I wish I had a girlfriend who was a cop."

"You just wish you had a girlfriend," Lenny fired right back.

"And why not? I'm not that picky," Vinnie replied, looking to his friends for support. "As long as she has a pulse, I'll be happy."

"Pulse?" John asked, jumping into the conversation.

"I thought that was optional."

They laughed at Vinnie, but Kate didn't find the comment funny. They seemed to like each other, but they were not above making fun at the other's expense.

"A pulse was optional," Vinnie defended himself.

"But then I met that vampire girl, and things just haven't been the same."

"She wasn't a real vampire, was she?" Kate asked, her brow furrowed.

Vinnie nodded his head. "She had the teeth. They were real enough. I still got the bite marks to prove it."

"That's just a hickey," John said, dismissing him.

"Women like that do it to mark their territory," Harold commented. "Sorry, but it's true, just like a dog pissing on a tree."

"So she's a dog now," Vinnie guffawed, the Rodney Dangerfield of fandom.

"Are there no women in science fiction fandom?"

Kate asked, looking around the room and spotting one or two shopping at the jewelry table.

Lenny stepped up to answer her question. "Fandom was largely made up of men. You'd see the occasional femme fan, like Leigh Brackett or Connie Willis, but they were outnumbered 10 to 1. Today, there are more women attending science fiction conventions than in the past, but the numbers still skew more men to women. Three or four to one."

"The problem is that they come with their boyfriends," Harold said.

"Or they're gay," John added.

"Or they're just insane," Lenny said, bringing it full circle.

"She wasn't a dog, you guys," Vinnie said, defending his former girlfriend. "Other than the teeth."

Kate nodded as if agreeing with him, but she didn't know. Here, they were complaining about women who attended science fiction conventions and how the women's demeanor towards them made them question their own desirability. She could have just as easily made that same statement about men and how they were unavailable to women like her. But then, when it came to relationships, she had never been careful, not about her choice of men or even about men in general. She was the last person in the world to offer them advice about dating.

While she was so entranced by their conversation, she lost track of the faces and people in her surroundings.

Kate didn't see the large dark figure come up behind her until she felt a heavy hand on her shoulder.

"Holy shit!" she screamed.

Darth Vader, the dark lord of the Sith from *Star Wars*, had emerged from the shadows and was bellowing with laughter at her.

"Did I scare you?" he asked with a deep, ominous voice. He knew he had frightened her, and that pleased him as he continued to enjoy his brand of merriment. Sebastian, the fifth member of Lenny's Docking Bay 94 group, lifted the black helmet and mask from his head, revealing the scarred face of Anakin Skywalker underneath. He achieved the look with make-up, spirit glue, greasepaint, and a huge amount of natural talent. Sebastian looked like a man whose face was burned by fire and volcanic ash.

"You should never sneak up on someone you know to be armed," Kate said, regaining her composure.

"That's how accidents happen. I've had to warn Lenny about that a couple of times."

"Darth Vader isn't exactly a character who sneaks up on people, Officer," Sebastian said, mounting his defense, "but your point is well taken. I thought I'd surprise you and make your first visit to a sci-fi convention a memorable one."

"Surprise me? You did. I thought I was going to have a heart attack when I turned around and saw you standing there."

"Mission accomplished," he said with an upwardturned thumb.

She gazed up at him, examining the minute details.

"I didn't know this much talent existed," Dawson said, amazed by his work. "You should be down in Hollywood working for one of the studios."

Sebastian shrugged Darth Vader's broad shoulders.

"I worked at Universal Studios for a week as a tour guide and tried to get into the make-up and costume departments, even brought my portfolio of work to show what I could do, but they weren't interested in talking with me. You see, I didn't have a degree from UCLA or USC. So, after a week of beating my head against the pavement, I came home and went to work at my dad's hardware store. I've been working there for nineteen years. There isn't a day that goes by I don't curse God for giving me a talent that doesn't mean shit in today's world."

"It's the same for all of us, Kate," Harold explained.

"I wanted to draw comic book superheroes, but now I work in the paint department at Walmart. John wanted to be an actor, but he sells life insurance for MetLife. Lincoln and Vinnie wanted to be costume designers, but now Lincoln works as a night watchman and Vinnie's unemployed. We thought life was going to be different—somehow."

Dawson stared at Harold for a moment. They started out with such huge dreams, and yet the story was always the same. Maybe that was the reason why they all found themselves in science fiction fandom. It was a safe place where they could still dream and not have the harsh realities of life confound their awesome talents. They had each found an outlet to showcase what they did best. Rather than knocking them for their immaturity, she was beginning to understand them.

Thinking and turning things over in her head, Kate remembered the invitation John had made to her about the open house for new members every fourth Sunday at his church. Tomorrow was the fourth Sunday of the month.

She looked back at Sebastian. "Do you think you could you change my appearance enough for some undercover work? I've been invited to an open house on Sunday afternoon, and I'd rather go as a complete stranger, if you know what I mean."

"Sure," he replied eagerly. "With a little greasepaint, a wig, and some different clothes, your mother wouldn't recognize you."

"What about tomorrow morning?"

Sebastian was silent for a moment, "I guess. I've got all of my makeup supplies with me in the room. I don't have a wig, but I've got a wash we could put in your hair to change its color."

"Great! You now have your first professional assignment with the San Francisco Police Department," she said, smiling.

"All right!" Sebastian cried, then collected high fives from each of the members of his circle of friends.

Kate turned to Lenny. "You brought the schematic?"

"Sure, it's back in the room," he replied. "Are you really going to do this? Go to the church compound in a disguise?"

She nodded her head. "For the last week, I've been trying to figure out how I'd get in there without being recognized, but now I think I got my answer. Your friend is going to provide me with the one tool I need to slip right in there. A new identity."

"He's a talented guy," Lenny said.

"Well, between the two of you, how can I lose?" she asked.

"Good, I'm glad that's settled," he replied, anxious, ready to get the show on the road. "Now, if you don't mind, let's get on with our tour of the convention and see if we can't catch Rebecca and her new boyfriend some place along the line."

"Why not?"

Kate and Lenny made a sweep of the Dealer's Room then headed out to make the rounds of panel discussions that sounded the most interesting. A panel on "Interstellar Empires" appealed to Lenny because novelist, Steve Golding, and scientists, David Helmsworth and Paula Quigley, concluded that the key to establishing various interstellar empires was to establish trade and trade routes.

Another panel, "The Implications of Artificial Intelligence and Sex," fascinated Kate. She wondered what it would mean to society if people no longer needed a partner to obtain a satisfactory sexual experience. Rusty Paulson and Sam Jaffe gave their ideas on the topic.

Both Lenny and Kate bailed out of the panel on "Hard Science." They found author Greg Bear interesting, but the subject matter was deadly dull. The discussion on "Why Fandom Is So White" featured funny moments from African-American author, Steven Barnes, who arrived late to the panel, crying "Where are the chitlins they promised me?" No one seemed to have a real answer as to why there were so few minorities in science fiction fandom.

They walked out of "Ecology in SF" when California's Green Party candidate, Dutch Richardson, decided to turn the panel discussion into a campaign speech.

Finally, they attended the memorial that recognized writers and artists who passed away throughout the year.

Kate didn't know their names, but Lenny kept wiping back tears, listening to the long list and trying to tell her something about each one.

When the art show opened just after twelve in the afternoon, the line to see all the paintings and exhibits was too long, and they skipped it. Later in the day, after they had made the round of the panels, the line was gone. Kate was impressed by Bob Eggleton's work, and she laughed each time Lenny pointed out his obsession with the movie *Godzilla* and the small dinosaurs in Eggleton's paintings. Kate liked Chouten's stony waterfall of stone nudes. She viewed them, taking in the impressive details. Several dioramas captured art in miniature and showcased the talents of sculptures made by Stanley Alison and Dana Rosa.

"The art show today is better than the previous years," Lenny said. "The early fans wrote fanzines to keep in touch with each other before the Internet made it easier to exchange ideas.

"Lenny, I'm impressed by the imagination here. I thought science fiction fans were a group of losers who were living in their parent's basements because they refused to grow up and get a job. I owe you an apology," Kate said.

At six p.m., people were lining up for the elevators, Kate and Lenny among them. Since the formal masquerade did not start until eight p.m., most fans used the two hours that followed the close of the Dealer's Room and the Art Show to eat dinner and re-charge their batteries for the evening's activities. Kate decided she had seen enough of the convention and was ready to pick up her car from the hotel's valet parking lot. She was a loyal friend to Lenny, staying by his side all day long. Even if they had failed in making Lenny's ex-girlfriend Rebecca jealous, Kate's presence at the event made her friend look like a rock star to his own circle of friends. She imagined that John, Harold, Vinnie, Lincoln, and Sebastian would be talking about her for the next few months and ribbing Lenny about his girlfriend who was a cop.

"I can't believe she didn't show up," Lenny said, disappointed.

"Don't be too upset." She patted his back comfortingly. "I'm sure that word will get back to her about the woman you were with at the convention."

Lenny thought about it. "You know, I had a good time today," he said while they waited for the elevator to arrive.

"I'm glad," she replied, looking away. "I also had a good time. I never had any idea there was so much creativity here."

"You're special, Kate. You're the kind of girl that . . ."

Kate slumped, blocking the rest of what he was saying. She had heard it all before and hoped that Lenny had moved far enough away from his puppy dog crush so they could be genuine friends. She felt sorry for him because he was such a nice person, but she did not need an emotional cripple weighing her down with his unrealistic expectations about male-female relationships. She had enough trouble on her own, dealing with broken dreams.

". . . I always thought you would be right for me."

"Why, thank you, Lenny, you're special in your own way."

"I don't suppose we could go out again?"

"Sure, but just as friends."

Lenny swallowed hard, remembering their past conversations. "I know, I know. You've got a boyfriend," he replied, fumbling for the right words. "I hope he appreciates you as much as I do."

Kate nodded. "He tries."

Lenny looked puzzled, trying to bring to mind what she meant. *Is that a note of cynicism in the tone of her voice? A sense she wasn't getting everything she deserved from this man? A desire for someone or something better?* He turned to her with all of the warmth and charm he could muster. "Because if you were my girlfriend, you'd never have to do a thing. I'd take good care of you."

"I'm sure you would." *Thank God I am a strong woman. This is most uncomfortable.*

His enthusiasm danced in his eyes.

"You're going to make some girl out there," Kate added, as another elevator whizzed right by them, "a very lucky woman."

"But I've already met—"

She changed the subject. "Would you like a breath mint?"

"Thank you," he said, taking one from metal tin in her hand. "You know, I read somewhere that when a woman offers a man a breath mint at the end of a date, it means she wants him to kiss her."

Kate took a deep breath and sighed. "Does this mean we're going to kiss?"

"It's just a breath mint."

Lenny stopped talking and they just stood there, the silence growing heavy between them. When the next elevator stopped, Lenny caught a glimpse of Rebecca out of the corner of his eye and reached for Kate with his right hand. He snapped her into his arms with a flick of his wrist, and said, "Rebecca," under his breath.

Kate grinned, then reached for him and pulled Lenny into a romantic embrace. She kissed him on the lips, long enough for Rebecca to get an eyeful, then pulled him into the elevator. Kate continued to hold him tight as the door slid shut, then let him go.

"Wow!" Lenny said, his head spinning like a top.

"If that doesn't convince Rebecca that she missed out on

something hot, nothing will," Kate said, fluffing her hair and re-applying lipstick. She smiled a big self-satisfying smile she kept to herself.

"That was amazing!" he added, out of breath.

The elevator door opened at the lobby and people filed out between the two of them. When the last person walked out, her smile had softened, becoming more congenial, friendly. Kate nodded at Lenny as if he was nothing more than an acquaintance, someone she barely knew.

"I'll see you first thing in the morning," Kate said over her shoulder and walked out of the elevator without a backwards glance.

The door closed behind her and the elevator zoomed upward to the seventeenth floor. When it reached its destination, Lenny stumbled out of the door like a drunken man, dizzy and disoriented. He struggled to reach his hotel room. When he opened the door, he collapsed to the floor, lying there until his friends returned several hours later from the masquerade.

CHAPTER ELEVEN

Disguised as a fifty-five-year-old spinster, Miss Lonelyhearts, Kate climbed out of the taxicab at the intersection of Liberty and Dolores and walked the block and a half to the First Pentecostal Church of God. A white lace handkerchief was in her hand, and she kept coughing into it. As she approached the storefront church, she saw John and was reminded of the moment she first saw him. He was flanked on both sides by two large men in black suits who she also recognized as the gorillas that George Friedman employed as his enforcers. They did not look friendly or welcoming, even though they pretended to distribute bulletins to those newcomers that John missed.

She did not react with fear or apprehension. She didn't react at all. She was confident Sebastian's disguise would get her through the front door, and the rest was up to her.

She walked up to the door, keeping John at a safe distance, and took a bulletin from one of the two gorillas.

Kate continued walking through the door, sitting in a pew near the back on the right-hand side of the sanctuary. She counted twelve rows of pews on each side of the church, with each pew capable of handling ten members. The wooden pews contained five slots to hold Bibles, hymnals, and other clerical materials. At the front of the church, there was a formal altar, pulpit, and two long pews for the lay leaders.

"Madam, you'll be much more comfortable towards the front," said one of the ushers, trying to take her arm and move her.

Miss Lonelyhearts coughed into her handkerchief.

"This recycled air is bad for my asthma," she said.

"What?" asked the usher, backing up slightly. She coughed again. "The chill always gives me a cold."

"Okay, why don't you stay where you are," he conceded.

"Thank you, young man, for your concern."

As the usher moved away, she sneezed into her handkerchief and wiped her nose. Kate added another loud sneeze to discourage the rest of the ushers from getting too close. For the time being, her disguise was beholding. After all the time she had spent in Sebastian's make-up chair, Kate expected the disguise to hold for several hours. When he transformed her into Miss Lonelyhearts, she looked in the mirror, but a stranger looked back at her. Lenny's friend was such a genius at his craft, she was surprised that he wasn't working professionally in Hollywood. She planned on doing something about that as long as she lived long enough to act.

Visitors from the storefront church filled in the rows of pews, and in the fifteen minutes before the open house service was scheduled to start, the number of people had swelled to over two hundred. Kate put her bulletin down, nodding at the person to her immediate right and left. As she glanced around the sanctuary, she saw mostly single men and women, but no couples and no families. They didn't display any unusual ticks or the idiosyncratic behavior she had often associated with members of cult groups. There was little doubt in her mind that the people sitting around her were desperate, poor, lost souls looking for guidance and something to believe in. They came to find out if religion was their magic cure.

The organist set the tone playing Bach's Prelude in C major on the small organ near the altar. Its beautiful harmonic sounds and three-and four-voiced fugues filled the sanctuary with voices of an angelic choir. Kate realized just how easy it was to get swept up by the music in such a small sanctuary and resisted the temptation by focusing her attention on other things. She watched the twelve church lay leaders, John among them, gather in their white robes on the left hand side of the church and proceed en masse to the altar. Nearly all of them were men, with Luisa Morales as the only female member of the group. They stood in front of wooden benches on either side of the pulpit, waiting for their cue to sit.

On the hour, without any of the pomp or circumstance that Kate associated with a traditional worship service, two younger lay leaders broke rank with the others and helped support the aging Charles Hampton Kenilworth who was struggling to climb the short steps to the pulpit. He did not appear to have the portable oxygen tank and nasal cannula shown in Internet photos. She wondered if it was hidden somewhere under his robe or near the altar. When he reached the pulpit, he fought to adjust the microphone with his arthritic hands then steadied himself in place.

For the last two weeks, she was speculating about the leader who controlled the End Times Ministries with an iron fist, and now he was standing right in front of her. Kate could hardly believe her eyes. She thought Kenilworth looked like one of T.S. Eliot's Hollow Men—a scarecrow figure of a man unable to stand on his dry parched limbs that had withered from a lifetime of complacency and neglect. His eyes were sunken deep into his head, and his facial features appeared to be stitched together like a leather handbag. He was a hollow man, stripped of all that had made him human, and what remained was a living corpse. *Was it any wonder he sought to turn the world into a wasteland where the dead men lost their bones?* Kate shivered at the thought of this old man controlling an atomic bomb.

"The scripture tells us that the day of destruction is coming," Kenilworth said, his voice like parchment paper brittle to the touch. "Brothers and sisters, I am here today to tell you it is upon us. The end is in sight. You have less than seventy-two hours to make amends with God and redeem your soul. It is time to awaken out of your sleep. Far too many believers have been slumbering, and paying no attention to what has been going on in the world. Christianity, our whole belief system, has been under attack for years by those who would replace it with secularism, that doctrine that rejects all things sacred. Even the President of the United States and members of his party have rejected God by declaring that we are no longer a Christian nation. Far too many of you have been asleep while this is happened. The Promised Land, which was once that bright, shining city on a hill, is now a commune run by the secularists, where the few support the many. But it's not too late. This generation need not die in sin without the forgiveness of God. You have to make a decision here, right now, at this very time, to renounce evil and serve God.

"Over the last few months, I have been telling you about the signs. These signs are leading us on this road to destruction. Daniel 12:4 talks about a period near the end times when an explosion of knowledge will occur. That explosion is the Internet. And while you think all this knowledge will help enlighten the world about the message of God, you'd be sadly mistaken. Secularists have no use for God or His kingdom.

They want to occupy His churches; they want to tear down His laws and replace them with new ones that do not bear His name."

Kate looked around the sanctuary, watching everyone gathered in the small storefront church, hanging on his every word. They were mesmerized by his mishmash of Biblical prophecy and fear-mongering rhetoric. She heard a few sermons in her day, but none constructed to push emotional buttons as this one. He was tapping into a primitive instinct for survival, promising safety and enlightenment for his select few. Kenilworth was masterful, diabolical, and even sympathetic as the sick and aging prophet. The only way he could have sold it better was to have his lay leaders nail him to a cross.

"Prophecy tells us that the world will plunge into the darkness of a final war, waged by the great deceiver on behalf of Satan. Most will perish in the flame of this final war. When the night is spent and the day is at hand, you will be called upon to account. Some of you will be in God's army, while others will be with the beast. On that day, when we meet God face to face, will you be able to stand tall and be counted with God, or will your soul bear the mark of the beast? Time is fleeting, passing ever so rapidly—so prepare. Judgment is at hand." He looked out at those gathered in the pews before he continued.

Kate thought it was time to get the show on the road.

She signaled for an usher and leaned across the back of the pew. "Young man . . ."

The usher hurried to her side, "Yes, ma'am."

"I'm in need of a restroom."

"Back this way, ma'am," he replied.

She gave him a closed-lip smile and patted his hand. "Don't you trouble yourself over me. Just point me in the general direction, and I'll find it myself."

"The restroom is back there, ma'am," the usher said, pointing to the lower right corner of the sanctuary.

"Thank you," Kate replied, moving out of the pew.

She took her time, and shuffled her feet moving out of view. By the time she reached the restroom, everyone had forgotten about her.

Kate moved carefully working her way out of the restroom area to the door at the rear of the storefront. She could hear Kenilworth talking to the crowd, hoping his voice would provide cover if she stepped on any uneven parts of the floor. She pulled back on the safety lock, opening the door into a courtyard; an open space connecting the three buildings and the storefront together as one large compound.

She looked from behind the door and saw the courtyard was deserted. She climbed down the steps from the storefront door, conducting a routine sweep of the compound. She bent down, trying to look into the cellar windows, but each one was painted black on the inside.

"Shit," she said under her breath, inching her way around. *Whoever built the compound had done so to protect the privacy of its owners.*

Kate climbed the steps of the first building and put her ear to a rear door, listening. No sounds. No sign of anyone. Everyone was at the open house, which is where she should have been. She eased the door open about an inch, three inches more, then opened the door wide, slipping into the next room. Kate turned for the stairs. She climbed the steps melting into the shadows, tense, and ready to spring. When she reached the upper landing, her eyes searched the darkness, but there was no sign of movement.

She snaked her way into the front room and looked around, trying to find some sign of what they were doing.

Instead, Kate found that the whitewash on the walls was chipping, the water-damaged curtains were fading, and there was an unpleasant smell of mildew in the air. The room was stripped bare, except for a handful of mattresses stacked near the window. She moved toward them, stopping when her footsteps creaked on the rotted wooden floor. The mattresses were lumpy, but they looked like they had been recently slept on. *Had the members of the church been quartered here, like soldiers in an army barracks?* She figured that John was one of them, one of the loyal soldiers of God who followed orders. Kate checked the closet. She found pillows, sheets, and blankets in a drab olive-green color stacked from the floor to the ceiling. In the next closet there were National Guard uniforms that were pressed, folded, and waiting for deployment. Just as she had suspected, this was an army barracks, and they were soldiers preparing for a great battle.

She searched the back room, but she could find no evidence that anyone, other than the soldiers, had lived there.

Kate found additional mattresses stacked in the corner and the closets were identical to the first room, except the uniforms bore the insignia of higher-ranking officers. There were several captains, two lieutenants, and staff sergeants.

Why National Guard uniforms and not Army or Coast Guard? Kate thought to herself. Then she realized the National Guard was the reserve military unit that would be called up to respond to a domestic emergency. In the chaos that followed the detonation of a bomb, they could easily infiltrate the National Guard with their authentic-looking uniforms and cause irreparable damage to the command and control centers. She thought that it was an inspired plan, but then she realized that there was probably much more.

Kate searched the adjoining rooms. In one she found a

makeshift communications center, with a map of San Francisco, the surrounding Bay area and a handful of SCR-536 walkie-talkies. In another room, she found medical supplies, including a stockpile of potassium iodide. She read the label. Potassium iodide, a common salt tablet, was a pill doctors used to treat radiation sickness. In the event of a nuclear attack, these pills would be worth their weight in gold. In a third room, she found an arsenal of weapons, standard issue M9 Beretta, the M16 rifle, M4 carbine, M50 pump-action shotguns, M84 stun grenades, and thousands of rounds of ammunition. It was a treasure trove of the finest in military weaponry. Kate took one of the M9 Berettas down off the shelf, removed the clip, and worked the slide. The handgun was a newer version of the one she carried on the Force and she liked how it felt in her hand. For a brief moment, she felt tempted to take the M Beretta for herself, but then she thought better of it. *Their quartermaster must be a real stickler for order, keeping an exact count of the weapons in their arsenal.* The ATF was going to have a field day when she reported her findings.

Creeping down the stairs of the first house, Dawson came out the back door. She moved into the courtyard that connected the four buildings together, sticking to the shadows like the fly on the wall. She was fortunate the sky was overcast and dark. It would have been much harder on a bright and sunny sky.

She hurried across the courtyard to the third house and ducked into the overgrown underbrush that covered most of the basement door with its long tenacious vines.

Kate ripped through the vines, hoping they weren't poison ivy. She reached for the bolt to the basement door, but it was rusted shut. She struggled for a couple of minutes, but it wasn't budging. Then she heard footsteps in the courtyard and froze in place. She watched from behind the cover of the overgrown bush and held her breath to keep from panicking. The man approached her location, looked around, and then continued walking away. When she was certain he had cleared the courtyard, she exhaled slowly and started breathing again.

Kate concentrated on the bolt. When it started to give way, she pulled it back. If anyone was waiting for her on the other side of the door, she prepared herself for what she would do. She applied gentle pressure to the door with her shoulder, let it open a few inches, pushed forward hard, and sprinted for the first cover she saw. She ducked down behind a concrete pillar and watched the basement door swing back and forth in the darkness.

Nothing moved around her.

Kate thought the place had the familiar stench of a slaughterhouse that hadn't been used in a long, long time.

Before long, she was overwhelmed by the smell of death in the basement and wanted to run back out to the fresh air of the courtyard.

Kate was trapped by her surroundings and struggled within herself to stay calm. She controlled her fear with a rational mind and used it to strengthen her resolve then relaxed and straightened up. She returned to close the basement door, gagging on the odor of hell itself.

Pinching her nose, she continued to move forward, feeling her way to the stairs. A zig-zag staircase threaded its way up three floors of the building with a touch of light from the overcast skies coming through the windows to illuminate her path forward.

She reached the third floor of the house and looked around. Like the other two houses, the whitewashed walls were chipping paint, and the draperies were water-damaged.

There were a few packing crates broken open. The packing material was spread across the floor with twists of random binding wire. Something big had come in those crates, but it was anyone's guess what was delivered to the compound.

Perhaps it was the centrifuge and the rest of the scientific equipment needed to turn the raw plutonium into a bomb? Dawson walked from crate to crate and kicked through the packing materials on the floor to see if there was a clue, but there was nothing. The fresh footprints in the dust showed that materials were accessed recently, at least in the last seventy-two hours.

She started back down, slow steps at first, faltering, like a child learning how to walk. Then faster, more secure, step after step, until her feet touched the bottom. When she reached the floor of the basement, Kate wanted to head for the exit door and the safety of the courtyard beyond. The stench was nauseating, her costume was stifling, and she longed to breathe fresh air again. *Did I miss something in the basement?* Kate pulled out her iPhone and used the light from the screen to survey her surroundings. The old wine cellar that figured prominently in the original drawings was converted a medieval torture chamber. *Why had the church created its own torture chamber? Were they punishing members? Was this where Philip was beaten to death?* The thought of another torture chamber, and the one from her recent past, terrified her.

She heard a noise and stopped dead. Kate turned around, lowering the iPhone and taking hold of her weapon that was nestled in the small of her back, ready for anything.

"Is that you, John?" Not ten feet from her, in the corner of the room, was a rat. John and a rat are one in the same. In a big city like San Francisco, she had dealt with more than her fair share of rats, including the kind that walked on two feet. As she turned away from the rat, something worse came into view, and the detective's heart skipped a beat.

"What in the world happened here?" Kate said in disbelief and horror.

She looked down a row of decomposed bodies of the three men and two women chained to the wall of the dungeon and bit her lip to keep from screaming. The bodies were naked, beaten in much the same way she found Ross's body. *Were they the ones that refused to follow orders? An example for the others?* Their faces were shrunken, wrinkled, and covered in dried blood. The skin around their temples was torn away by a sharp instrument, their hair was gone, and their lips had shrunk back, exposing gray, cracked teeth. Their chest cavities had an incision the size of a cannonball, and through it, she could see a gray-black mass of twisted ribs and rotted organs. Limbs were twisted and bent into impossible directions for their bodies. What was left of their flesh was yellow and rubbery, grazed upon by parasites. One of the men was staring at her with his remaining open eye. Why the five of them had been murdered and hung up here to rot was a question beyond her understanding. Fear was the measure they used to maintain control over the members of the church.

Kate backed out of the third house, closed the basement door, and hid again in the overgrown bushes. She waited and listened and watched for any signs of movement, and then looked across the courtyard at the main building. She desperately wanted to find something, some minor detail, that connected the church to the plutonium theft, but it wasn't in the first two buildings. That left one more building to go.

Kate scrambled towards the stairs of the main building and stepped upon the first step, but when it creaked loudly, she stopped moving. She looked down and saw the boards were rotted. Between the boards were dirt and mildew where water had seeped in. She carefully placed her foot on the next step, and using the wooden railing, she pulled herself up. It creaked again, but she continued on up to the rear door of the house.

Kate slipped through the door, locking it behind her.

She worked her way through the kitchen and saw that it looked more like a mess hall at an army base than a family kitchen. Trays were stacked near the sink, and the flatware was in huge bins. MREs and large urns of coffee lined the kitchen cabinets.

She walked through the dining room and down one of the corridors to the front of the house. The house was darker than the other two, with all the shutters and drapes drawn shut, and she took advantage of the shadows to edge herself along. The front room was normal, with an eclectic mix of new and restored Victorian furniture. She noticed a pair of tire tracks that ran from the front door to the stairs. *A truck making repeated deliveries to the stairs?* The deliveries were heavy enough to have required the use of a hand-truck. *What had been in those deliveries?*

Kate climbed the steps to the next floor, melting into the shadows. The schematic she received from Lenny showed that there were three large rooms on the second floor, and that one of them registered bright green with its enormous power consumption. She walked down the corridor, listening at the first door for any sign of life.

Nothing.

She opened the door and glanced around the room.

Again, several mattresses were stacked near the window, but nothing seemed to be out of the ordinary. She moved to the next room, and with her ear pressed against the door, she heard a loud humming noise. She cracked the door open a few inches. A man and a woman in their mid-thirties sat in front of two computer terminals with headphones, like air traffic controllers. They were lost in another time and place and didn't notice the door had opened by itself.

Kate crept around the corner of the door to get a better look. The room was full of computer terminals set up on desks with chairs. Each terminal was wired into the huge mainframe computer at the back of the room. A giant map of San Francisco covered the wall, with each neighborhood highlighted in red marker by a square grid. The grids were designated by a station number. She recalled the conversation in the elevator about the city's problems with its antiquated power grid, and then the map made sense to her. They were planning to crash the city's power grid, sending San Francisco back to the Stone Age. *But what was the point of the bomb or those National Guard uniforms—unless it was part of a three-pronged attack?* First, trigger the bomb, then wreak as much havoc out of the firestorm, the electromagnetic pulse, and radioactive fallout as possible. Then, when the city most needs its emergency medical and fire-fighting resources, crash the power grid and cripple those resources. When the city was completely dark, send in units to sabotage and destroy command and control centers. In the aftermath of the destruction of an American city, the United States would mobilize its armed forces against the terrorist nation that took credit, and the world would erupt into flames. Kate had to stop it—and quickly.

She moved back down the stairs and turned slightly in the direction of the rear door, but she heard voices coming from the courtyard. The open house must have ended, and people were dispersing. Damn! She cursed to herself, looking for a place to hide. She had hoped to use the open house as a cover to make her escape, but now she was trapped inside the main house with no apparent exit. *Do I have time to make it around to the front door?* No, they were already on the porch, turning the key. She pressed herself into dark recesses and waited. She ran several scenarios and their outcomes through her head. Kate risked another hurried glance at the front door, but it was too late. Several members had stepped into the foyer.

Drawing a few deep breaths, she screwed up her courage and sprinted into the library. It was a dead end. Kate reached around to the small of her back and took her gun out. She didn't want to shoot her way out, but if she had no other choice, she would. People would die unless there was another way. She looked around the room again, spotting a closet door. She scrambled to it and climbed in, just as a group of church members came into the library. Kate holstered her weapon, pressing her ear against the door, listening and waiting.

"We've been over this before," said Thomas Grey, as he circled around the great Ottoman desk, his well-manicured fingernails gliding along the edge. He pulled the over-sized leather chair out and sat down, tugging on the pleated fronts of his trousers like an old-school gentleman.

Thomas was a handsome man in his middle forties, with dark hair and a thin mustache. Well-polished and groomed, he adjusted the French cuffs on his white Turnball & Asher shirt, pulling them one quarter of an inch from his jacket sleeve. As he sat back in the leather chair, dressed in an expensive, black pin-striped Brioni suit, he could have been mistaken as the chairman of a great corporation. But he was neither rich nor an entrepreneur. He didn't have a position or title. He aspired for something much more, and he was ruthless enough to take it. "I've already made my decision, and I expect you to comply."

"I can't kill my babies," confessed Susan Peters, a young woman in her thirties with dark, sullen eyes that made her look much older.

"Simon, will you please explain to your wife that this is no longer a matter open for discussion," Thomas instructed one of his men. He did not raise his voice but was firm.

"I've tried, Thomas. Believe me, I've tried," Simon replied. The thirty-five-year-old man looked like he had reached the end of his rope.

Thomas glared at him. "Well, you've not done a very good job, have you?"

"I don't know what more to say." Simon shrugged.

"Leave us. Immediately," Thomas said.

Simon Peters didn't move. He looked at Thomas then to his wife Susan and then at the other men in the room, swallowing hard. Finally, he marched out of the library.

"Other men and women in this congregation have complied with those orders, what makes you think you're so special?" he asked, rising to his feet and putting his hands on the desk for balance.

"Ask me anything else, Thomas, and I'll prove my loyalty to you. But just don't ask me to do this," Susan said, pleading.

"When God instructs Abraham to take Isaac to the top of Mount Moriah and sacrifice him, does Abraham offer God a counter proposal? No, he does what he is told."

"I won't kill my babies," she persisted.

"You don't have a choice," Thomas said, coming around from behind the desk. "You must take the lives of your children by midnight tonight or you and Simon will be cast out of the church. You will lose God's grace and be forever damned to the infernal regions. Your children will die at the hands of a stranger who has no regard for them, and you and your husband will spend the last few minutes of your life in agony as you are being beaten to death."

Susan's eyes narrowed in anger, flashing him a look that

warned him to proceed with extreme caution. "You can't force me to do this. I'll have a word or two with Pastor Charles and settle this once and for all."

"The old man is no longer calling the shots," Matthew Foster interrupted.

Thomas shot him one of his patented steely looks.

"Charles has lost his way," he said, with a great deal more diplomacy and feeling. "He's like a shepherd who can no longer keep track of his flock."

"I don't believe it," Susan replied.

"Oh, I'm afraid that it's true," Thomas said, his voice softening. "The Holy Spirit has left him, and what remains is a weak man. We'll be fortunate if he survives the night."

Susan shook her head. "You must think I am a fool. I watched Pastor Charles give one of the most inspired sermons of his life today."

"His last sermon," Matthew said.

"His last sermon," Thomas repeated. "He collapsed right into my arms after the service was over—an apparent stroke. I had James rush him to the hospital."

"You're lying," she said.

"Well, I guess you'll never know," he replied, turning to one of the two men who worked as an enforcer for Friedman. "Take her home and do whatever needs to be done."

Susan threw herself at him, her hands raised into claws, her ruby red nails, talons. He caught her wrists in mid-air and held her at bay, feeling her hot breath bearing down on him like a caged lioness that turned on its master.

She wanted to scratch his eyes out. She wanted to tear his heart out of his body and taste the blood on her lips. She wanted to hurt him more than she had ever wanted to hurt another living being.

He fought back, struggling to keep her claws at bay.

One of the men grabbed Susan by the shoulder and tried to pull her off Thomas. She pushed back and elbowed him in the groin. Another gripped her around her throat, but she snapped at him with her teeth, and he let go. The third seized her around the waist. The four men brought her down to her knees on the carpeted floor.

"It's over," said one of them, holding her in a choke hold.

"Calm down, Susan," said another.

Thomas hauled himself upright, his face bright red with surprise and hurt pride. He straightened the lines of his expensive suit, and then pushed the knot in his tie to his shirt collar. Once he had regained his composure, he looked down at Susan and shook his head.

"Let her go," Thomas said. "Let her go, Matthew. Nice and easy. We are not at war with this woman."

They complied, released her, and climbed to their feet, then took up flanking positions to Thomas.

Still huddled on the floor, Susan buried her face in her hands and trembled as she thought about her attack on Thomas. She was an obedient, well-disciplined wife, and her actions surprised her more than they had the men. If she felt animosity towards them, it was only for an instant.

She knew deep down in her heart they were messengers reminding her of an obligation she owed to the Lord. No one was more aware of the Biblical story of Abraham and Isaac than her. She had studied it many times in her short life.

"No tears, or we'll mistake you for a blasphemer," Matthew reminded her.

"I'm sorry," she whispered. "I'm sorry. I don't know what got into me. I don't act like this."

Thomas looked at her with pity. He pulled her up into his

arms in a brotherly embrace. "God understands that we all experience doubt in our lives from time to time. It's only human. Think about my namesake, Doubting Thomas. He was a skeptic. He refused to believe the Lord was resurrected and demanded to feel Jesus's wounds before he was convinced."

"I'm sorry, Thomas, but I had to raise the question."

"Yes, dear sister, I understand," he replied, comforting her. "But remember that faith is believing in something when you don't have proof. It means putting your trust solely in God and allowing Him to control what happens to you. When we surrender our will, we are asking Him to guide us in all aspects of our lives. He leads us to the best for us. You have to realize that He sees the big picture and knows what's ahead, so you can trust Him as He guides us."

Tears were pooling in the corners of Susan's wide brown eyes, and she struggled to keep from crying. "But what is to become of my babies, Thomas? You can't expect Simon or me to put them to death."

"I do," he said. "We have important work ahead and can't be distracted by concerns about our children."

"They're babies," she continued to plead with him.

"Then you of all people will want to spare them the horrors that will soon follow—pestilence, war, famine, and death . . ."

"I just wish there was another way," she said.

"There is only the way of the Lord," Thomas reminded her, his voice soft, almost a whisper.

"I'm not sure I can do this."

"Remember the lesson from Ecclesiastes that Pastor Charles once taught us," he said, looking into her soul.

"There is a time to plant and a time to uproot what's planted. Well, now is the time to uproot what you have planted."

"Uproot what I planted," she repeated, her eyes faraway.

"A time to plant and a time to uproot," Thomas said it again.

"A time to plant and a time to uproot," Susan repeated.

"Your garden needs tending, dear sister," he whispered to her.

"My . . . garden needs tending," she repeated. Thomas turned to one of Friedman's enforcers.

"Please see that Susan and her husband make it home safely," he ordered, a distinct change in his voice. "Matthew, why don't you go with them?"

"Whatever you say," Matthew replied.

They escorted Susan out of the library between them.

She walked with them, tired and defeated. She didn't know or care where she was or where she was going.

George A. Friedman, Esquire, did not seem surprised to find Thomas sitting at Kenilworth's desk in the library when he returned to the church compound late that afternoon. It was as if he were expecting the forty-five-year-old lay leader to be seated there when he walked in.

Thomas was unapologetic about his assuming the leadership role.

"That desk fits you," the overweight attorney said, holding his hands up in front of his face and squinting through the imaginary picture frame that was formed by the thumb and forefinger on each hand.

"Yes, it does," Thomas replied, "and I intend to keep it."

Friedman shrugged. "And why shouldn't you. To the victor goes the spoils."

"You are cheerful, considering we're against the clock on this one. Do I need to remind you of all the things that could go wrong in the next fifty-three hours?"

"No. Is there anything I should be concerned with? You aren't going back on our deal, are you?"

Thomas stared at him for a moment then shrugged.

"No, your plan is still a sound one. I don't think anyone will see it coming. But then, if they do, it will be too late to do anything about it."

"So, is everything else on schedule?"

"Yes, just a few minor details to iron out, but we always knew there would be some desertions right at the end. You know, people who lost their nerve—that's the reason why I doubled up on the critical tasks."

"Morales?"

"No," Thomas sighed. "I was never worried about her loyalty. She'll go to her death triggering the nuke, and all the while thinking that her actions are for the greater glory of the Lord."

"I don't trust her. She graduated from West Point and spent a couple of years in the army. For all we know, she could be spying on us right now."

"Her loyalty is beyond question," Thomas reassured him. "Who do you think has been out in San Juan Bautista shooing away all those nosy tourists? She is an expert marksman."

"Still, if it were me, I'd have a backup in place," Friedman said. He walked over to the door of the library and signaled for his man. "We've spent far too much time and money planning this for anything to go wrong."

"Don't worry so much about it, Friedman. I already told you I've doubled up on the critical tasks. I've got every location covered."

Friedman nodded his head. "Well, I hope you're also taking care of those desertions. I've always considered it prudent to eliminate one associate in order to keep the others in line."

"I sent men with Susan and her husband. They're going to take care of the children and the two of them if she refuses to honor her commitment. I think one of your guys went with them."

"Good," Friedman said, breathing easier. "Her death as a would-be deserter will serve as a strong example to the rest. No one will dare desert their post, or worse, give us up to the authorities."

"I told you I had everything under control."

Friedman smiled. "I never doubted you, dear boy. Just think, in less than three days' time, you'll be the richest man in the world. You'll be wealthier than Kenilworth ever dreamed."

"Yes, poor devil."

"You're not having second thoughts, are you?"

"Not at all," Thomas replied, smirking. "I was thinking about how much money you are going to earn from this little venture of ours."

"A modest finder's fee. That's all."

Thomas hesitated, "Your modest finder's fee is costing me over a hundred million dollars."

"I do hope we're not going to quibble over this," Friedman said, alert and on guard. "What is a mere hundred million dollars compared to the billions of dollars you'll be making. I was the person who brought the idea to your attention. I deserve my finder's fee."

"Make sure your private jet is fueled and ready to take off when I get to Stockton. We're not going to have a lot of time before the FAA closes off the air space over the San Francisco Bay area."

"We'll be ready."

"You had better be," Thomas warned him.

Friedman put a finger to his lips to silence him, but he kept talking as he ambled around the room. "I don't think I ever told you about my special gift. It's like a sixth sense, only I don't see dead people," he said, nodding at his black-suited enforcer. "I developed a subtle perception ability when I was in college. It gave me the ability to detect subtle changes in the environment that most people never see. Carpet fibers on a brand new carpet that have been pressed down by the boot of some unknown assailant, a wet dishcloth when the owners use a dishwasher, and dust that's missing from a door handle. By themselves, insignificant, but when taken together as a whole, the work of a clairvoyant."

He threw the closet door open, and his enforcer grabbed Kate by the shoulder.

"Take it easy," she ordered, struggling with the large man.

"What the hell?" Thomas said, jumping to his feet.

Friedman pointed to the door handle. "For a room, like this one, that gets little usage overall, I was surprised to see the door handle was free of dust. That either meant your non-existent housekeeper was meticulous in cleaning this room, or someone had opened and closed the closet door recently and was likely still inside, listening to our conversation."

"Well, who is she?" Thomas demanded.

"I think you'll find," said Friedman, wiping the grease-paint from her face with his handkerchief, "under this clever disguise, the redoubtable Inspector Dawson of the San Francisco Police Department."

"Son-of-a-bitch! She'll ruin everything!" Thomas exclaimed angrily.

"Not quite," Friedman said, with a shit-eating grin on his face. "You're forgetting the most important factor in all of this. She's our prisoner. She's not going anywhere."

"What? Kill a cop?" asked Thomas.

Friedman shook his head. "Dear boy, your morals astound me. Here we are, hours away from launching an attack on a city that will kill millions of people, and you're concerned with the life of one cop. Extraordinary! Well, if you're that squeamish about it, I'm sure that one of my men will be more than happy to take care of it for you."

"You had better get it right the first time," Kate said defiantly. "For if you miss, I'm coming back here and kill each of you myself."

"He never misses, Inspector," Friedman said.

"Someone screwed up to allow me to get this far," she said, planting seeds of doubt. "Or I had help on the inside."

"Or maybe, you got lucky," Thomas added. "But that's one mistake that is easily correctable."

"The same way that you took care of Charles Hampton Kenilworth?" Dawson fired back at him.

"I loved that man like a father," Thomas said, easing back down into the huge leather chair. His eyes had a faraway look in them as he reflected back on the old man. "I was running a home-school umbrella program in Harrisburg, Pennsylvania, reading student portfolios at a hundred dollars a pop when we first met. The work wasn't hard, but I had trouble making ends meet. I had to live in the back of a restaurant and eat the scraps off other peoples' plates. He offered to take me away from all that; said that he saw something special in me and recruited me to be the first of his disciples. Back in those days, you didn't need a ministry or a church. You needed a calling, and some good Christian was always there to take you for a meal. We traveled all over the country and Canada, preaching about the end of times and looking for lost souls that needed saving. Of course, what I didn't know, until much, much later, was that every donation we received, Charles invested it in technology stocks. He made over $30 million before the dot.com bubble burst.

"When George Meador died and Kenilworth first took over Meador's ministry, he had an ambitious plan to take the battle right to Satan himself. He realized the only way we were going to beat the devil was to fight fire with fire, and we all agreed with him. We built an army for God and started planning guerilla attacks against targets that were clearly in the hands of Satan. I felt a sense of purpose when we bombed our first abortion clinic. Think about all those babies' lives we saved! But that was also when Charles had his first stroke. He grew weak and tired and retreated back into his own mind, back into the rhetoric of the past, while the rest of us hungered to strike a real blow against Satan and the deceiver he's put into the White House. That's when we started working on our master plan."

"It must have taken a lot for you to betray him." Kate had to push to get the truth.

Thomas nodded his head. "It was one of the most difficult things I ever did, but when a great leader like Charles loses his way, there's really no other choice. I've taken consolation in the fact that great leaders throughout history have always been deposed by their protégés when they reach that point they're no longer effective. Like Brutus and Caesar, my name will be forever bound to his."

"Was it also part of Charles's plan to funnel millions of dollars out of people's bank accounts into one central account?" Kate asked.

"No," Friedman said. "That was my idea."

"You're really quite clever, Inspector. You overhear a two-minute conversation between the two of us about making millions, and you put it all together by yourself. Brilliant."

"Now, you see why we have to kill her. She knows too much."

"It's going to be a real pity watching you die."

Kate glared at Thomas. "So after all of your posturing, all of your lofty speeches, this is nothing more than a robbery. What would your 'great' leader think about that?"

"Charles wanted to reshape the world; to bring the word

of God to every living soul on the planet," Thomas replied. "Well, I still believe in that vision. I'm just going about it in a different way."

"And how many millions of people have to die first?" she asked.

"Does it matter?" conceded Thomas. "In a few hours, we're going to make history here, and shaping the world for the next 100 years to come."

"I want to know one thing," Kate said, shooting him a sideways glance. "How much money is enough? I know you've got $30 million of Kenilworth's fortune, and Friedman is loaded. How much is enough? How many more millions do you need? What more can you buy that you can't buy already?"

Thomas smirked. "You can never have enough money. Whoever says differently is a fool."

Friedman directed his attention at the enforcer, "Lock her up in the dungeon until we decide what we to do with her. And if she gives you any trouble, do whatever it takes to get her under control."

He pushed Kate out of the room with her arm twisted behind her back. She struggled to break free from his grasp, but the pain shooting up her arm was more than she could bear. She bit down hard on her lower lip, fighting to keep the scream inside, as she was led away.

"I'm concerned she knows too much about the operation," Thomas said.

"Yes, it would be rather inconvenient to have all of our plans unravel because one Homicide detective was good at doing her job."

Thomas was worried. "Maybe she blundered in here on a detective's hunch. There may not be any others involved."

"I don't think we can afford to take that chance."

"Agreed."

"We discussed a contingency plan," Friedman reminded him.

"You're right," said Thomas. "Let's push all the time tables forward and dispatch everyone to their designated stations."

Kate leaned against the cold, wet limestone of the dungeon wall, her arms chained above her head to a heavy iron ring embedded in the wall. She pulled defiantly on her bindings, but her wrists were bound by an iron manacle that was hooked to a ten-inch chain to an iron ring connected to the wall. All she could do was stretch her arms out straight.

The weight of the chains was too much. She couldn't keep her arms outstretched for any length of time. Kate's ankles were locked in leg-irons, with a short six-inch chain connecting them. The nauseating corpses next to her made her vomit, and she struggled to keep it together. Just out of her reach was a narrow cot with a thin mattress and an empty tin bucket. She could not sit or lie down and was forced to remain on her feet.

Immobilized, was forced to slump in her chains against the dungeon wall when she could doze.

Several hours later, the bolt to the basement door slid open. She was blinded by the light from the exterior courtyard that flooded the basement. When her eyes recovered, Kate looked at where she was. There was a damaged desk across from her, several wooden tables, chairs stacked in the corner, and a large chest with broken handles lying on its side. The basement was the dumping ground for all discarded furniture from the house.

Kate thought she heard John Mitchell's voice, but the noise from her heavy iron chains clanking together drowned out all other sounds as she struggled to see who was there.

She tried to stop moving and listened closely. And there it was again, as he hurried to her side.

"Kate, thank God, you're all right!" He wrapped his arms around her body and kissed her. She kissed him back, looking into his eyes. It was difficult to doubt the concerned look on his face.

Kate opened her dry mouth and tried to speak.

"See if you can find a key for these," she said, pulling on the chains. "Try the desk. It's a big brass key."

John randomly pulled drawers out of the desk, dumping the contents on the floor, while looking for the key.

He sifted through the contents, rummaging through papers stacked next to the desk. If the key was hidden there, he was determined to find it.

"How did you know I was down here?" she asked.

John looked at her briefly, then resumed his scavenger hunt. "I heard several of them joking about the police detective they caught. They said she was chained in the dungeon with the rest of the freak show."

"Then you knew it was me?"

"I hoped it wasn't," he replied, slowing down.

"Why didn't you trust me, Kate, and get out of town?"

"I'm a cop, John, with a job to do."

They held each other's eyes for another moment. He went back to ransacking the room, turning everything in the room over, searching the drawers and cupboards, the forgotten chairs and tables . . . everything.

"There's no key here," he reported to her. "Damn! He must have taken it with him."

John walked over to her side and took hold of the iron chain with both hands. He spit in one hand and then the other. He pulled on it with all of his strength, leaning in with the weight of his body, but he couldn't budge it.

"Okay, so I'm waiting to hear your idea," he said.

Dawson rotated several thoughts through her head.

"Look around and see if there's something you can use to break the lock or the chain."

Mitchell scrambled around the basement, looking for a bolt cutter or crowbar or hammer or a hunk of metal he could wedge between the links of rusted iron, but he found nothing.

"I'll be right back," he said. "I'll be here."

Minutes later, John returned with a fire-axe he liberated from an old-fashioned fire emergency case in the church sanctuary. As he came walking back into Kate's view with the fire-axe, her gaze fixed on John. She looked at him with admiration, smiling, picturing him in her mind as the Norse god Thor returning to Valhalla with his mighty hammer. How appropriate that her long-haired lumberjack would return with his tool of the trade—an axe!

"Let's see if this will work," he said, drawing the axe with both hands.

"But they'll hear out in the courtyard," she protested.

John shrugged his shoulders. "I bolted the basement door behind me. It's a solid wooden door, so we might just be okay."

"Okay, let's do this," she said.

Kate pulled down on the iron chain, stretching it taut, between her and the iron ring about her head. Her exposed wrist was out about shoulder high; the chain flat against the limestone wall. John swung the axe hard, bringing it down on the chain. THUNK! He hefted the axe a second time, bringing it down hard again. THUNK! The third time, he swung hard and brought it down. THUNK! John stopped swinging the axe and examined the intact iron chain.

"The iron in the chain is much too dense for the tempered steel," he said. "We're going to have to figure something else out."

There was a sound at the door—the sound of the bolt sliding open.

"He's coming back," Kate whispered.

"Distract him. Keep his attention. Let me handle the rest," John whispered as he moved to get under cover.

The heavy wooden door swung open, hitting the basement wall as one of Friedman's enforcers pushed his way into the basement. He slammed the door shut behind him and slid the bolt lock. Dressed in a black suit, he looked like a black gorilla from the Congo. His three-hundred-pound mass was moving menacingly towards her, obscuring the few sources of light that kept the basement dark as he lumbered on. The black shadow came into view.

"I got orders to give you the full treatment," he said.

"But that doesn't mean we can't have a little fun first."

"It's hard to have fun when you're chained," Kate replied, holding her arms out.

"You should learn how to relax."

The gorilla moved in tight on Kate, and as he placed his huge paws on her shoulders, she flinched. He massaged the tendons beneath her skin, leading her to believe he was trying to relieve the tension in her muscles.

She knew all too well what he planned and struggled to maintain her composure. But when his hands moved down, massaging her breasts, squeezing the nipples tight, Kate barked the word "No!" in his face and squirmed to get out from underneath him. His caresses, at first feigning tenderness, turned more violent as his hands wrapped around her delicate neck, and he began to squeeze her throat. She fought to break free, making his grip tighten more. The three-hundred-pound man nearly smothered her with his body as he began to ravish her inch by inch.

John came out of hiding, tapping him on his shoulder. As he turned, John raised the axe over his head, setting the blade between his eyes. The gorilla shuddered then belly-flopped to the floor.

"That's no way to treat a lady," he said.

Kate had fallen back against the limestone wall, coughing, choking, and trying to catch her breath. Her neck was adorned with red fingerprints where he had had tried to strangle her.

"What have you done, John?" she demanded, her voice hoarse.

"I never liked that guy anyway. C'mon, let's get you out of those chains."

John rolled the gorilla over on his back and patted down the pockets in his jacket and pants. Once he had located the brass key in the large man's suit, he made fast work of unlocking Kate's manacles and leg-irons and threading the chain through the iron ring in the wall. She was trembling as she leaned back against the wall and kneaded the black and blue marks around her wrists. John moved toward her, putting his arms around her, holding her close.

Kate had tears in her eyes. "I've never seen a more beautiful sight in my whole life than that sight of you coming through the door to rescue me."

He pressed her closer, guiding her head into his chest. He held her in his arms and caressed her hair. "I wasn't about to let them hurt you no matter what I had to do."

"I love you," she whispered and kissed him passionately, urgently.

He kissed her back with equal passion. "I know," he replied, and he held her tight in his arms for another moment.

A noise outside the door in the courtyard brought them back to reality. It sounded like a big truck that had backed up and opened its loading gate.

"We've got to get you out of here," John said. "Come with me," she said.

He shook his head. "No, someone's got to stay here and cover your tracks. Besides I've got to figure out what to do with that body."

Kate walked away, starting for the basement door.

When she reached the door, she pulled off the ridiculous make-up appliance that was still on her nose and fluffed her hair. He hurried after her.

"Tell me, John," she called over her shoulder.

"Honestly, will I ever see you again?"

"I hope so, Kate. I really hope so."

"I don't understand any of this," she replied, angrily.

"You're not one of them. You're not some lunatic out to destroy this city. What do you hope to gain from staying here?"

"Maybe I can do something about this," John said.

"Don't be ridiculous!" she shouted, squeezing back her tears. "You're just going to get yourself killed!"

He seized her by the shoulders and looked her right into the eyes. "Trust me, Kate, I'm going to be all right. I'm worried about you. We need to get you out of here while we still can."

"Okay, okay. So what's your plan?"

John reached into his pants pocket for a few dollars.

He put the money into her hands. "There's a light rail station a block over on Liberty. You can take it down to Market Street. Just give me a minute, then run. Run like you've never run before."

Kate reached over and kissed him. He gathered her into his arms and kissed her back. She groaned, melting into his arms. He placed his right hand on the back of her head and pulled her tight against his mouth. Their bodies pressed hard together in one long embrace.

Kate pulled away. "I'm trusting you, John. Don't disappoint me."

"I won't."

John slid the bolt on the door back gently, pushing the heavy wooden door open. He stepped out of the basement, emerged from the overgrown bushes, walked over to the truck, and ordered the two men to follow him.

They acknowledged him and followed John into the darkness of the church sanctuary.

After listening and watching several moments for some sign of him, Kate decided that she couldn't wait anymore. She climbed to her feet and moved through the door. The court-yard was dark with no sign of movement around the truck. No sign of movement at all. She craned her neck around the corner of the third building and ran for the cover in the neighbor's garden. She took off running as fast as she could, scrambling down the street. Kate crossed the main thoroughfare against traffic at Dolores Street and ignored several approaching cars as she ran to meet the sidewalk. She ducked down Liberty Street and vaulted up the stairs to the light rail station as the train approached from the south.

She purchased a ticket from the conductor, settled into a seat, and when she was on board, breathed a sigh of relief.

CHAPTER TWELVE

As the cold drizzle of rain fell on Dolores Street, Kate turned up the collar of her London Fog trench coat and waited for Lieutenant Roberts and the Chief of Police. It had been a few hours since her escape from the church compound, but in that short amount of time, the might of the San Francisco Police Department had descended on the peaceful neighborhood sandwiched between Noe Valley and the Mission District. Uniformed police officers in patrol cars cordoned off a ten-block radius around the compound and went door-to-door warning people from the neighborhood to stay indoors. Members of the elite SWAT unit deployed to manage the volatile situation, and the Chief of Police was called upon to supervise operations as the highest-ranking member of the SFPD.

"This had better be good, Dawson," snapped the Chief of Police as he stepped out of the back of a Lincoln Town Car. The stocky man in his early fifties was dressed like a stockbroker in a black pin-striped suit, partially visible under the full-length Burberry woolen car coat. "I passed on a very important Sunday dinner with the Mayor and his wife to be out here in the cold. You damn well better not disappoint me."

Lieutenant Roberts followed him out of the car. He had heard what the Chief said and felt it necessary to intercede on her behalf. "Inspector Dawson doesn't press the panic button unless it's serious, Chief."

The Chief offered a noncommittal grunt and surveyed the situation. Members of SWAT lurked in the doors and entryways around the compound, their black suits and body armor a stark contrast against the white wash of A the buildings. A handful of others knelt on the top of the rooftops with grappling hooks and cables while other SWAT members flattened themselves on the neighborhood roofs with their sniper rifles and high-powered scopes. Their weapons drawn, uniformed policemen crouched down behind the row of cars that formed the perimeter, waiting for the show to begin. Other cops scrambled along the edges and shadows of the area. The air was filled with the snap of weapons and breeches as members of the SFPD made ready for the siege.

With Roberts standing next to him, he turned from the store-front church and looked up and down Dolores Street, where a half a dozen other businesses stood alone.

A few late evening curiosity seekers had stopped and were peering over the makeshift police barricade as well as a few dozen members of the press. The police, wrapped in their heavy blue rain gear, nudged them back behind the safety tape with their batons.

The Chief shot a glance over his shoulder at Kate. "I hope you've alerted the local business owners and cleared away any civilians within a block radius of the compound."

Kate nodded. "Yes, sir."

There was a slight edge of disdain to her voice, suggesting she did not care for the man. It was due more to his predecessor than the office. Captain Ruiz Aguilar, the former Assistant Chief of Police and the Mayor's personal hatchet man, went out of his way to make life hell for her. Even after he showed up dead in Kate's bed at the Mark Hopkins Hotel, Aguilar continued to strike at her from beyond the grave with his alleged connections to a development corporation that was bilking the city out of billions of dollars in revenue. It was nothing personal, just a lot of shit that had rolled down hill on Dawson.

"Excellent," he remarked, moving past police technicians and walking forward to join a group of officers, including William and Jawara. "Poor devils. We'll give them a chance to surrender. I'd hate to have another Waco on our hands. But we're also not going to let these scumbags have any quarter. If we get the chance to take them out, they're as good as dead. Understand?"

"Aye," the group of officers replied in unison. "No quarter," William repeated to Mikhail.

"I got it," Mikhail said, clearing the empty chamber in his handgun.

"Chief, we're just about ready," said one of the SWAT unit commanders as he stepped forward and saluted.

"I'm coming," the Chief replied, walking over to the front line.

Another unit commander with a walkie-talkie stopped him. "I've got Myers on the radio, Chief. He's in the first assault group."

"Myers," the Chief spoke into the radio.

"Yo," was the only response Myers gave.

"Get ready to kick some ass!" the Chief ordered then handed the walkie-talkie back to the unit commander.

The Chief marched up to the Mobile Command Center with Kate and Lieutenant Roberts nodding at the two operators sitting behind two computer consoles, looking at four separate monitors. The Mobile Command Station (MCS) was an over-sized, Chrysler-built, sport utility vehicle. In keeping with

Special Ops that required the deployment of SWAT personnel, the MCS was the first vehicle on the scene because it could be setup and operational in minutes. Contained within the SUV were multiple nineteen-inch LCD monitors, power receptacles, communication ports with dideo and Data applications—including real-time video and satellite imagery—and two separate IP networks, all housed on a framework chassis.

Within minutes, the C2 operators had real-time eyes on their mission.

"Have you noticed any movement at all between the buildings?" the Chief asked one of the two operators.

"People going back and forth?"

"None, Chief," the first operator replied.

"Sir, everything looks quiet over there," the second operator added.

"Okay, time to get this show on the road," the Chief said.

Another SWAT unit commander stepped forward handing the Chief a portable bullhorn. He slung the boom box over his shoulder and keyed the microphone several times to test that it was working. He nodded his approval moving with the SWAT commander to the sidewalk, leaving detectives Kate and Lieutenant Roberts standing at the Mobile Command Center.

The Chief spoke into the microphone. "Attention! Attention! This is Chief of Police Nelson Gates of the San Francisco Police Department. You have one minute to put your weapons down and exit the compound with your hands held high in the air. We have a legitimate warrant, issued late this afternoon by the Attorney General of the state of California, that authorizes us to search the premises and seize any illegal weapons. You have one minute to stand down and comply."

Kate swallowed hard; her throat dry and aching. She watched as SWAT members took up flanking positions outside the storefront with two additional SWAT officers working their way down the alley on the left side. They weren't just moving into new positions. They were getting ready to assault the property. Kate's thoughts turned to John and any other noncombatants that may be held in the compound.

"What's going on?" Kate asked, approaching the Chief from behind.

"What's it look like, Inspector?" he replied, watching the seconds tick by on his expensive Swiss watch. "We're going in."

"Going in? Are you out of your mind? There could be hundreds of women and children in that church compound," she said.

"They knew the risks when they joined up," the Chief said. "Besides, we gave them plenty of time to surrender."

Kate was terrified. "I hope you know what you're doing, Chief. Tomorrow's headlines could read that we massacred some Bible study group."

"Weren't you the one that made it out of there alive?"

"Yes, sir," she replied, with a nod, "but I didn't know you had planned to come back here and exterminate them."

"That's what you do to rats, don't you? You exterminate them," he said with a cold stare.

"Please, sir, not like this."

"Anytime you want to go home, Inspector," said the Chief, turning away, "consider yourself dismissed."

Kate and the Chief of Police exchanged glances, like the crossing of swords.

"No, sir. You couldn't drag me away," Kate said, putting her foot down.

"Something's happening, Chief," one of the operators said, shouting out of the Mobile Command Center truck.

The door to the storefront church opened and a beautiful

young woman in her thirties with long white hair and pale skin stepped forward. She was carrying a Bible in one hand and what appeared to be a small black plunger in the other. When she opened her mouth, she unleashed an unfamiliar language.

The Chief glanced over his shoulder and said, "What language is she speaking?"

"I think it's Aramaic, sir," Kate said. "She's speaking in tongues."

"What is she saying?" he asked, mistaking her for an interpreter.

"I don't know, Chief. People who speak in tongues don't know what they're saying either. It's the word of the Holy Spirit, of God, being channeled through them, and they need a member of the congregation to interpret what they're saying."

The Chief fixed her with a glance. "Dawson, that sounds like double-talk to me."

"Sorry, I was just trying to explain what it is," Kate replied.

"Well, is it hostile? Belligerent? Is she telling us to go fuck ourselves?"

"No, sir. It's a manifestation of the Spirit of God."

"It sounds like a load of crap," the Chief concluded.

"Anyone with a clear shot is authorized to shoot. Bring her down!"

"No!" Dawson screamed, but it was too late.

One of the SWAT snipers on a rooftop opposite the storefront church fired his AR-15 sniper's rifle once, the report of the gun echoing through the small collection of buildings lined up in a row on Dolores Street. BLAM! The bullet hit the young woman's chest and threw her backwards and down on the sidewalk. As she fell to the concrete, she dropped her Bible, the small black plunger rolling out of her hand. Anyone within a few yards of her location, including Kate and the Chief, could see it was a dead man's detonator that triggered if the human operator became incapacitated.

BOOM!

The roar of an explosion shook the block and tore through the old wood-framed two-story houses like a blast of wind through a house of cards. The main building in the church compound lifted from its foundation then came crashing down to earth in burning splinters. Black smoke mushroomed into the cold and rainy night sky, and the swift March breeze whipped the hot ashes into the air, touching off secondary fires in the other houses of the compound. A fireball rolled through the courtyard, bursting into the church sanctuary and setting the wooden pews aflame. The painted windows in the storefront blew outward, showering the sidewalk with glass.

Kate dropped to her knees and covered her head as flaming fragments rained upon her. The SWAT members and police officers raced back and forth to contain the fire.

Some in the blast tried to get to their feet while others lay dead. The scene was a bloody mosaic of chaos and mass destruction.

Kate crawled away from the conflagration. After she had reached a safe distance, she climbed to her feet and looked around. Flames from inside the compound danced over the roofs of neighboring houses, and she saw on one side of the block, eight family dwellings were ablaze. The sight reminded her of the devastation a nuclear blast in the city of San Francisco would bring and made her sick to her stomach.

A few hours later, after the Fire Department gave the 'all clear', a group of plain-clothed detectives and police officers walked through the skeletal remains of the church compound. The group included Lieutenant Roberts, William, Mikhail, and Balardi, as well as some patrolmen. Kate said nothing but led the way through the burned-out church sanctuary to the charred courtyard that once connected the four of the buildings together. SWAT members maintained flanking positions on both sides of the courtyard. Two policemen stood at the top of what was left of the steps to the first building, helping members climb the stairs, despite the missing wooden railing.

At the top, they were met by two plain-clothed detectives. The men nodded at Kate and led the way down a corridor of blackened and smoldering wood. They paused outside the door frame to the library.

They walked into the room. The leather chair and Ottoman desk were there, just as Kate described, but what remained were two molten clumps of iron and wood.

"This is it?" asked Roberts.

"Yes, sir," Dawson said. "This is where I witnessed Thomas and his men intimidate a young couple into agreeing to kill their own children, and also where I overheard Thomas and Friedman discussing their final plans."

"We've got an APB out on the Peters," William said, glancing at his notes. "So far, there's not been a report of another murder-suicide involving kids. We're hoping that we may have dodged the bullet on this one."

"So you heard them say that Tuesday was the target day?" Roberts asked Kate.

"Not specifically, sir," she replied, thinking back, trying her best to remember. "I recall Thomas warning Friedman to get his private jet fueled and ready to take off from Stockton Airfield just in case the FAA closed off the air space over the San Francisco Bay area. I'm sure they mentioned Tuesday night as the next time they were going to meet."

Dr. Brogan and one of his investigators from the ME's Office had been asked by the Chief of Police to compile a list of casualties for the official report. On their rounds, they stopped to bring Roberts and his team up to speed.

"Edgar, what did you find out?" the Lieutenant asked.

"We've scoured the ruins of the four burned-out buildings for other bodies, Jim, but there's no one else here," Brogan reported.

"Looks like the woman was the only casualty from their group, sir," the investigator confirmed.

Kate sighed in relief. Their news meant John was still alive.

"We found evidence of heavy tire tracks in the courtyard and in the grass in front of the other buildings.

They may have used large trucks to haul away the weapons and computer equipment before we got here," Brogan added.

"We've talked with neighbors, and they remember seeing a lot of moving activity late this afternoon," the investigator said.

"Thanks, guys. Good luck with your report to the chief," Roberts said. He was tired and needed sleep.

"Nice and neat," William said, recording the data in his notes.

"They knew we were coming," Balardi added. "Well, that's just it. This whole thing was a big set-up. Designed to take out as many of our people as possible," Roberts growled.

Mikhail folded his arms across his chest and looked at Kate. "I hate to point out the obvious, but they're still after Kate."

The Lieutenant did not respond but stared hard at Kate. William and Mikhail could see him thinking, planning his next move, figuring out how to best protect her. There was a sense of plodding about James Roberts. He appeared to be a thorough and hardworking person, but he also lacked imagination when it counted.

"Well, what do you think?" Mikhail pushed him for an answer.

"Dawson, for the remainder of this investigation, you should be sequestered for your own protection," Roberts said.

"Lieutenant!" she protested. "I've put a lot into this investigation. This is my investigation. Don't pull me from it now."

"It's for your own good, Dawson," William added.

"You won't be safe until those scumbags have been rounded up."

"Just think of it as a couple days off to rest and relax," Mikhail said.

"To hell with that!" Kate was not happy. "I'm not walking away from this case. Everything you know about this cult is because I brought it to you. I sweated out the research and put in the leg work. This is my case."

Roberts put his hands up and cut off the discussion.

"It's settled, Dawson. You're being sequestered! Now you can do this the hard way or the easy way. You'll find yourself in a holding tank, or you'll find yourself in a comfortable hotel room. Either way, you're being sequestered, under twenty-four-hour guard."

"Damnit, this isn't fair," she cursed.

"Sir, I think you missed a third option," Balardi said, glaring at Kate. "She could always turn in her badge and resign from the Force."

"Fuck you, Balardi," she said.

"Fuck you, Dawson," he shot back.

"All right, that's enough! Knock it off!" Roberts ordered.

"I want Clark and Jawara to go back to Kate's apartment with her while she packs an overnight bag.

Then check her into the Fairmont. I'll be over in the morning with an officer to replace you."

"I'll be expecting your call, Lieutenant," William said.

"We'll be expecting the call," Mikhail added. Kate's eyes blazed with anger and embarrassment. She'd agreed to go along with sequestration until she could find a way to escape and back on the trail.

By the time Kate arrived at the hotel, she was tired and weak. The day had caught up with her, and for the time being, she was trapped inside the hotel. She lay on the bed, struggling to stay awake, but the pain and drowsiness overtook her as she fell asleep. The Fairmont Hotel was a luxury hotel on Mason Street, high atop the famous Nob Hill. Built in 1906, the hotel survived the great earthquake because of its innovative use of reinforced concrete, suffering minor damage from fire. Exterior and interior shots of the hotel were used as a stand-in for the fictional St. Gregory from the 1983 television series, *Hotel*. Kate watched the show growing up. Her room was on the seventh floor and was large enough to be considered a suite in other hotels. When Kate woke, soft light from the morning sunrise bathed the room with rich spring-like colors. Kate thought she could have done a whole lot worse.

There was a hard knock on the door, and Roberts entered the room, flanked by William and Mikhail. He surveyed the room with patented disinterest until he reached Kate.

"Not bad, not bad at all," the Lieutenant commented, walking around. "How are you holding up?"

She turned off the television and slid off the bed.

"Better than I expected," she lied. Kate looked out of place in the luxury suite, but if she felt uncomfortable, it didn't show. She was still upset that Roberts had pulled her from the case. But masking her emotions from her boss had become second nature.

"Good," Roberts said with a nod of his head.

"Considering the taxpayers are footing the bill for all of this, we wouldn't want your stay to be an unpleasant one."

"Be sure to thank the taxpayers for me," Kate quipped.

Mikhail leaned forward and smiled. "We thought you might like to know that Ramirez is being released today."

"When you see him, tell him I'm thinking about him," she said.

"Ahh-choo!" Mikhail contained his sneeze in a handkerchief.

"*Gesundheit,*" she replied.

"Thanks, Dawson. I think I caught a cold last night standing out in the rain," he added.

"Well, take care, Jawara. This is the cold and flu season."

William opened his notebook. "Is there anything special you need, Dawson?"

"No," Kate replied, looking around the room. "I miss my office computer."

"Can't stop working, can you Dawson?" Roberts said.

Kate turned to Roberts. He was hovering near the hotel room door, looking uncomfortable. "Lieutenant, is there any word about that young couple I reported as being a potential flight risk?"

"They were picked up about an hour ago in Lake Tahoe, hiding out in a cabin with their two young children," he said. "The authorities are working with the Nevada courts to expedite their return to California."

"Oh, thank God. I thought they'd be another statistic."

"No word on the two men sent with them. We can hope they're dead and buried in a shallow grave," Roberts added.

Kate nodded in agreement.

Roberts pulled the heavy hotel room door open and directed Kate's attention to the policeman sitting outside in the corridor. "There'll be an armed officer outside this room twenty-four hours a day."

"Is he there to keep people out or keep me in?"

"He's there for your protection," Roberts said.

"We'll be back to check on you. C'mon, Clark, Jawara. We're going."

William and Mikhail walked over to the door after hugging Kate. Once she had closed the door behind them, Kate peered through the peephole and saw the policeman sitting in one of the hotel's deep, comfy chairs. He was a regular cop who walked a beat, but she knew that getting around him wasn't going to be easy.

For hours, Kate sat at the desk in her hotel room, scribbling notes on the stationary, trying to make sense of the much larger whole. She looked at the paper circling key words: religious cult, end of days, cyber-attack, power grid, atomic bomb, firestorm, National Guard, plague, sickness, army of God, final battle, theft of millions. She was certain they had planned a three-pronged attack: First, they would detonate an atomic bomb. Second, they would crash the city's power grid and transfer billions of dollars to some off-shore account. Finally, they would send in their members dressed as National Guard troops to sabotage and destroy command centers. In the aftermath, people would react, and blame would be on a terrorist nation in the Middle East. US officials would be forced to take action and thus launch World War III. She thought the plan was a brilliant one and had every chance of succeeding. If Kate knew the "when" and the "where," she could stop it from happening.

Kate had a vague notion it was happening on Tuesday, but without the "where," she was powerless.

She awoke several times during the night, her mind filled with horrible images of the end of the world. Dreams of firestorms, earthquakes, demons, monsters, chimeras, halfhuman animals, men being eaten by monsters, and the Four Horseman of the Apocalypse swept through the dark recesses of her mind. Kate tried burying her face in the pillow, but the dreams continued. No one was more aware of the dangers of losing control than a police detective on sequester.

When she woke for the day, Kate found crumpled up tissues around her nightstand and on the floor next to the bed. She had been crying throughout the night's ordeal, and the streaks of tears were all over her face. The bright light in the bathroom hit her like a blow from a hammer.

She looked pale and drawn, the flesh around her eyes loose and sickly.

"Fuck!" she swore at her own reflection in the mirror.

As Kate was feeling tearful, the water from the tap felt cold and reinvigorating on her face. She cupped the water in her hands and doused her head with it. She was just two days into sequester, but she was already losing it.

In order to distract herself, Kate sat down at the desk and compiled a list of the names of the cult members. At the top of the list, she wrote the name Charles Hampton Kenilworth then crossed it out, replacing it with Thomas Grey. Kate wrote the names of the three couples: Philip and Wendy Ross, Thaddeus and Luisa Morales, and Simon and Susan Peters. She added John Mitchell, Matthew, and George A. Friedman—even though she considered him a peripheral figure. She knew there were many others. Kate studied the list and looked for a pattern. That's when it hit her. She opened the desk drawer and pulled out the Gideon's Bible that rested inside. She opened to the New Testament and thumbed to the Book of John where she found her answer.

Except for Friedman, the men who had served Charles Hampton Kenilworth and the End Times Ministries were named after the twelve apostles who followed Jesus Christ. Kate knew it made sense because Kenilworth had fancied himself as a great leader, like Christ, and gathered men to him as disciples when he first started his ministry.

She thought about John and wondered where he was and where his true loyalties lay. Kate reached for the remote control on the nightstand then clicked through the channels to find any local news. Kate shifted her position on the bed and reached up to adjust the lamp sitting on the table next to her. She eased back, focusing her attention to the newscaster on ABC-7 News.

The news reporter stated: "Authorities say that there are no reports of damage after an earthquake with a magnitude of 4.3 hit near the sleepy hollow of San Juan Bautista, California on Saturday morning around ten o'clock. The US Geological Survey says the quake hit about eighty-nine miles southeast of San Francisco at 10:07 a.m. A USGS seismologist says the quake was recorded in an area that is considered seismically active, but the earthquake itself was considered rather mild. Geologists warn that the next big one, or an earthquake with a magnitude 7.0 or greater, is likely to happen in the same area, near the San Andreas Fault. This could create a serious shift in the continental plates, triggering large-scale devastation up and down the California coastline. Two powerful earthquakes, one in 1857 and one in 1906, had their epicenters located in the San Andreas Fault. If a future earthquake were to occur here, there could cause substantial damage to the coastal area."

Kate knew when she saw the image of the Old Spanish Mission that she missed the location for ground zero. *The San Andreas Fault*, Kate said to herself. The last piece of the puzzle fell into place. Now all she had to do was get out of the hotel room.

She swung to the side of the bed, head down, thinking, working through possible scenarios. Then Kate looked up. Her room was connected to the adjoining room by a private door. She walked over to the door and opened her side. Kate listened at the other door and used her penknife to release the latch from the strike plate. The door swung open, and she hurried through the empty room to the main door. She saw the policeman through the peephole; turned about fifteen degrees in the other direction.

She'd get out of the door okay, but he'd stop her unless she changed her appearance.

Kate went back to her room, looked at the jeans, skirt, sweatpants, tops, and her trench coat in the closet, realizing she didn't have much to work with. Kate spotted the extra pillow on the top shelf and made a plan. She painted her face with blush and powder to give herself a glow then applied a palm of hair gel and slicked her hair back into David Bowie-look, topped off with a white scarf.

Then she fashioned a pair of buck teeth from the off-white plastic binder that held her room service menu, cutting them to a precise fit with her nail clippers. Finally, she stuffed the down pillow into the frumpiest clothes she had in the closet and climbed into the trench coat. The finishing touch was rolling her jeans up to mid-calf and turning her socks down over her flats.

In the mirror, Dawson looked like a pregnant stoner heading off to an Iron Butterfly concert. The buckteeth sold the image. She wouldn't be mistaken for a police detective.

The last thing Kate needed was a distraction, and when her eyes hit upon the remains of the menu, she knew what to do. She placed a call with room service to have a juicy steak, baked potato, asparagus, salad and cold Coke to be delivered to the policeman who was guarding her room. She also convinced room service to add a person note that read: *Thanks for protecting me. Kate.* While he and the waiter were sorting it out, she'd slip out the other door and get to the elevator.

After she had placed the order, Kate added another layer to her plan. She started a hot shower running, then turned up the volume on the television. If the cop let himself into the room, he would hesitate before bothering her in the shower. That moment of hesitation might be all she needed to get away. Kate returned to the door in the other room and waited for her cue. She didn't have to wait long.

On schedule, the waiter pushed his metal cart down the hall and paused outside her hotel room. Kate used that moment to exit the other door. As the hotel waiter pulled the metal covers off the meal, she lumbered by, pretending to be a pregnant woman. The policeman glanced at her but seemed more concerned with the luxurious meal that was delivered to him. He rubbed his hands together in delight, stuffed the cloth napkin down his shirt, and sat down in front of the feast.

Meanwhile, Kate caught the first elevator, and within a few minutes, she was out the door collecting her car from the parking lot.

CHAPTER THIRTEEN

By the time Kate reached the Old Spanish Mission at San Juan Bautista, night had descended and turned the grounds into a realm of shadows created by the half-moon. It danced from one side of the large grassy plaza to the other in a fanciful imitation of life. She parked her BMW coupe with the blown windshield several blocks away to maintain the element of surprise and crept along the forgotten byway in silence, using the walls of the monastery and mission for cover.

When she came upon the historical marker, the words *San Andreas Fault* glared at her. She missed them the first time around, but this time they resonated in her head.

They planned to detonate an atomic bomb as part of their maniacal obsession with triggering a third world war, but what she had never considered was the location of ground zero. By detonating the bomb in the San Andreas Fault, they would not only get the firestorm, electromagnetic pulse, and radioactive fall-out, but it would trigger one of the most devastating earthquakes in history. The damage and loss of life up and down the west coast was more than she could imagine. Failure to stop them was not an option.

Kate came around the corner of the mission and ducked down in the cloisters; that long corridor of arches that ran along the southwest side of the adobe building.

Ahead of her, she could see the mission's bell tower that stood tall and silent like a forgotten sentinel against the night sky. She pictured the trap door at the base. It had not been in any of the original architectural plans, like the cellar that existed as a place for the nuns to store perishable goods.

When the mission was repaired after the 1906 earthquake, the cellar was sealed for over a hundred years. Pictures of the bell tower steps in the brochure show no trap door. They must have dug out the cellar and added the trap door when the documentary film crew came through, then tunneled to the fault in the intervening months. Who would have noticed? With such a distant location, well off the beaten track of most tourists, the Old Spanish Mission was the perfect choice for ground zero.

As she slid behind the first arch, Kate saw a man out of the corner of her eye. He was standing on the other side of the grassy plaza in front of the saloon, smoking a cigarette; each time he puffed, she saw the glowing embers of tobacco. He must be the backup Thomas revealed to Friedman, and that meant one thing: Luisa Morales was already inside the tunnel waiting to trigger the bomb.

Kate ventured another look, but as she raised her head, an alarm went off in her mind, followed by the sound of a gunshot. BLAM! She threw herself sideways into the cloisters. She came down hard, rolled, and compressed her body against the wooden planking that made up the sidewalk. BLAM! BLAM! Two more shots rang out, and as one bullet whizzed right past her head, she summersaulted forward and grabbed for her weapon. With her Beretta drawn, she scrambled down the long row of arches, using each one as cover. When Kate hit the last one, she flattened herself against the adobe wall, gun cocked and ready to fire.

She was listening for some sign of the man when something moved in the saloon window. She aimed low and fired twice. BLAM! BLAM! Both bullets slammed into her assailant's chest. The impact threw him backwards, crashing through the saloon window. Dead.

As Kate straightened up, she looked across the grassy plaza and could just glimpse the dead body folded over the front windowsill of the saloon, broken glass shattered. She didn't know who he was or what brought him to this sorry state. She was glad to be alive and counted herself lucky at that. In the back of her mind, she heard John Monroe mocking her. *When did you first realize you could kill? That you could take a human life?*

Kate pushed her way into the mission through the rear door that led to the bell tower, pausing with her gun drawn. She surveyed the room, sharpening her eyes to cut through the darkness. *Not a creature was stirring*, she thought to herself, *not even a mouse.* She circled the floor, keeping the trap door at arm's length. When she made a complete circuit, she walked over to it and crouched down.

After her experience at the compound, the last thing she wanted to do was go down into another dark cellar, yet she knew that she didn't have a choice. All of her years of training and experience had come down to this single moment. She closed her eyes, took a deep breath, and pulled the trap door open.

She focused on the cellar, her eyes moving through the darkness. She couldn't tell whether Morales was hiding down there or further on in the tunnel, but she knew she wasn't getting any younger standing there. It was time for her to climb down and face her demons.

With her gun held at eye level, Kate eased down the first rung of the ladder, placing her foot onto the second rung when the cracked and rotted wood gave way under her weight. She grabbed hold of the ladder and held on while her feet went out beneath her. She scrambled to find a foothold with her right foot then her left foot. Finding the third rung, she was able to pull up on the ladder. She clung to it for a moment to catch her breath. She took several deep breaths, holding the last one, then started back down, descending one step at a time. When Kate touched down on the dirt floor, she let her breath out in relief.

She moved slowly, scanning the cellar. The walls were made of limestone, making it look like a dungeon, not unlike the one she had experienced firsthand. At the far end, facing the San Andreas Fault line, she stumbled upon an opening, large enough for a man, cut out of the wall.

Beyond, she could see evidence that someone had been digging three separate tunnels, perhaps weeks or months earlier. All but one had collapsed under its own weight. The one remaining was long, expansive, and reinforced with a rough wooden framework. She slumped against the cellar wall, exhaling deeply. She didn't want to go down into another dark place, but there it was, waiting to swallow her whole and she was running out of options.

Kate flattened herself against one side of the tunnel opening, her eyes casting out into the darkness like a fisherman casting a line in a stream. From where she stood, she could make out minor details of the underground passageway, such as its down-ward sweep, but she could see no sign of Morales or the bomb. She waited another few minutes, disappointed by the dead silence. *Son-of-a-bitch*, she swore to herself as the panic rose in her stomach. Kate never liked small, dark rooms. It wasn't a phobia, but a reasonable fear. She was staring down into the depths of the earth; her nerve slipping away while the anxiety got bolder, stronger.

Kate screwed her courage to a sticking place and started down the tunnel; weapon drawn and ready. She moved along, listening to her heart pound, feeling the muscles in her stomach tighten. Several times, she stopped dead, peering into the darkness, losing her way, as well as her nerves. The blackness in front of her was starting to play tricks with her head. John Monroe, Crystal Rose, Bradley Rutherford, Stephen Collins, and the others lunged at her, pulling her into their twisted reality. The Four Horseman of the Apocalypse galloped into view; the riders wearing the face of someone she had killed in the line of duty. Kate was running a few steps ahead of the sickle and the sword. On either side of her, she imagined dismembered corpses, ravenous cannibals, and horned beast-men racing along to keep pace, like a cavalcade of the damned from Dante's lowest circle of hell.

She kept reminding herself that none of this was real, but they drew strength from her wild imagination.

Half way down the tunnel, as she fought her way through the demons, Kate felt a trip-wire bite into her ankle. *Shit, it's booby trapped*, she realized, a little too late. BOOM! She was blinded by the flash of an explosion. The thunderous shock-waves racked the tunnel, bringing the walls of earth and timber crashing down upon her. She braced her muscles to take the full impact of the blow, but the force knocked the breath out her and sent her tumbling.

Kate fell forward about ten feet then was buried under a ton of earth.

Everything stopped. Kate lay motionless.

"Kate, when did you first find out?" John Monroe whispered in her ear.

Kate stirred, struggled to move, to rouse herself from the collapsed tunnel, but her body was immobilized. She was alive—barely. Lying in the rubble, she fought to make the long, agonizing climb to consciousness. John Monroe was there. She listened helplessly as he taunted her from the shadows.

"You know, Kate, we all have the killer instinct in us," he said, his hot breath on the back of her neck. "Ten thousand years of evolution may be all that separates us from our beastly ancestors, but the mindless primitive is still there.

We pretend that we have civilized ourselves with our laws and our religious beliefs, but all we've done is make it more enraged."

She strained against the crushing weight on her back pinning her to the ground. It felt like the entire tunnel was sitting on her, and she could not budge it.

"We all carry that mindless primitive within us," John Monroe continued to taunt and tease her with his words. "We all can kill, struggling to keep the urges in check. But what happens on that day when we all realize we can no longer control the beast? I guess we won't have to wait very long to find out."

"Not if I have anything to say about it," she said, her voice restored. "Now get the fuck out of my way!"

Gritting her teeth, she raised her head and gasped for breath. Kate sucked in a mouthful of air and dirt, coughing, waiting for the blood to pump again through her limbs. She struggled to maintain an edge. Her ears were deafened by the shattering booms, and her eyes watered, unable to focus. She knew that it would take more than a few minutes to feel the life creep back into her body . . . if she had the luxury of time.

Her second thought was that Morales had panicked in the chase and detonated the bomb, but it wasn't an atomic blast.

No. She shook it off. Morales or one of her confederates must have wired a percussion grenade, like the ones the police used to control riots and looters. The blast would have been enough to seal the tunnel off from any outside interference, but not enough to bring the whole thing crashing down. And if the big bomb went off before Kate could dig herself out, neither she nor the world above would have any more worries. She shuddered at the horrendous twists in her thoughts and worked to stay calm and in control.

All this, and a hundred other thoughts and fears, went racing through Kate's mind in the first minutes she was buried alive in the tunnel. She felt the sickening suffocation of being smothered to death by the darkness around her and struggled to hold down the scream building inside her. Ten seconds was ten hours. She was going to explode, and the scared little girl inside the woman screamed and kept screaming until the sound was choked off by a rush of earth in her mouth.

Kate spit up the dirt and gasped for breath, but as she struggled for air, the pressure on her lungs was too much.

She was drowning in earth and uttered a quick, solemn prayer for what may have been the first time in her life. Then she twisted her body to the left and came up to an air pocket, gasping. Lying at full stretch in the collapsed tunnel with her head turned to one side and her cheek pressed against a fallen timber, she knew the explosion had thrown her forward. But how far forward? She could only be a few feet from the other side.

Kate then reached forward, closed her hand around a clump of dirt, and pulled it towards her, digging a path for herself. Stretching out her arm in pain, she gritted her teeth and again twisted her body. Her first thrust brought down an avalanche of loose dirt, but she continued to dig. She edged herself along, one inch at a time, freeing the earth with her bare hands then moving it behind her with a sweeping motion backwards, like swimming through the center of the earth.

She hauled herself along, burrowing through the dirt like a mole. She fought against her diminishing strength for every inch until she reached the end of the collapsed tunnel and freedom. The advantage was now hers. Morales had to have heard the explosion, and was content that she had stopped a would-be assailant from reaching her. Kate was there to prove her wrong, but she had lost her weapon in the cave-in. Yet, she now possessed an even more important tool: the element of surprise.

Kate ached, but she climbed to her feet and made her way down the tunnel. She wondered, in such weakened condition, if she still had the strength to beat Morales hand to hand. If Morales had a handgun, Kate was facing eight shots, possibly nine, from the barrel of a gun. She refused to let her mind dwell on that and focused her eyes forward. As she came upon the light at the end of the tunnel, she knew what she had to do.

Within minutes, Kate blew into the last chamber like a grenade. She body-slammed Morales against the wall, catching the Latina off guard. Morales was back on her feet in seconds, pulling a gun from her duffle bag. Kate threw herself sideways and came down hard on Morales's body.

The gun exploded, with a single bullet racing out, creasing Kate's arm. Kate thrust her knee into Morales's groin, and her right hand grabbed for the .9mm Beretta. They struggled for control, tumbling to the ground and rolling over each other. Again, the barrel of the gun narrowed its focus on Kate, and Morales pulled back on the trigger to fire, but Kate twisted her body to the left, getting out of the path of the bullet. Then she slashed sideways in a karate chop with the edge of her hand. Morales's forefinger slipped away from trigger, and Kate continued to hammer harder until the gun fell free.

With an elbow jab to the ribs, Morales came back fighting. She broke free of Kate's tentative hold, trading places with her then grabbed the back of Kate's head and slammed it to the ground several times; her face red with anger.

Kate was stunned and fought back the urge to black out. Shifting her weight, she body-slammed Morales again, Morales's head smacked against the wall. Then in one sweeping motion, Kate took both of her hands and executed a shoulder throw. Morales came down hard, and got the wind knocked out of her. Kate was ready with her follow-up, but Morales anticipated the next move and rolled to one side to grab her opponent. She grabbed Kate by the throat, pulling her to the ground. The two women came to their knees, fighting, grappling with one another like wrestlers.

For an instant, their two sweating faces pressed against each other. Kate saw the rage in Morales's eyes. Fear pulsed through her—the fear of what might happen if that bomb went off—and sharpened her determination. Morales had little strength left for herself, but what she did have went into every blow. Kate was on the edge of exhaustion, having spent it all in the tunnel, digging her way out of the cave, and she wasn't certain how much longer she could hold out against the younger woman.

They continued to exchange blows, hammering punches, kicking at limbs, and clawing at one another; then Kate saw an opening. She arched her back, slipping by her opponent and avoiding another jab to the ribs. She slashed two-handed backwards with the mother of all karate chops.

The blow caught Morales on the back of the neck, near the collarbone, and her body went limp. She tottered from side to side, like a children's top out of balance, and then fell over, looking at Kate in disbelief.

"You're too late. The countdown's already started," she said between clenched, bloody teeth.

"Then help me stop it," Kate demanded, kneeling beside her, but Morales never heard her demand.

Kate staggered to her feet and wiped the blood from her mouth as she stared down at Morales's motionless form. She couldn't tell whether the woman was dead or unconscious, but she didn't give a damn. Kate cared about one thing: stopping the bomb. She reached down for the Beretta and tucked it into her belt for safe keeping. She scanned the rest of the chamber. Other than a few wooden barrels—identical to the ones at the Old Spanish Mission—and Morales's duffle bag, there was nothing unusual or out of place. She didn't know what the bomb looked like, but she had a damn good idea of its size and makeup. The duffle bag was much too small to contain it. That left the barrels.

Working rapidly, her hands shaking, Kate pushed through the large barrels and examined the contents of each for some sign of the bomb. Next to the last barrel, she heard a metallic rattle against its wooden interior. Thomas and the others must have smuggled the bomb in one of them then placed it into the tunnel. Kate placed her ear against the side and listened for the sound of the detonator. The barrel was beeping. Taking a deep breath, she slowly unlatched the outer casing of the barrel and carefully removed the bomb. It looked like a gumball machine— a large opaque globe on one side and a metal box on the other.

Kate placed it gently on her lap and studied the arming mechanism, forcing her to deal with the long sequencing of numbers. Nervously, she watched as it continued to count down to zero.

"So, you've found the bomb," a voice said.

Kate nearly dropped it as she swiveled around and came face to face with the person she had tied to the voice.

"Fuck! You scared the shit out of me."

John Mitchell emerged from the shadows. Nothing about him was the same. The last two days had changed him somehow. His hands were filthy with dried blood and earth.

His flesh, cracked, blistered and covered in dirt. He couldn't see well, couldn't even walk without stumbling. He looked like he had spent the last two days inside a cement mixer. He had a military-grade Beretta holstered on his belt and a two-way radio tucked in his pants.

"John, what are you doing here?" Kate asked, pulling the Beretta from her belt and pointing it directly at him. Her mind flashed on something that Thomas had said about his contingency plan. *Maybe the man I shot in the saloon wasn't the backup. Maybe the backup person was John Mitchell. Otherwise, how would he have known where the bomb was?*

"I don't have time to explain," he said.

"Well, you better make time," she replied.

Mitchell lumbered towards her. "I've got to disarm the bomb."

"Freeze! Not another step!" Kate yelled, holding the gun out in front of her. Her back was against the wall with the muzzle trained squarely on John Mitchell's chest.

He turned pale white and recoiled, his hands moving back and forth, palms out, like a policeman trying to stop an oncoming automobile. "Hold it! Hold it! Don't shoot. I am here to disarm the bomb."

"Put your hands up!"

"Kate, you've got to listen to me. We only have a few minutes, at best. I've got to disarm that bomb," he pleaded, taking a step forward.

"Put your fucking hands up!" she screamed. "Don't move!"

"Kate, please . . ." He advanced another pace.

"Don't! Don't move!" Kate cocked the gun.

"How did you know the bomb would be here? At this location?"

John was as pale as a white linen shroud. "Trust me. We don't have a lot of time."

"Why should I trust you? Gimme one good reason."

"You love me," he said as he took another step toward her.

Kate wasn't buying it. She kept the gun on him.

"Look, I warned you not to move. Take another step, and I will shoot you."

"Kate, please, we don't have a whole lot of time."

"You haven't given me one reason to trust you," she said, her hands shaking.

"Do you know anything about disarming an atomic bomb?"

Kate looked down at the mechanism in her lap. The long sequence of numbers had gotten shorter since she had last looked, and with each passing moment, they were getting shorter and shorter. "No," she confessed.

"Then, for Christ's sake, let me do my job."

"I don't even know what your job is," Kate said, shaking her head. "Are you one of Thomas Grey's cult members? Or are you that sweet man I introduced to the Moody Blues? Who are you John Mitchell? Who are you really?"

"Kate," he said in his deep croak of a voice. "My name is not Mitchell. It's Prescott."

Kate felt like her head was about to explode, and she struggled to maintain focus on her target. The gun was growing heavy in her hand, and she could no longer keep it steady.

"I'm with the Justice Department. I work directly for the Office of the Attorney General. I've been working under cover for the last two years on a probe into the End Times Ministries. The probe has been looking into allegations of fraud, money-laundering, illegal weapons sales, murder, and intimi-dation. You name it."

"You're going to have to do better than that, John," she said. "The first time, you told me you were a lumberjack from Washington."

"I am telling you the truth, Kate."

She stared at him but was unable to keep the gun trained on him. She let her arm drop to her lap.

John moved toward her, knelt down, and took the weapon out of her hand. He then placed his arms around her, holding her close. "John Mitchell, the lumberjack, was just my cover identity. Not a creative one, I'll admit, but it got me inside their organization."

"Was everything else a lie?"

"No, not everything," he replied, with a smile. "But right now, you've got to trust me. We don't have a lot of time."

John reached down into her lap and took the device in hand. He punched a few buttons in the sophisticated computer panel and waited for the bomb to stop, but the numbers keep reducing themselves. "Someone's overridden the fail-safe mode. We're going to have to disarm this manually."

"What do you need me to do?" she asked, struggling to find the energy.

"I'm removing the section that contains the plutonium from the detonating device," he said, "then if it explodes before we can disarm it, it won't start a nuclear chain reaction."

John Prescott rotated the outer cylinder until he heard a click. Then he gently unscrewed the arming mechanism from the body of the atomic bomb. He screwed it three times counter clockwise, slowing his rotations until he heard a second audible click. The upper half containing the pluto-nium was removed from the detonator. John wiped away the sweat on his brow and smoothed the long hair back away from his eyes.

"Done," he said, taking a deep breath and giving her a grin.

"Then it's over?" Dawson asked.

John shook his head. "No, not yet. We still have a bomb that is ticking down to explode."

"Okay, what do you need me to do?"

He pulled the wires from the bomb casing, examining the red, black, yellow, and green leads. Then he removed a small penknife, opening it in her hand.

"Two of these lead wires control the bomb. One set disarms it. The other primes it to go off. At headquarters, I was told to cut the red and black wires, but if I was dealing with a clever individual, he might have switched the two lead wires to prevent someone from doing what we're trying to do."

"John, you've got to be kidding me," Kate laughed.

Not because it was funny, but because it was the only way to release the tension in their predicament.

"I wish I were," he replied, holding the two sets of leads in his hands.

Kate shivered. It was hard to tell whether it was from fear or being in a cold, darkened tunnel chamber. "Tell me one thing."

"What's that?"

"Was romancing me part of your mission?"

"Kate—"

"Just tell me the truth, and I'll believe you."

John smile. "I didn't start out to fall in love with anybody, Kate. It happened along the way."

"Good." She looked at the two sets of leads and puzzled with the dilemma. Thomas was a clever man. He arranged for backups when he thought his plan was in danger. He would have conceived of a similar contingency here. She examined the yellow and green leads. They seemed just as promising as any of the other wires. She looked down at the counter: 20, 19, 18, 17 . . .

Gripping John's penknife, Kate raised the sharp blade to the yellow and green leads. She gulped down a deep breath of air, held it, and cut through the two wires. A moment of silence followed, then the machine started buzzing. Her heart skipped forward until she realized the familiar sound was the broken power source.

Kate fell into his arms. John wanted her. He held her tight and kissed her deeply, slowly.

"Why didn't you tell me you were with the Justice Department?" Kate asked, finally, entwined around him.

"I didn't want to take the risk. This group has its tentacles in local and federal offices. Judges, Kate. They control a few judges. I had no way of knowing if you were one of the officials they were paying off."

"And later?"

"Well, I did warn you, Kate. I begged you to get out of the city to someplace safe. Just in case things went bad."

Her eyes were bright with mirth. "The John Mitchell that I knew was single and straight, but I don't know a thing about John Prescott. Is he single? Straight? Is there a Mrs. Prescott?"

"Yes, as a matter of fact, there is a Mrs. Prescott. She is a very beautiful woman who means the world to me," he replied, smiling wryly.

Dawson frowned. "Oh—"

"She's my mother," John said, laughing. "Then you're not married?"

"No, I'm divorced. She never wanted to take my last name."

Kate looked into his eyes. "And what about your feelings for me?"

He didn't reply right away. "My feelings for you are real.

You're like a bulldog. You bite down on something, and you don't let it go."

She ignored his flippancy and pulled him close to her for a kiss. They came together again, kissing each other as soft waves of pleasure washed over them like waves breaking at the shoreline. Kate felt a swell of sexual passion, and she moved her hands over his body, reaching down for his manhood.

John tried to pull away when the Motorola CP11 two-way radio tucked in his belt rang, but she held him to her side. "Let it go," she said.

He broke away from her and answered the two-way.

He listened for a moment, then said, "It's done. The bomb's been neutralized. You can commence with mop-up operations. Oh, and one more thing, I'm going to need a couple of guys from the Army Corps of Engineers to dig us out."

"Who is it?" Kate asked, knowing full well who.

John cupped his hand over the microphone. "It's the Attorney General."

She grinned. "Tell him we're not in any hurry."

"Kate says we're not in any hurry," he repeated.

"Over and out, sir."

"I love you," she whispered and kissed him.

EPILOGUE

Kate drove through the front gate at Bayside Village Apartments and pulled into a parking spot near her building. As she walked across the parking lot, she spotted Lenny's Mini Coop and smiled. His help with the compound's architectural blueprints made the difference for her investigation. She decided to stop by his apartment and say thanks before continuing onto her studio apartment.

Maybe she'd suggest they go out some night, get dinner, and catch a movie. She was feeling good, and nothing was about to dampen her spirits.

As she huffed and puffed her way up the steps, Kate thought she heard voices outside Lenny's apartment and paused in the shadows. From her vantage point, she could make out a beautiful young woman dressed in a short black cocktail dress. She was holding a bottle of Sangria in her hands.

"Well, are you going to open the door, Lenny, or are you going to leave a poor girl standing out here all night?" she demanded.

"Rebecca?"

"I don't like being stood up," she answered.

"Were we supposed to meet? I don't remember—"

"I don't like being second choice either. You had a lot of nerve to bring that other woman to the convention!"

"I don't understand," he confessed.

Rebecca turned her back on Lenny and stared out over the apartment complex. Kate saw the naughty glint in her eyes. She knew Rebecca was not angry or upset with Lenny, and she smiled. She was toying with him, playing hard to get, but she doubted whether Lenny had the sense to know it.

"You told me you had a new boyfriend."

"What are you talking about?" she said, turning back around. "I never said anything about a new boyfriend."

Smiling, Rebecca handed him the bottle of wine while moving across the threshold of the apartment door.

Lenny closed the door behind him and followed her with the wine.

Kate rushed up the rest of the steps, walking on tiptoes towards her friend's apartment door. She put her ear to the keyhole to listen. Kate did not think of herself as a voyeur, but she wasn't about to be cheated out of the rest of this scene. She had to know what Lenny would do.

From what she could tell, Rebecca had sat down and kicked off her high-heel shoes. He must have been still standing dumfounded, holding the wine, unaware of his next move.

"Come here, big boy," she said, tapping on the edge of the couch. "Get that wine open! Let's get wasted and fuck our brains out."

"Whatever you say, Rebecca," Lenny said.

"There's nothing like getting what you want," she purred, "except perhaps getting more of what you want."

"I couldn't agree with you more," he replied, twisting the cap on the Sangria and pouring two glasses.

In the dark recesses of the corridor, outside Lenny's apartment, Kate tiptoed away, smiling.

At nine o'clock the next morning, Kate paid Dr. Glass a visit. She was surprised to find him in the secretary's outer office, standing over a file cabinet with a handful of files in his hands. The odd contrast of the older, balding man with the white beard and the bright, colorful Hawaiian shirt and deck shoes made her think she was entering a travel agency that catered to the geriatric crowd instead of a therapist's office. After all she had been through in the last couple of weeks, Kate could have used a quiet vacation.

"Dr. Glass?" she asked, not meaning to start him. He turned to her and frowned. "Inspector Dawson, you missed your regular Tuesday appointment with me. I hope you have a good explanation for missing a mandated therapy session."

"I was sequestered and there might have been other things I was busy doing," Dawson spouted back.

"Oh, yes, that's right," Glass said, looking over the top of his wire rim glasses. He had stopped filing the manila folders in his file cabinet, looking at her with admiration.

"I hear the Chief's office is awarding you the Gold Medal of Valor for outstanding bravery above and beyond the call of duty. Good job."

"Thank you," she said with humility. "You know, I heard there was a serious debate going back and forth between the various offices about giving me the award or suspending me for three months' time."

Glass grunted. "You can thank the Justice Department for that one."

"Really?"

"And the local news outlets," he continued with a thin smile.

"They all wanted a hero to pin a medal on for saving the city from the brink of atomic destruction. Once all the dust settled from those rascally cultists, there was only one police officer still standing—Inspector Kate Dawson."

"I still can't believe it."

"Well, don't go claiming all the credit," the doctor said, bringing her down to earth. "I also heard your partner Jorge Ramirez is receiving the Bronze Medal of Valor for the shooting in the museum."

"Ramirez is a good cop. He deserves to be recognized for his bravery in chasing down those thugs. You know, if it hadn't been for him, I wouldn't be around today."

"Dawson, you're such a bad liar," Glass pointed out to her. He picked up a couple of manila folders and filed them in the filing cabinet. "I read the file."

"I suppose little escapes you, Doctor."

"You'd be surprised," he replied. "What do you know about filing? I can't make heads or tails out of this system, and my secretary's away on maternity leave."

"I spent two years filing papers in the file office down in the basement. But then you knew that, didn't you?"

"I did," Glass said with a grin.

"The system is not all that complicated. You have to remember that all case files are filed by the first four letters of the arresting officer's last name, followed by the case number," Kate said, pointing to the first four letters in the name "Brown" and the case number. "This one is BROW7780147."

Glass shot a look at the folder then back at her and nodded. "Good, I think I got it. But then, you didn't just stop by the office to give me pointers on filing. What can I do for you today, Inspector?"

Kate hesitated then she said, "I came here today to apologize to you, Dr. Glass. I'm not good talking about my feelings, and when you started in on me about my daughter last time, I guess I lost it. I want to open up to you."

"Why don't we go into my office?" he asked.

"Thank you," she replied. Kate settled on the couch.

"First of all, I recognize how hard it is to admit you're wrong and to offer an apology to someone you've had an adversarial relationship with. That takes a tremendous amount of courage and personal fortitude," Glass observed.

"Second, I'm impressed with your willingness to open up, to deal with the issues at hand. That shows a person of great character and learning."

"Well, I know the mandatory routine," Kate confessed with the slight nod of her head. "The sooner I spill my guts, the faster I get out of here. But that's not why I came back."

"Third, what is mandatory is to discuss the trauma you went through during your investigation of John Monroe and to work through those issues. The first step begins with being able to admit you've got a problem."

"You know, that's very hard for me to do as a police officer, Dr. Glass."

"In this room, it's just Barry and Kate," he said, trying to reassure her.

She studied his face then looked away. "And what about Internal Affairs?"

"Well, I have to write a final report that's submitted to IA. But what goes into that report is determined by you," he said. "If you're angry and refuse to talk with me, then you've got anger management issues. If you are open, then you're a credit to the Force. It all depends on you."

"What about details of my personal life? Relationships?"

Glass shook his head. "Who on earth have you been talking

to? I don't care about that. Those details are only relevant if you worked in Vice, or if you had somehow blurred the lines between reality and fantasy."

"So then, you're saying it's safe for me to talk to you?"

"Yes, Kate, it's safe."

She closed her eyes trying to summon the violent images that were haunting her dreams. She imagined seeing the bloody, violent demise of Stephen Collins, the final moments of Rosemary Murphy's life, and the look of surprise in John Monroe's face when she shot him. She opened her eyes and glanced at Dr. Glass for comfort.

"I have been having horrible dreams about John Monroe . . ." she started.

In the afternoon, after Kate received her Gold Medal of Valor from the Mayor and the Chief of Police in an official ceremony, she climbed into her BMW 5.25i, still dressed in uniform, and headed south on Interstate 280. She drove along the highway with the sunroof open and the windows down. The early spring sun felt warm on her back, and she enjoyed the wind blowing through her hair.

At the exit for the sleepy little town of Colma, Kate pulled off the interstate then drove several more miles to the entrance for Woodlawn Memorial Park. The groundskeepers were planting flowers. She drove around the outer ring and parked near the section set aside for the graves of fallen policemen. Kate got out of the sporty coupe and walked along a narrow path, reading the names and dates on the markers and thinking about her fallen partner.

When she reached Miller's gravesite, she brushed away leaves, twigs, and grass clippings. The plain stone tablet read: *Frank Miller. Inspector. San Francisco Police Department. Killed in the Line of Duty. November 11, 1954–September 22, 2016.*

She still felt responsible for his death. If she hadn't convinced him to take on that one final case, Frank Miller would still be alive. Kate felt the emotions of the last few weeks welling up inside her, but she fought to keep them all in check. Instead, she wondered what he would have thought of her on this day, receiving the Gold Medal of Valor. If he would have been proud of the young detective he nourished and mentored, or not.

Kate stood at attention in her dress blues at Miller's gravesite saluting her fallen partner. She removed the medal from around her neck, placed it on the gravestone around Frank's name, and stepped back away. "I miss you, Frank," she said.

After a few moments of silence, she turned and walked away from his grave without looking back. Kate climbed into her car and drove back to San Francisco, thinking of John and the night to come.

Kate watched John pace up and down the corridor outside her apartment for fifteen minutes, trying to summon the courage to knock on her door. She seemed to know that the longer he paced, the more he realized his courage wasn't there, but she was determined not to make it easy on him.

Only a couple of days before, the two of them faced a crisis that may have triggered the end of the world. Now, as she looked out from behind the curtain, he appeared to be just a bundle of nerves. What had happened to that confident, attractive lumberjack that captured her heart? Had his swagger deserted him or was that all part of the act that went into making John Mitchell a desirable hunk of man?

He walked up to her door one final time and paused.

The door opened with Kate waiting for him in the entrance, wearing a black negligee that revealed all of the wonderful curves of her body.

"Do you mind telling me how much longer you intend on pacing outside of my apartment?" she asked with a grin.

"How did you know?"

"I've been watching you, love," she confessed.

John shook his head. He seemed to be both pleased and a little annoyed to be transparent to her. He lingered outside of her door for another moment, a grin forming on his face.

"You know, you remind me of a girl I dated in college before my wife."

"Really?"

"She was very beautiful," John explained. "She also confused me. A lot."

Kate's beautiful lips formed a lovely beaming smile.

She beckoned him into her apartment then took him into her arms as he crossed the threshold. She leaned forward and kissed him. It was tentative at first, but then she opened her mouth and kissed him deeply, passionately.

She whispered, "I hope you've come here to show me how confused you are."

He pulled her closer and kissed her again. Then, looking into her brown eyes, he said, "I have a surprise for you. But you need to give me a moment to set it up."

"Oh?" Kate replied, raising her eyebrows.

"And no peaking," John said, as he walked away towards her bedroom, carrying a plastic bag she had missed.

"Don't be long," she sighed, as she slid onto the couch, the edges of her nightgown floating down through the air like flower petals. Kate ran her fingers through her long, brown hair, listening to him humming "Nights in White Satin," now their signature 'first song'.

John returned with a smile on his face. He took her by hand and said, "Close your eyes."

As she took the first step, she caught the scent of lavender and let out a pleasurable, "Hhhhhmmmm." Kate turned her face up to his, eyes still closed, and kissed him deeply, passionately. Breaking away, she buried her face in his neck; his cologne a catalyst aphrodisiac. "I'm glad you're here," she whispered in his ear.

"So am I." John slid his hand down her back and cupped her buttocks, squeezing firmly.

He reached under the straps of her negligee pushing them away from her shoulders, letting it slip through his fingers, falling to the floor at her feet. She stepped away from it without hesitation. Naked, Kate smiled and ran her hands from her belly to her breasts, inviting John to take her. He ripped his shirt over his head and let it drop next to her gossamer. He pulled her to him and kissed her bare shoulders lightly cupping her breasts in each hand. Kate moaned then pulled him against her. As she curled around him, he sighed and held her tight. Her breasts pressed sweetly against his strong, hairy chest. Her long, luscious legs wrapped around his large muscular legs.

"Oh, John," she breathed with a heavy sigh. "I love you—I need you!"

John broke their embrace just long enough to kick his shoes to the other side of the room and peel his jeans off, then put a finger to her lips and pushed the bedroom door open to reveal his surprise.

Kate's tiny bedroom had been transformed into a wonderland. Small votive candles flickered all around.

Lavender from the diffuser filled the air. Rose petals had been scattered all over the room. A bottle of champagne and two glasses sat on the nightstand; bubbles rising to the surface, popping, as the Moody Blues serenaded them.

She buried her face in her hands and her eyes teared up. "Oh, John, it's beautiful!"

He handed her one of the glasses of champagne, gently touching the two together. "To beginnings." They sipped and then he took hers from her hand.

"And this is not all. *No*, this is not all," John proclaimed, guiding her to the bed. "Lie on your stomach for me."

Kate obeyed.

He climbed on the bed, straddling her from behind, his large cock rubbing against her back.

She closed her eyes, listening to the soft music. "I'm not a big fan of champagne," she remarked, "but that is really good."

"I'm glad," he said, smiling, pleased with himself.

Pouring an ample amount of lavender massage oil into his hands, he let it drizzle down her spine. His strong hands worked the oil into her shoulders, her arms, and down her back. At that point, both lost control and her took her from behind, melting into her.

Kate rolled her eyes back into her head. She quivered as her body stretched and contracted. They pulsated in orgasmic bliss, and rode the wave of passion washing over them like pounding surf at the beach.

Kate collapsed into the bed. His arms wrapped around her, holding her tight against him, he rolled them into a spoon, refusing to leave her. Drifting off, listening to the sweet lyrics of the "Tuesday Afternoon," they were finally both content.

As the soft light from the morning sunrise bathed the room in rich colors of yellow and gold, Kate awoke in her bed, lying in John's arms. He was softly snoring as she maneuvered cautiously to the edge of the bed. She got up and sidestepped her way through the wreckage to the bathroom.

When she returned, John was still snoring, but suspended in that gray area that existed between sleep and wakefulness. He rubbed against her as she slipped back into bed. She stroked his body as she climbed back into place.

"I love you," he murmured, half asleep.

Kate pulled his arms back around her like a cozy, winter blanket and snuggled against his chest. "I know," she whispered, closing her eyes and drifting back to sleep.

ACKNOWLEDGMENTS

As the author of this book, I would like all to know that books are not produced successfully in a vacuum. There are many people along the way who help make the idea become a reality. I would like to acknowledge several people who helped me with their love, words of advice, or listening ears to write *Architects of Armageddon.*

First, I want to thank my friends and family who listened to me almost endlessly talk about the book. No doubt you've recognized yourselves in many of the characters who are based upon the people in my life. Thank you, Claudine Biggs, Pam and Bob Peay, David Nixon, Brad Johnson, Matt Sherman, Bob and Diane Blackwood.

Thank you, Rosanna Tufts. Rosanna is one of my favorite talk-show hosts, and has had me on her radio program a number of times, talking about the writing process and my Kate Dawson books.

I also want to thank my agent Jeanie Loiacono. Jeanie was a trooper in dealing with my obsession about writing this particular book and in making certain that it was the best book we could produce. In addition to marketing my books to publishers, she has worked tirelessly behind the scenes as an uncredited editor, reviewing and editing scenes until they were perfect for submission. I could not have managed on my own without her, and liken her tremendous input to that muse we all seek out for inspiration and guidance.

In researching the background for the book, I read extensively about cults, cult leaders, and other groups on the fringe of mainstream Christianity. During that research, I kept reading accounts of one, truly amazing individual who had been part of a cult group but managed to escape. Her name is Joni Cutler, a former State Senator and now a Judge from South Dakota. Her account made for excellent reading, and in turn, helped inspire me to be as authentic as possible when documenting what really happens within these groups behind the scenes.

At the same time, I did not want to alienate Christians, in general, and sought the advice of my brother Robert "Bob" Flynn. We were both raised Christian, but he has actually lived every day of his life as an Evangelical Christian, doing what is right for his family, friends, church, and community. I have often kidded my younger brother Bob about wanting to grow up and be just like him some day. Fact of the matter is I admire him tremendously and know the world would be a much better place if everyone lived by his example.

And finally, I want to thank the city of San Francisco, another major character in the piece. My father John Johnson lived most of his life there and shared his love of San Francisco with me on each of my many visits. My love and life will be forever tied to the sights and sounds of that grand city by the Bay.

ABOUT THE AUTHOR

Born in Chicago, Illinois, in the 1950s, Dr. John L. Flynn is a three-time Hugo Award–nominated author, psychologist, teacher, and college dean. In 1977, he received the M. Carolyn Parker Award from the University of South Florida for excellence in creative writing. He received his Bachelor's and Master's degrees in English from the University of South Florida and worked as an English teacher in Baltimore, Maryland. He published his first book *Future Threads* in 1985. In 1998, he earned his PhD as a clinical psychologist from the University of Southern California. He has published nearly twenty books and dozens of articles. He currently resides in Lake Worth, Florida.

THE KATE DAWSON MYSTERIES

FROM OPEN ROAD MEDIA

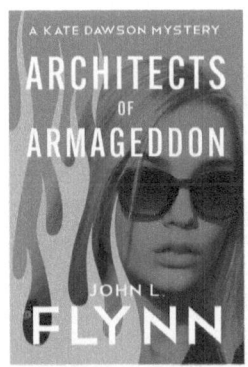

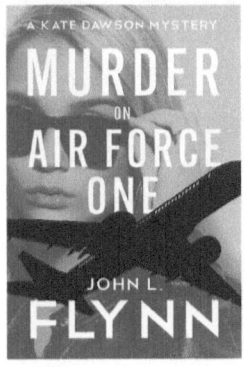

INTEGRATED MEDIA

Find a full list of our authors and
titles at www.openroadmedia.com

FOLLOW US
@OpenRoadMedia

EARLY BIRD BOOKS

FRESH DEALS, DELIVERED DAILY

Love to read?
Love great sales?

Get fantastic deals on
bestselling ebooks delivered
to your inbox every day!

Sign up today at
earlybirdbooks.com/book

www.ingramcontent.com/pod-product-compliance
Lightning Source LLC
Chambersburg PA
CBHW060427030726
47495CB00003B/765